MURDER AT
THE ELMS

Books by Alyssa Maxwell

Gilded Newport Mysteries
MURDER AT THE BREAKERS
MURDER AT MARBLE HOUSE
MURDER AT BEECHWOOD
MURDER AT ROUGH POINT
MURDER AT CHATEAU SUR MER
MURDER AT OCHRE COURT
MURDER AT CROSSWAYS
MURDER AT KINGSCOTE
MURDER AT WAKEHURST
MURDER AT BEACON ROCK
MURDER AT THE ELMS

Lady and Lady's Maid Mysteries
MURDER MOST MALICIOUS
A PINCH OF POISON
A DEVIOUS DEATH
A MURDEROUS MARRIAGE
A SILENT STABBING
A SINISTER SERVICE
A DEADLY ENDOWMENT
A FASHIONABLE FATALITY

Published by Kensington Publishing Corp.

MURDER AT THE ELMS

ALYSSA MAXWELL

KENSINGTON
PUBLISHING CORP.

www.kensingtonbooks.com

KENSINGTON BOOKS are published by

Kensington Publishing Corp.
119 West 40th Street
New York, NY 10018

All Kensington titles, imprints, and distributed lines are available at special quantity discounts for bulk purchases for sales promotion, premiums, fund-raising, educational, or institutional use. Special book excerpts or customized printings can also be created to fit specific needs. For details, write or phone the office of the Kensington Special Sales Manager: Attn. Special Sales Department. Kensington Publishing Corp., 119 West 40th Street, New York, NY 10018. Phone: 1-800-221-2647.

Library of Congress Card Catalogue Number: 2023936104

The K with book logo Reg US Pat. & TM Off.

ISBN: 978-1-4967-3619-2

First Kensington Hardcover Edition: September 2023

ISBN: 978-1-4967-3620-8 (ebook)

10 9 8 7 6 5 4 3 2 1

Printed in the United States of America

For Erin

MURDER AT THE ELMS

Chapter 1

Newport, RI, 1901

The aromas of ink and newsprint. The rumble of the presses emanating from the rear of our little building on Spring Street. The murmur of voices and the tap-tapping of my colleague working away on his latest article, his shoulders hunched and his dark hair flopped over his brow as he hunted and pecked faster than most people typed using all ten fingers.

Home. The word filled me with overwhelming satisfaction and a sense of peace. After weeks away, I was back where I belonged. Where I felt most myself. Where I presided over the news stories that would inhabit the pages of the *Newport Messenger*, the small but growing paper owned by my husband and myself. I was now officially the news reporter, but that distinction, of course, was tempered by my being the *only* news reporter on staff. My colleague, Ethan Merriman, currently engaged in capturing the tastes and textures of the latest to-dos along Bellevue Avenue, was our society columnist.

Wait. Did I say husband? Yes, indeed I did, for I was now

Mrs. Derrick Andrews, although here, in these offices and in the byline that accompanied the articles I wrote, I continued to be Emma Cross.

We were married in October of the previous year in a quiet, heartfelt ceremony at St. Paul's Church in town, attended by close friends and family, followed by a luncheon in the meeting hall below the sanctuary. My parents had been unable to travel here from France, so my half-brother, Brady, had walked me down the aisle, and my longtime friend Hannah, who was also Brady's sweetheart, had served as my bridesmaid. At Derrick's request, darling Nanny, my housekeeper, friend, and surrogate grandmother, had made her special apple ginger cake in several layers and iced it with snowy cream frosting. My aunt Alice Vanderbilt had attended, as had her daughters Gertrude and Gladys, and sons Alfred and Reggie. In their jewels and finery, they'd appeared the teensiest bit out of place against St. Paul's plain surroundings, but they had done their admirable best to pretend otherwise. Alice's eldest son, Neily, and his wife, Grace— *dearest* Neily and Grace—had stayed away so that the other family members would come, but the schism in the Vanderbilt family is another story altogether.

Derrick's parents had vowed to boycott our wedding, a threat that his mother had made good on but that his father, in the end, had not. It had been our first meeting, and I found him distinguished if a trifle austere, gracious if somewhat melancholy. He had kissed my hand and wished us well and gifted us with a lovely set of china that had belonged to his mother.

At the suggestion of a friend, a trek to the beautiful, rugged Adirondacks had served as our wedding trip. Then, when spring came, we boarded ship and ventured across the sea to Italy. The voyage had been touch and go for me, but Derrick had plied me with chamomile tea and oyster crackers to settle my stomach, and somehow I made the crossing without an excess of misery.

We disembarked in France and spent time with my parents, who were overjoyed to see us. Tuscany, our eventual destination, was glorious, as was visiting with Derrick's sister, Judith, and reuniting with a small friend from several years ago, her precious five-year-old son, Robbie. Upon learning that, as an infant, he had spent time at my home, Gull Manor, he had professed to remember me, but I knew that to be impossible at his tender age.

Now, on my first day back at the paper, I stepped into Ethan's and my cramped office, made even smaller by the two desks, chairs, and typewriter table. His index fingers went still on the keys. With a swoop of his head to flip the hair back from his brow, he glanced up and broke into a beaming grin. "Miss Cross. Um, that is, Mrs. Andrews. You're back."

"Yes, I am. And it's wonderful to see you. But really, Ethan, Emma will do."

His eyes filled with mild alarm. "Oh, now, that wouldn't be right. I couldn't."

No, we had established that some months ago and Ethan was nothing if not consistent.

"Why, you're the boss's wife," he went on, still enumerating the reasons we must avoid undue familiarity. His agitation widened a grin of my own. "And I'm . . . I'm just . . ."

"Just the best society columnist Newport has ever seen." I included myself in that assessment. I'd once held the very position he did, except at a different publication. But where I had bristled at assignments covering the antics and excesses of the Four Hundred, Ethan relished them and put all his energy into recording every detail. "Tell me, how did it go for you covering hard news while I was away?" A sudden qualm gave me pause. "Will you miss it terribly, do you think?"

"Not a speck. It's all yours, Miss Cross." He caught himself at the last minute. "Mrs. Andrews. Anyways, speaking of hard news, there's something already here for you. Mr. Sheppard brought it in a few minutes ago." He waved a hand toward my desk and the torn piece of paper that sat square in the middle. "Seems there's trouble brewing down the avenue."

He meant Bellevue Avenue, of course, that long, straight thoroughfare that traveled the southeastern portion of Aquidneck Island overlooking the cliffs and the Atlantic Ocean. Once mere farmland, one by one the families of the Four Hundred had built their summer cottages—palaces, really—and transformed the area into their exclusive playground for eight to twelve weeks each year.

I picked up the paper and read the terse message in our editor-in-chief's sharp, tilting handwriting. An instant later I slapped it back down on the desk. I'd already slid the pin from my straw boater. Now I slid it back through, securing it to my coiffure, and headed out of the office. "Ethan, we'll catch up later."

At the front of the building, in the room that served as both our administrative office and lobby, I stopped long enough to tell Derrick where I was off to. I started to explain the situation, but he stopped me as he rose from the desk that faced out over Spring Street. "Stan told me. He stepped out for a minute. Do you want me to come with you?"

"Don't be ridiculous. You've got your own work to do." I took advantage of having the front office to ourselves, albeit with the risk that passersby might swing their gazes in our direction, and gave Derrick a quick peck on the lips. "I'll see you after. Now I'm off for my first-ever look inside The Elms."

"You probably won't get farther than the kitchen, but good luck." He grasped my arm as I started toward the door. "Be careful."

"I always am," I replied, and ignored his grunt of skepticism.

The weather being fine and clear, Spring Street teemed with activity. The sidewalks were jammed with pedestrians while the street juggled carriages, wagons, and the oncoming streetcar. I almost left my buggy where it was along the curbstone, thinking it might be quicker for me to walk the block up to Bellevue and then head south on foot.

One look at the heat waves shimmering from the dusty road convinced me to take the buggy rather than arrive at The Elms covered in a sheen of perspiration and my skirt and shirtwaist a study in wrinkles.

Its construction only recently completed, The Elms sat along the upper portion of Bellevue Avenue only a few blocks from town. Once I drove past the Casino with its row of shops, the trees, mostly elm, closed overhead to offer sweet, reviving shade and a cooling breeze. Kingscote, a neo-Gothic structure with an almost fairy-tale aspect, stood to my right. I wondered if the Kings were back in town after spending the winter and spring in Europe. I thought about leaving my calling card but decided I'd best be about the business that had brought me to this part of town.

The Elms came soon after. Designed by Horace Trumbauer in the style of an eighteenth-century chateau, the house comprised a columned center section flanked by long, recessed wings on either side. The façade revealed only two stories, but a limestone balustrade along the roofline concealed a third story that housed the servants.

It wasn't to one of the three front doors framed in columned arches that I went, but instead I turned down Bellevue Court, a side street that skirted the north side of the property. I parked my buggy and entered the property at the service driveway. Approaching the delivery entrance was like venturing into another world entirely from the one the owners, Edward and Herminie Berwind, inhabited. Gone were the statues, the exotic trees, and the carefully designed flower beds that graced the elegant lawns. Here, it seemed the sun ducked behind thick clouds. That was only an illusion. Dense and tangled vines of wisteria grew like a roof above a circular drive, shielding the delivery carts and wagons from the view of anyone gazing down from the first- or second-story windows. Likewise, coal deliveries were made at the mouth of a tunnel that opened onto Dixon Street beyond the stone wall on the south side of the house. As far as the family or any of their guests were concerned, The Elms ran as if by magic.

Yet it wasn't magic that had brought me there that morning. As soon as I passed through the delivery hall and into the cold-preparation kitchen, the tension wrapped like tentacles around me. The house had been open a mere few weeks, but even so, by now the staff should have fallen into a seamless rhythm as they went about their tasks. I felt no such rhythm, no harmony of a well-tuned orchestra.

Footmen, maids, kitchen staff—even the butler and housekeeper, judging by their clothing—stood gathered two and three deep around the long, zinc-covered table used for the preparation of cold dishes. A quick glance through the wide windows looking into the main kitchen—normally the heart of any great house—revealed a stillness I found astonishing, especially at that time of day. Only one man hovered over the cast-iron range with its many burners and oven doors. His white tunic and tall hat identified him as the Berwinds' chef. No assistants chopped vegetables or mixed ingredients at the worktable, no scullery maids collected used pots and pans to scrub at the long sink.

If I hadn't known better, I'd have ventured to guess that nearly all the servants, over forty of them, were planning to . . .

"That's it, then," the butler said with a sigh and a yank at his necktie. "We are going to strike."

I swallowed a gasp.

"Do you think that'll get through to 'em, Mr. Boreman?" someone asked.

"Yeah, what if it doesn't?" another challenged.

"It has to." The assertion came from somewhere in the middle of the crush. "Where will they find enough servants to replace all of us on such short notice?"

Despite the butler's assertion that "this was it," the debate raged on around the table while I watched, listened, and took notes. I tried to be discreet, keeping well to the back of the assembly, but it wasn't long before a housemaid spotted me.

"You're Miss Cross from the *Messenger*, ain't you, ma'am?" At that, the room fell silent.

"Aren't," the housekeeper corrected, then turned her sights on me. "Do you intend running this story in your newspaper?"

"I . . . uh . . ." Suddenly feeling cornered, I took a half step backward. My shoulder blades came up against the cold surface of the rectangular white tiles that lined the walls.

"I certainly hope so," the butler said with a sniff. "It's the reason I telephoned your office. Come closer, Miss Cross. Or . . . did I hear you'd married recently?"

"Miss Cross will do." The crowd parted and I stepped up to the edge of the table. "You're truly planning to strike? You know it's never been done before. Not by house servants here in Newport."

"We have as much right to air our grievances as any longshoreman or rail worker or coal miner," a liveried footman said.

I couldn't help frowning as I remembered the violent results of a miner's strike only last September. I set my notebook and pencil on the table in front of me. "I was led to understand that your wages here are among the highest in Newport. And that many of you enjoy rooms to yourselves,

and two full bathrooms with hot and cold running water at
your disposal. Forgive me if I inquire what it is you're asking for."

"A little time off, is all." This angry retort shot at me from
a young woman in black serge sporting a crisp white pina-
fore and frill-edged cap.

"You're a housemaid?" I took up my writing implements
once again.

"Head parlor maid," she said with an Irish lilt. Her chin
lifted proudly.

"And the Berwinds allow you little time off?" I queried.

"Little? How about none?" Fiery color swept her porcelain complexion from chin to hairline.

My pencil went still. Had I understood correctly? "None?
As in . . ."

"Never," the housekeeper clarified. She was a stout woman
with severely swept-back hair, round spectacles, and a digni-
fied air. "When we are not sleeping or eating, we are working. Seven days a week, with time off only for meals and
church Sunday morning."

"I worked eighteen hours yesterday," the head parlor
maid supplied. "As I do most days."

Murmurs of agreement rose in volume, echoing off the
tiled walls.

"We've had about as much as we can take, Miss Cross,"
said a handsome young footman. "A fella needs some time
to himself once in a while."

"And to *her*self," the parlor maid added.

"I certainly agree." I addressed my next question to the
butler: "Have you talked to the Berwinds, tried to reason
with them?"

"On more than one occasion." Mr. Boreman shook his
head sadly. "I'm afraid my words have fallen on deaf ears."

"There's nothin' left to be done but walk out." The parlor

maid spoke as if ready to lead the charge out through the service entrance doors. "We'll see how they get on without us."

"You do realize that once you leave, there's no guarantee you'll ever enter this house again." While my sympathies lay entirely with them, my hopes for their success were rather less enthusiastic. Call me a realist. I hated to see anyone put out of work.

While they continued their planning, working out exactly when and how they would walk off their jobs, I noticed one young woman backed off into a corner by the electrical circuit box. Her frightened eyes darted from one colleague to the next, and her hands fisted around her cotton apron. I went to stand with her.

"You don't look particularly confident about this plan."

She shook her head rapidly and spoke with an accent I recognized as Portuguese; there were many families from Portugal, or of Portuguese descent, living on Aquidneck Island. Her dark hair and eyes spoke of her southern European origins. "Only ill can come of it, ma'am."

"And you don't wish to follow their lead," I guessed.

"No, ma'am. No trouble. I wish only to work."

"You're from Portugal?"

"I am, ma'am."

"You're far from home. I understand your trepidation. Have you family here?"

"No, ma'am. No family. No one. Only me. I am Ines."

"I'm Emma Cross." I almost corrected myself, until I remembered that since I'd come here in a professional capacity, my maiden name would do. "I'm pleased to meet you, Ines. Your English is quite good for someone who hasn't been here long." I stopped myself from adding that her language skills would help in securing another position, should it come to that.

Her eyes grew large with fear, as if I'd accused her of

something. She backed up until she came up against the glass case that housed the circuits. "There was a wealthy English-woman in my village. My parents worked for her. She taught English to many of the children on the *propriedade*." She shook her head again, then translated, "On the estate."

"I see. That must have made things easier once you arrived in this country."

"Yes. But now . . ." She shook her head. "Miss Cross, I do not wish to strike. I am afraid. I don't want trouble," she repeated. She was shorter than me by several inches. She tipped her oval face up at me, the cheeks wide and smooth, the chin gently pointed, mouth bowed pleasantly. An exotic beauty, by American standards. Behind a thick fringe of lashes, her eyes reddened and she blinked away tears.

I reached for her hand. "You can't be forced to strike, Ines. They are doing what they believe is right. You must do the same, even if it is to remain behind when the others leave."

She returned the pressure of my hand, holding on tightly. Almost desperately. "May I truly?"

"Ines, you are free to make your own decisions."

"What's this? What are you tellin' her?"

The cross voice startled us both, and we glanced up to see the parlor maid standing close, her features taut with anger. Ines pressed herself farther into the corner and half behind me. I let her use me as a shield as I stared the housemaid down. "I'm simply confirming that she has choices, just as the rest of you do."

The maid held up a fist. "It's all for one and one for all. Everyone must agree to strike. If one of us backs out, the rest of us will fail." Her Irish accent thickened as she spoke.

"That's not fair," I told her calmly but firmly. "Ines has no family in this country and nowhere to go should she lose her position. Are you prepared to help her if you're all fired from The Elms?"

"We won't be fired if we stand together," she insisted. I noticed that several servants were watching us. She half turned and spoke to them. "Isn't that right?"

Heads nodded, but I shook my own. "That's not how it works. The Berwinds might accede to your requests or they might send you all packing, as they see fit. It won't matter to them if one or all of you decide to strike."

Yet, even as I spoke, I again recalled the miners' strike of last autumn. Those men were quickly replaced by nonunion workers. An easy solution for the mining company—one that ended tragically when the union miners opened fire on their replacements at a terminal of the Illinois Central Railroad.

Was I helping to put Ines in a similar position, with her coworkers so resenting her that they would take out their anger and frustrations on her?

I pointed into the main kitchen. "What about the chef? He doesn't appear to be interested in striking either."

"Monsieur Baudelaire is an exception," the maid informed me in a tone that implied I was something of an idiot. Her lips flattened in disapproval. "He has time off whenever he isn't cooking, and he's never considered himself one of us."

I turned back to the Portuguese woman. "Ines, if you should lose this position, you can come to me for help. You're to go to Gull Manor on Ocean Avenue and tell whoever answers the door that Miss Cross sent you. Do you understand?"

She nodded vigorously. "Thank you, Miss Cross. But I hope it will not be necessary."

"I hope not too."

"Traitor." Scowling, the housemaid started to move away, but I placed a hand on her shoulder.

"The same goes for you. For any of the women here who might find themselves in need of shelter. They'll be welcome at Gull Manor."

The maid pressed her face close to mine. Her complexion turned so red I fancied I could feel the heat wafting off it. "No one here needs your charity. Not them, not me, and not her." Her finger shot out as if to pin Ines to the wall. "We're willin' to work for our livelihood, and work hard. All we want is a bit o' respect and working hours that wouldn't kill a donkey."

"I'm only saying that you'd be welcome, if you needed," I tried again, but she cut me off.

"Besides, I've a family on the island, and family sticks together. Just as everyone here is a family, or should be." She aimed another spiteful look at Ines, who cowered with her chin to her chest.

"Bridget," the handsome footman called over, "leave Ines alone and come over here if you want in on this vote."

"Did I hear something about a vote?" A man in street clothes pushed his way in through the delivery entrance and stood poised with a notebook and pencil. He wore a brown tweed coat with patches at the elbows and a battered derby, his pale blond hair in such need of cutting it stuck out in tufts all around the brim.

"Hello, Mr. Brown," I said with a sinking feeling. Orville Brown owned—and almost single-handedly staffed—the *Aquidneck Island Advocate*, a newspaper I had found to be of more sensationalism than substance. If Mr. Brown didn't believe a story had what it took to sell newspapers, he had no qualms when it came to exaggeration, embellishment, and, I had seen with my own eyes, downright fabrication.

"What have we here, hmm? I hear tell there's worker discontent here at The Elms." His weaselly gaze took in the room. "It seems everyone is here. So, who is going to give me tomorrow morning's front-page story?"

I wished the little man would go away. Behind him, other reporters filed inside, among them a journalist from the

Newport Daily News, one from the *Mercury*, and Ed Billings, my former coworker and, to put it honestly, my nemesis at the *Newport Observer*. I put Ed Billings in the same category as Orville Brown, but with rather less creativity.

Ed walked in my direction. "Emma," he said in terse greeting. "Always the first on hand, aren't you?" He spoke with his typical resentment, prompting me to shrug.

"Sorry, Ed. Can I help it if I got the scoop earlier than you? From what I understand, the staff here called me in specifically. How did you find out about this?"

He looked me up and down. "I see marriage hasn't improved your manners." I didn't rise to the bait but stood waiting for his next comment, a faint smile on my lips. He harrumphed. "Word always gets around."

Yes, that was Newport. I couldn't have expected to keep a story like this all to myself, as nothing stayed confidential for long. Tell one person, and you've told everyone. I gestured to the group around the table. "Would you like to listen to them, Ed, or do you want me to fill you in later?"

It was a subtle poke at how he had often taken credit for stories I'd fleshed out when I worked for the *Observer*. His excuse had always been that he held the *Observer*'s official news reporter position, while I was merely the society columnist.

He scoffed and moved away. I set my pencil to paper, ready to record what happened next.

The butler held up his hands for silence. "All in favor of going to Mr. Berwind this very day and presenting him with our demands and ultimatum, raise your hands."

"One moment." The French chef leaned in from the kitchen, his arms crossed over his chest. In his thickly accented English, he asked in a mocking tone, "Do the women get to vote, too?"

"I say no," a footman said.

"Oh, you do, do you?" The housekeeper challenged him with a heft of an eyebrow.

"Well . . ." The young man compressed his lips and seemed to deflate. In the next moment, he regained his bravado. "Women aren't allowed to vote, generally."

The housemaid, Bridget, raised her fist once again. I didn't doubt she'd use it if she felt the circumstances warranted it. "We're in this as much as any of you men."

Mr. Boreman raised his hands again to halt the debate. "That will be quite enough. Mrs. Sherman and I are still in charge here. Everyone will vote." At the titters of disagreement this roused, his eyes blazed. "Everyone or no one. Is that clear?"

Once again titters filled the air, but these were a slightly more agreeable kind.

"All right, then," Mr. Boreman said loudly. "All in favor of carrying on with our plans today, raise your hands."

Everyone did. Except Ines, who had remained in her corner, not exactly cowering, but not with conviction, either.

"Well, I'd say the ayes have it." Mr. Boreman sighed deeply and clasped his hands behind him. "There's no sense in putting it off. I'll go up now."

He started for the service staircase but stopped when a small voice cried out his name. "Mr. Boreman, may I come, too?"

He turned, searching for the source of the voice. His gaze lit on Ines. "You, Ines? Why?"

Her arms hugging her middle, she stepped forward timidly. "I wish to tell the Berwinds that I do not strike, sir."

"Why, I should . . ." Her fist again curling, Bridget whirled on the Portuguese maid. I stepped between them.

"That's enough threats from you." I held out the flat of my hand. Anger rose in several of the faces around me, and I braced for their outbursts. None came. They turned away and gathered among themselves to speculate on what the next minutes would bring.

Mr. Boreman held out a hand to beckon to Ines. "Come along, then, I suppose." He didn't sound happy about it, but at least he didn't forbid her to go.

Ines started toward him looking like a convict walking to the gallows. The chef put his feet in motion as well. "I am going up, too. I must make clear to the Berwinds that I am not a part of this nonsense."

Mr. Boreman nodded, then faced his coworkers one last time. "Wish me luck."

He looked as though he believed he would need it.

Chapter 2

It seemed an eternity before we heard footsteps descending to the basement. Just as he had led the way up, Mr. Boreman now led the other two down. Their faces didn't give a hint as to what happened above stairs. Such a simple request: time off, a few hours to oneself each day before going to bed and starting all over again the following morning. A servant's life was one of the most difficult I could imagine, physically and mentally. To work so hard and know that it was all for someone else, that you would never profit from your toils, that the best you could hope for was a modest pension in old age—but even that was never guaranteed.

"Well?" Mrs. Sherman's brittle voice revealed her impatience.

Before Mr. Boreman answered, Ines spotted me and hurried to my side. I tried to read her expression. I saw the same fear and apprehension as earlier. What did that mean?

"We are fired," Mr. Boreman pronounced in his authoritative baritone, the same voice he must have used daily to speed his underlings to their work.

"What?" This came from several mouths at once. The rest seemed frozen, suspended in disbelief. I was among them. While I'd known in theory this could happen, I realized now that part of me had dismissed the possibility as simply too cruel.

Someone said, "Surely not."

"I'm afraid so." Mr. Boreman bowed his head. "I reasoned, I pleaded, I tried to bargain with him by saying we would even accept a monthly rotation of time off." He raised his chin and met each horrified gaze in turn. "I am sorry. I have failed you."

Orville Brown raised his derby in the air for attention. "You're not going to take this sitting down, are you? You've got to fight back—all of you."

"Mr. Brown," I called to him, "there is little they can do if they've all been dismissed."

"Exactly," Mr. Boreman concurred. "We no longer work here. Nothing we say is of any account anymore."

"That, sir, is rubbish." Mr. Brown squeezed his way between shoulders until he reached the preparation table. He set his palms flat against the zinc surface and leaned forward. "You *can* fight back. I'll help you. We'll picket the house. We'll send your story to all the newspapers in the northeast. We'll appeal to the governor." He slapped the table for emphasis.

"The governor?" Bridget let out a harsh laugh. "Men like the governor are in the pockets of men like Edward Berwind. He won't lift a finger for the likes of us."

"I wouldn't put it quite that way, but yes, it's unlikely anyone will intervene for us." Mr. Boreman looked at the floor, schooled his features, and gazed back up with a sad smile. "The summer is young yet. There may be new positions to be had, either here in Newport or back in New York. We'd best be getting on with finding them."

"But . . . when . . . ?" Mrs. Sherman wrung her hands, suddenly looking older than she had only minutes ago. "I never for a moment thought this would happen. When must we leave?"

"Today. Now." Mr. Boreman put his hand in the air in a gesture of futility. "We are to pack our things and go."

A grunt brought attention to the chef, who had colored to a ruddy shade that stood out starkly against his white uniform and chef's hat.

"You too, Mr. Baudelaire?" a footman asked. "But we thought you said . . ."

"I could not stand against you. And now I am sacked, too."

Ahs of appreciation came from all corners of the room.

"It won't take but an instant for a man of your talents to find a new position," Mr. Boreman assured him. "If not at another great house, perhaps in one of New York's many fine restaurants."

"You're awfully quiet, Ines." Bridget thrust a finger at the maid. "I'll wager you didn't change your mind. You stood against us, didn't you?"

"I . . . You know I did not wish to strike," the maid murmured, her eyes downcast.

"And so they're keepin' you on?" Bridget nearly spat the words, more a statement than a question.

Ines nodded, still avoiding eye contact with the others.

"Why, you . . ." Before anyone could stop her, Bridget launched herself at Ines. Standing so close to both of them, I also felt the brunt of the Irishwoman's attack. Her hands flew at whatever they could connect with, slapping, whacking, shoving. I found myself on the floor, unhurt but for the indignity of landing on my rump. Ines, I saw, had backed once again into a corner.

The shock that had held the group immobile wore off with a shudder of alarm, and several servants, both male and female, closed in on the scuffling pair. I struggled to my feet and found my path to the two maids blocked by both Ed Billings and Orville Brown, who had shoved their way around me. They scribbled madly in their notebooks.

"Let me by," I commanded them, to no avail.

Orville Brown cast me a glance over his shoulder, revealing a delighted grin. "Serves her right. She shouldn't have gone against the rest."

By now Bridget had been hauled off Ines. While two of her fellow maids held her in check, a small circle of her peers spoke quietly to her, trying to calm her. I put a hand on Ed Billings's shoulder and nudged him aside. Before he could protest, I brushed past him and went to stand with Ines.

"Whyever did you come back downstairs?" I whispered to her. "If you're not dismissed, you can go back to your room for now."

"You are right, but I wasn't thinking, Miss Cross. This is all so confusing. So upsetting." Her brow furrowing, she bit her bottom lip. "I did not want this. I am sorry for them. Perhaps I should have . . . but where would I have gone?"

I nearly repeated my offer of Gull Manor, but that might have made her feel more guilty about not going along with the strike. She had made her decision and she would be allowed to remain in her position at The Elms. As for the rest, they quietly began retreating up the staircase, to their rooms, presumably, to pack their things. Bridget cast a dark look backward before continuing up.

One man refused, however, to be quiet. "Why are you taking this without a fight? What are you, a pack of lemmings?" Orville Brown darted from person to person in line waiting to climb the stairs. "You've got decency on your side. Use it. Expose the Berwinds for what they are. Refuse to leave until your demands are met."

His pleading had no effect. Each servant kept walking, filing up the staircase. I heard weeping and realized it was Ines. I put an arm around her shoulders. "They'll be all right. What Mr. Boreman said is true, that it's early in the season and they'll find new positions."

"But they've been sacked. What if no one will hire them now?"

"That reporter"—I pointed at Orville Brown—"is right about one thing. They do have decency on their side. It isn't right to expect people to work every waking hour of every day, and prospective employers will realize that. I'm sure of it." In truth, I wasn't at all sure. But perhaps I could be of help. I thought of several wealthy friends and acquaintances, such as my distant Vanderbilt cousins and others for whom I had performed favors over the years. Some of them might have openings in their households or might know of families who did. I simply couldn't sit by and do nothing.

With a heavy heart I drove back to the *Messenger* and told Derrick what happened. He was as appalled as I.

"Could there be a misunderstanding? I can't believe the Berwinds would fire an entire staff, especially not with the summer season about to get under way."

"There didn't seem to be any doubt about it." We had my office to ourselves, as Ethan had gone out on an assignment. I removed my boater and slid my gloves from my hands, then slapped the bundle down onto my desktop. "I don't know who to worry more about, everyone who lost their jobs today or Ines, who's staying on. One woman in particular seemed bent on punishing Ines for not joining the strike."

He perched on a corner of the desk, his arms folded in front of him. "You don't think she'd go back to The Elms and try to hurt her, do you?"

"I hope not." I considered, then added, "I don't see how

she'd be able to enter the house again after today. Once a new staff is in place, no one there will know her. She'd be like any other trespasser."

"That may be so, but it might be a good idea for this Ines not to venture into town for a while." He picked up a pencil and twirled it between his fingers. "Or anywhere off the estate, for that matter. Until things blow over."

"Yes, you're right and I should have warned her." I lowered myself into my chair and pulled my notebook out of my handbag. I needed to have this story typed up before we left the office for the day.

Derrick leaned to brush a kiss across my lips. "My darling, it's not up to you to save everyone in the world. I'm sure Ines is capable of seeing for herself the wisdom of staying put for a time."

I nodded. "Yes, but I think I'll check on her tomorrow, all the same."

That evening, we drove together to Gull Manor. Ordinarily I would have said we drove *home* together. Surely Gull Manor had been my home for nearly ten years, ever since my great-aunt Sadie had passed away and left me the property in her will. Before that, even, since when my parents had moved to France, Aunt Sadie had invited me to move in with her. So yes, home. Except that now it felt different.

Or perhaps it *didn't* feel different when it *should* have. It should have been *our* home now, mine and Derrick's, but it wasn't—it still felt solely mine and having Derrick there was, for me . . . awkward. As if I couldn't quite think of the house as equally his. I felt the same way about his flat in town, on the Point, despite it being in the very house I had grown up in. My parents had sold it to him when he first came to Newport, believing I no longer needed it and finding themselves in need of funds. To me, that flat, even the entire house, felt like *Derrick's*. His bachelor's digs. Not a place for a married couple to set up housekeeping.

So then, two houses, but neither quite a home. Since returning from Italy we'd split our time between Gull Manor and the house on the Point—mostly the Point, using the excuse that it was closer to town and more convenient to our work at the *Messenger*.

Still, the people at Gull Manor were family. Nanny, who had been my nurse when I was a child, lived there as my housekeeper—more in name than in deed, for at her age I didn't wish her to work too hard. There was also Katie Dillon, our maid-of-all-work. Barely out of her teens now, she had come to me in dire need several years ago. Just as Nanny was like a grandmother to me, Katie filled the role of younger sister.

As we turned up the front drive, I couldn't help noting how many repairs had been accomplished in recent months. The shutters hung straight, worn shingles and roof tiles had been replaced, and the trim was freshly painted. Where the house had once shown a decidedly shabby face to the world, it now wore an aspect of gentility, one might almost say affluence.

In truth, the passing of Cornelius Vanderbilt, a cousin I had considered more of an uncle, *had* left me relatively affluent. My marriage to Derrick Andrews had elevated me yet more, economically, to a level on a par with many members of society's Four Hundred.

I could afford to fix a shingle or two.

The front door opened and Nanny filled the doorway, her girth blocking our view of the hallway within. Swathed in flowered muslin, her corset worn loosely these days, she came out and down the step, waiting with a delighted smile for us to alight from the carriage. From the open door behind her streamed a brown and white spaniel, who added his excited yaps to Nanny's welcome. Once Derrick and I had touched ground, Patch bounded around us in glee as Nanny embraced each of us tightly and bustled us inside.

"Something smells wonderful," I said, inhaling deeply the savory aromas drifting from the kitchen at the back of the house. To my right, the dining room awaited us with the linen tablecloth Aunt Sadie had embroidered herself, and the lovely china Derrick's father had given us at the wedding.

"I have a pork shoulder roasting along with potatoes, carrots, and all the trimmings." Nanny's grin had yet to fade. "And a nice bottle of Madeira to go with it."

"Sounds like we've come to the right place," Derrick commented with feeling, and gave Nanny another hug and a kiss on her soft cheek.

"Good evening, Miss Emma, Mr. Andrews," Katie called from the kitchen doorway. She had a towel in each hand and held a pan of something that steamed. Strands of red curls that had escaped her bun coiled like tight springs from the damp heat.

I waved to her. "Set that down and come say hello properly, Katie."

"Oh, Emma, before I forget." Nanny went to the hall table and retrieved an envelope from the post tray. "Here you go. It came yesterday."

Patch leaned against me with his forepaws propped against my leg. I absently stroked his head as I glanced at the embossed envelope and raised my eyebrows in surprise. "It looks like an invitation."

"I expect we'll see a great many of those now that society knows we're back." Derrick moved to glance at the missive over my shoulder.

"It's from the Berwinds." I broke the seal and slipped a sheet of glossy vellum from inside, also embossed and framed in silver foil. "We're invited to their musicale, which is to take place a week from this Friday night." I lowered the hand holding the invitation to my side. That the Berwinds would invite me to their new home, I found astonishing, but it was something I must get used to as Derrick Andrews's wife. "Oh, but they'll call it off, of course. They can't possibly hold an entertainment only a week after dismissing their entire house staff."

Nanny slid her half-moon spectacles lower on her nose, as if that might help her better understand what I had just said. "They what?"

We all made ourselves comfortable, Patch curling up at my feet, and Derrick and I spent the next several minutes explaining to both Nanny and Katie what had occurred at The Elms that morning.

"Well, I never," Nanny murmured when we'd finished. She fingered the lace antimacassars draping each arm of the chair she sat in and shook her head. "An entire staff."

"I'll admit I don't know what I'd have done in Ines's place." Katie absently played with one of those fiery springs framing her face and went on in her light brogue, "When I first came here from Ireland, it was the same for me as for her. In a strange country with no one to help me. No family. Not even a friend, not at first. I'd have been afraid to make any sort of trouble, never mind strike." She gazed over at me, the fondness in her sky-blue eyes plain to see. "Trouble found me anyway. If not for you, Miss Emma, I don't know where I'd be today."

Our gazes connected a long moment, hers brimming with gratitude, my own conveying, I hoped, that I felt as lucky as she that our paths had converged.

Nanny slapped her knees and struggled to lift herself out of the tufted parlor chair. Derrick came to her rescue with a supporting hand. "Thank you, love. Come, Katie, let's get dinner ready to serve."

I stood too. "I'll help."

"As will I." At a look from Nanny, Derrick chuckled. "Don't you dare tell me no, Mrs. O'Neal. If I'm to survive in a houseful of women, I must learn to pull my own weight."

"All I'll tell you, then, is that it's high time you started calling me Nanny." She pivoted with the grace of a much younger woman and disappeared into the hallway, leaving us to follow.

I left the Berwinds' invitation on the sofa table. As I had said, they would have to call off the evening; I felt no obligation to reply.

Except that, as I learned two days later, they did not call off their musicale. A footman turned up at Gull Manor to inquire if Mr. and Mrs. Andrews would attend.

"Stop fussing. You look beautiful." Derrick held the reins in one hand and put his free hand over my own to stop me from fidgeting. "And if you'll pardon me for saying so, you know it too. Nanny certainly did when she put the final touches on your hair."

"Nanny is as talented as the grandest lady's maid from New York, London, or Paris," I agreed. I also acknowledged how handsome he looked in his evening attire, cape, and top hat. "That's not what's got me jumpy. Do you think the Berwinds will realize I was at The Elms the day of the strike?"

"I don't see how. You said they never came downstairs. And the only person working there now who saw you is Ines, and I don't think she'll be exposing your secret."

"Still, they could have read the story. They'll know that Emma Cross and Emma Andrews are the same person."

As we proceeded down Bellevue Avenue, we exchanged waves of greeting with the passengers of passing carriages. All were on their way to various functions, from the opera to a ball at the Casino, to soirees at the various summer cottages. The Elms loomed ahead to our left. Derrick turned to me, his face in shadow but his dark eyes gleaming with moonlight. "If they took issue with your article, they wouldn't have sent their footman to inquire if we were coming tonight."

"Hmm . . . ." I wasn't so certain. Perhaps they wanted me at their musicale expressly to put me in my place in front of their guests. A public shaming.

"And it's not as if you editorialized," he went on. "You wrote the facts, plain and simple. If anything, Edward Berwind is proud of his actions in dismissing his striking servants."

"None of their futures is certain now." I sighed. "Some may end up on the street. How can anyone be proud of that?"

"My love, you surely don't need me to explain the ruthless nature of the average American industrialist."

"That's true." I adjusted the hood of my cloak carefully around my curls to ensure they arrived at The Elms intact. Derrick steered the carriage onto the driveway that swung around to run parallel to the façade. There were several carriages ahead of us, but disembarking went quickly at the house's triple front doors.

In the marble-tiled foyer, a footman took our cloaks, along with Derrick's top hat. A few steps, wide and set between two giant bronze urns, brought us up to the long gallery that ran the length of the house. There, a double-sided staircase on either side of the entry hall swept away to the second floor. Electric lights shined from above and along the walls in elaborate bronze and crystal sconces, lighting the way directly ahead of us into the ballroom. Guests mingled up and down the gallery and in the public rooms of the first floor. I spotted several familiar faces, including my cousin, Gertrude, and her husband, Harry Whitney.

Though less ornate than The Breakers, where the Vanderbilt family spent their summers, this ballroom boasted intricate plaster carvings that framed the doors, arched windows,
and gilded sconces, and climbed across the ceiling, where a
medallion circled the immense crystal chandelier. Though
normally empty of all but a few pieces of furniture, the room
held rows of chairs, all facing the musical instruments that
waited before the French doors overlooking the garden.

"Mr. and Mrs. Derrick Andrews," the new butler announced as we entered the room. He surprised me, as we
hadn't given our names. Were we as famous as all that?

Mr. Berwind, a distinguished middle-aged gentleman with
a drooping mustache and abundant hair threaded with silver,
shook Derrick's hand and raised mine to his lips. "Fine article, Mrs. Andrews. Fine. But you should have let us know
you were here that day."

"Oh, I . . ."

"Indeed, Mrs. Andrews." His wife reached to shake my
hand as well. At face value, Herminie Berwind, Minnie to
her friends, presented an unremarkable aspect. Her features
were not beautiful and she wore her hair in an unadorned
coiffure. But this simplicity was adequately balanced by her
gown of elegant lace, the sleeves dripping with loops of
pearls and the bodice pinned with jewels. "We feel terribly
that we didn't invite you upstairs for some refreshment."

I held my features firm to prevent revealing my thoughts
about taking refreshment while others were cast out of their
positions. "I came in a professional capacity, with a job to
do, you understand. I wouldn't have dreamed of imposing
on you."

"A shame. Still, I thought your interpretation of the subject spot on." His evening coat unbuttoned, Mr. Berwind
hooked his thumbs in his vest pockets and leaned back
slightly as he surveyed me. The gesture revealed something
rather telling about him. Edward Berwind didn't hail from a

monied family. No, he was a self-made man, he and his brother forging their own way in the coal business, and he made no apologies for it. He reminded me of J. P. Morgan, another hard-hitting businessman with little inclination toward compromise. But where John Pierpont Morgan tended toward bluster, Edward Berwind delivered his unwavering pronouncements with deliberate composure. "Straightforward and unsentimental. The cold, hard facts. Not like that wretched Brown fellow at the *Advocate*. What a lot of rot *he* publishes."

"Told you," Derrick murmured in my ear.

Yes, he had, yet I found the Berwinds' complacency hard to fathom. "Then you don't mind the *Messenger* running the story?"

"Good heavens, no," the man said with a sharp laugh. "Let it be a lesson to all of them. Haggle with Edward Berwind, and you'll find yourself out on your ear. I never bargain with my employees, Mrs. Andrews. *Never.* If they don't like my terms, they can work elsewhere."

Did he believe that declaration earned him my admiration?

"It *is* as simple as that," Mrs. Berwind concurred. She wasn't from money either, but her father had been a diplomat stationed in Italy, where she had learned self-confidence and the intricacies of maneuvering through society. "Although, to avoid future inconveniences, we've decided to allow our new staff some free time each day along with the occasional day off." She raised her eyebrows. "Such an unpleasant business that was, all around. We've no desire to repeat it. But thank goodness the new staff consists of some highly competent individuals who were able to accommodate us for tonight. We'd have loathed canceling. Why, we've even hired on a new chef. A Monsieur Pelletier. He came very highly recommended by Delmonico's in the city."

Her disclosure left me stunned and speechless, so much so

I barely heard the rest of what she said. To dismiss an entire group of people whose demands the Berwinds had refused to meet, only to hire new servants and bestow the benefits of those same demands before they'd even asked for them? And to do so without an inkling of the unfairness of it? I let Derrick do the talking for the next few moments, while I pretended to smile and bit back everything I'd like to have said. My cheeks began to ache. . . .

My mind returned to Ines and how she might be faring among the new staff. Had she received any further threats from the parlor maid, Bridget? Would Orville Brown continue to berate her in his articles? I wished I might catch a glimpse of her tonight, perhaps approach her to see how she was getting along, but I knew that to be an impossibility. She would not be anywhere near this part of the house, nor could I devise any excuse to search for her through the servants' quarters.

Finally, the Berwinds moved on to other guests, and Derrick and I drifted back into the gallery, where we chatted with acquaintances and partook of champagne and hors d'oeuvres. When a gong sounded, we filed back into the ballroom to take our seats alongside Gertrude and Harry.

"Don't you look splendid tonight, Emmaline," my cousin said with enthusiasm. For once, I didn't wear one of Gertrude's cast-off gowns. For years she had supplied me with finery she had worn once or twice, which Nanny had pared down to fit my shorter, slimmer figure. I had appreciated every one of Gertrude's gestures, and sometimes sold them after wearing them to enable me to make extra donations to St. Nicholas Orphanage in Providence. The dress I wore tonight, a Jeanne Paquin design, was of cream silk embellished with beaded roses, with short sleeves and a wide, square neckline. I had chosen it not only for its artistic simplicity but also because it had been designed by a woman.

I thanked Gertrude, confirmed her guess that it was, indeed, a Paquin gown, and we settled in to listen to the entertainment. Situated in front of the three sets of garden-facing doors, the chamber ensemble consisted of a first and second violinist, a violist, a cellist, and a harpist, the latter being a woman. Though a small group, their music filled the room and resonated off the walls and ceiling, lulling me into forgetting everything but the lovely melodies. Sometime during the performance, my hand found its way into Derrick's and stayed there, warm and contented. Gertrude noticed, for she leaned toward me with a feline smile and murmured something about newlyweds in my ear. I paid her little mind and didn't care if anyone else noticed.

The music went on for about forty-five minutes. Bach, Vivaldi, Mendelssohn, Mozart. Then Mrs. Berwind announced there would be a short intermission during which the guests could stretch their legs and enjoy some refreshment. Little did we know the musical portion of the evening had ended for good.

Chapter 3

The guests drifted onto the terrace through the French doors. Derrick and I followed. It was a clear night, the sky inky black and full of stars, and from the distance came the echoes of the fog horns and buoy bells in the harbor. The rear lawn tumbled away to a sunken, French-inspired garden, where electric lights strung from the trees silhouetted statues, urns, and two matching follies whose white stone walls rose like ghosts amid their surroundings. Halfway between the garden and the house, a European beech draped its branches over the grass, their slight undulations in the breeze reminding me of the swaying skirts of a dancer.

Although some of the guests paired off or went in small groups down the steps to the graveled walkways and the lawn, many remained on the terrace. After accepting glasses of champagne from a passing footman, Derrick and I stood at the stone balustrade in a circle of acquaintances that included Gertrude and Harry; Alfred Vanderbilt and his new wife, Elsie; and another newly married couple, Harry and Elizabeth Lehr.

"I find the musicians extraordinarily talented," Elizabeth Lehr was saying in response to Alfred's inquiry about how we were enjoying the evening. She spoke in a cultured murmur, her gaze soft and her expression serene. Gertrude and I agreed with her. The others nodded without comment. "This evening is a rare pleasure."

"I understand they're from London," I said as I admired not only Mrs. Lehr's Worth evening gown, but her astonishing beauty.

"It was brilliant of Silvie Morton to sponsor their way to America," she replied to my comment. I recognized the Philadelphia intonations in her speech, tinged with an almost European lilt. "Where is Silvie, by the way? Or Rex, for that matter." She glanced about her but, apparently not spotting her friends, she returned to the topic at hand. "Newport is only a beginning for these musicians. I understand they have their sights on New York. They hope to play at Madison Square Garden and the Academy of Music. I do feel they're a bit small, however, for the new Metropolitan Opera House. Wouldn't you agree, Gertrude?"

"I can't help but wonder if the Academy of Music will allow them to perform there," Gertrude replied. "They're so terribly exclusive." The merest hint of bitterness edged her voice. Her family, and others considered new money, had been denied the privilege of purchasing boxes at the Academy of Music Theater. This had been what inspired the building of the Metropolitan Opera House, a project my aunt Alva Belmont had been heavily involved in. She had even had a hand in the architectural design.

"How did you find Italy, Mrs. Andrews?" Mrs. Lehr asked me now, and we spent several minutes comparing our impressions of the Tuscan weather and the virtues of the Italian countryside versus the cultural amenities found in cities like Florence or Rome. From the corner of my eye I saw Gertrude stifle a yawn. She and I had previously discussed our experiences in that country, and now, after she exchanged a brief word with her husband, they drifted away.

"I particularly enjoyed the tranquility of the wine country," Mrs. Lehr said with a wistful gaze onto the shadowed expanse of the lawn. "It was so delightful to be away from the bustle of New York and even here. I never wanted to leave. . . ." A slight frown marred her high forehead. She turned her aristocratic profile toward the south wing of the house. I suddenly noticed what had caught her attention as raised voices poured over the south perimeter wall.

"What is that . . . ?" Derrick craned his neck as he peered to the south end of the walkways below the terrace. There was nothing unusual there to see; only the marble statue of three cherubs and, on a level below it, a bronze tigress fighting a crocodile.

Harsh voices continued to echo beneath the trees somewhere beyond the south boundary of the property. That we could hear them over the high garden wall said something about their volume.

"Except for coal, deliveries are made on the other side of the house," Derrick mused aloud. "And I don't think coal would be delivered this time of night. What could be the matter?"

"I think we should have a look." I started for the terrace steps, but Derrick stopped me by catching my hand.

"Wait. Look there." He pointed into the ballroom, where Mr. and Mrs. Berwind stood talking with their new butler. The brightness of the electric lights revealed the alarm in their expressions, the knotting of their eyebrows. Then a scream spilled through the open doors, rendering the guests outside immobile.

My gaze locked with Derrick's. "That was Mrs. Berwind."

"Perhaps one of their workers was injured."

Perhaps, but why would that make the woman scream? I raised my hems off the ground. "Let's see what happened."

Gertrude blocked our path to the nearest door. "What's going on? Was that a scream? Was it Minnie?"

I nodded to her. "It was. We're going in to find out why."

I expected her to follow, but instead she stood rooted to the spot, her husband's arm wrapped protectively around her waist. As we entered the ballroom, the lights temporarily put dancing spots before my eyes. I blinked them away. Mrs. Berwind sat in one of the chairs facing the instruments, as if she alone waited for the continuation of the evening's music. A maid I didn't recognize crouched in front of her, offering her a snifter of brandy.

Mr. Berwind continued to talk in rapid whispers with his butler while a footman who had been standing with them suddenly scampered from the room. Voices rose in volume as curiosity drove the other guests inside. Mamie Fish came storming into the ballroom as though leading a charge.

"Ned, what the blazes is going on in here?" The dyed feather in her jeweled hair band bobbed erratically. "And what's gotten into Minnie?"

Mr. Berwind shut his eyes and squeezed the bridge of his nose. Then he signaled for Mrs. Fish to come closer. When she did, he aimed a frantic whisper at her. Derrick and I hadn't been noticed yet. I stole closer.

"Mamie, can Minnie and I depend on you to keep the others calm?"

"Calm? Is there a reason we should not be calm, Ned?" Mrs. Fish pulled back and studied Mr. Berwind from head to toe. With a gesture over her shoulder, she called her husband's name. "Stuyvie, get over here. There's trouble afoot."

While Edward Berwind hastily shushed her, Stuyvesant Fish strode to his wife's side. He might be the president of the Illinois Central Railroad and a powerful businessman, but when it came to his wife, he followed her lead no matter the circumstances. "What is it, Mamie, darling? What's happened?"

"That's what we're about to find out. Ned, if you want us to intervene for you, you'll have to tell us why." Mrs. Fish folded her arms and spoke with her usual doggedness, indicating she wouldn't budge another inch until she had her answers.

I waited breathlessly while Mr. Berwind thought it over, which took all of a few seconds. He leaned closer to the pair. "There's been a death. Out by the coal tunnel. Apparently the doors to the bulkhead were left open. Someone fell through."

"Fell, or was pushed?" Mrs. Fish's expression quickly went from shocked to resigned. She had been through a similar ordeal before, at her very own home, Crossways, the night of her Harvest Festival two years earlier. Somehow, her gaze found me and adhered. She beckoned me closer.

"I suppose you heard that?"

There was no use denying it. "I did."

"*We* did," Derrick corrected me. He, too, had been through similar ordeals over the years, due to his association with me, I'm afraid.

"What is it about you, Miss Cross? Er, Mrs. Andrews, I mean." Mamie's sharp-eyed scrutiny held me for several seconds while she apparently reached a conclusion. "Well, I suppose it's not your fault, but it sure is a highly odd coincidence you always seem to be on hand when something like this happens."

I couldn't disagree with her, but apparently Derrick felt differently. "All Mr. Berwind said is there's been a death. There's no reason at this point to suspect foul play. It sounds like the bulkhead was accidently left open from this morning's delivery. Unfortunate, but not sinister."

We all nodded, yet I didn't believe any of us was convinced. Not even Derrick. "We'll know soon enough," I said, and discreetly tugged on Derrick's sleeve.

"The police have been sent for," Mr. Berwind told us. He raised a hand as if to plow it through his pomaded hair, but let it drop to his side. "I can't see why they would wish to speak to any of the guests, but perhaps no one should leave until the police give their permission. A formality, I'm sure."

"Sounds about right." Mamie Fish patted the dark curls at the side of her head. "You might want to order some food brought up to the dining room, Ned. Substantial food, not more of those flimsy hors d'oeuvres. And more champagne. And something stronger, perhaps."

"Are you sure that's a good idea, my dear?" Mr. Fish frowned in concern. "People might become inebriated and lose their heads over this."

"Stuyvie, the best way to *prevent* them from losing their heads is to get them tipsy and keep them well fed."

Derrick and I left them to debate the merits of champagne versus whiskey. Before we left the room, I approached Mrs. Berwind's chair. The maid pushed to her feet and moved aside, and I crouched in her place. "Are you all right, ma'am? Can I do anything for you?"

Clutching the brandy snifter in one hand, she gripped my forearm with the other. Her manicured nails dug into my flesh, but I didn't react. "Find out what happened, Mrs. Andrews. I know you can. And then come back and tell me. You see, I fear my husband will try to protect me. . . ."

"I understand." I rose, tugging at my hem when it caught under the heel of my satin shoe. "I'll be back."

Derrick and I exited from the front of the house and strode to the corner of Dixon Street. The voices were quieter now, but a knot of workers, male and female, stood grouped in a tight circle beside the property wall. At the sound of our footsteps, their circle widened and they turned toward us.

"Where exactly was the body found?" Derrick asked them without preamble. For a long stretch no one said anything. I waited for Derrick to assume his authoritative voice, the one he used when he wanted answers or something done. But he didn't; he merely waited.

One of the men, dressed in the coarse clothing of a laborer, stepped forward. He spoke with a light brogue. "You're not a copper." He looked me up and down. "And the lady here . . ."

"The police are on their way," Derrick informed him. "Where is the body?"

He pointed behind him. "In the coal tunnel." He wiped his soot-stained hands on his trousers. "It's a lass."

The gathering shifted to reveal the iron bulkhead that should have been shut tight this time of night. The doors stood gaping, the blackness of the tunnel darker than the night sky. A shiver ran up my spine. "Who is she?"

"The one that stayed on," replied a woman in a kitchen maid's white cap and apron. She had come around the corner unnoticed and stopped several feet away. "The girl from Portugal."

Ines. An ache began in my heart; it spread and spread.

Derrick's hand found mine and curled tightly around it. One of the servants held a lantern above the opening to the tunnel, and we leaned to peer inside. The faint illumination gilded the walls around a cart directly below us. As I stared in, I began to make out the twisted shape of a figure at the bottom of the conveyance.

"How did you find her?"

"We're expecting a delivery tomorrow morning," said the worker, who apparently decided to do the talking for the rest. "A little while ago I went into the tunnel to make sure the cart was in place. It was. But it wasn't empty like it should've been. Then I noticed the bulkhead hadn't been properly closed, much less locked."

"Let's go inside." Derrick gave my hand a little tug and we retraced our steps. Once inside, we hurried down the long gallery to the servants' corridor and took the stairs down to the basement. A footman met us at the landing.

"Excuse me, sir, ma'am, but you shouldn't be down here." While the inappropriateness of guests descending to the kitchen area needed no clarifying, he felt obliged to add, "There's been some trouble."

"We know. That's why we're here," I replied, and hoped we didn't need to explain ourselves. Would this new footman be familiar with us and know we owned the *Messenger*? To ensure we weren't summarily escorted out, I clarified, "Mrs. Berwind wishes to know exactly what happened, and she sent us down to find out."

The footman shuffled in his uncertainty, prompting Derrick to square his shoulders and assume his full height. "Which way to the furnaces?"

The young man gestured for us to precede him through the cold-preparation kitchen. "In the subbasement, sir. But I don't think—"

"It's all right, we assume full responsibility," I assured him.

He took us through a wide corridor and through a second door. This brought us into the vast laundry room with its many washbasins lining the walls, clothing racks, ironing boards, and everything else needed to keep the Berwinds' wardrobes in fine form. At the far end, a rumbling sound penetrated a third door, the sound increasing when he opened it and led us down a narrow set of metal steps. Waves of heat rose to envelop me, making breathing difficult.

We were now in the deepest bowels of The Elms, vault-like—no, crypt-like—in structure. The room at the bottom of the steps housed a wall of cupboards and drawers, along with two tall, cylindrical pieces of machinery such as I had never seen before. I hadn't long to wonder what they were as we quickly proceeded through a vaulted doorway into a large, rectangular space, coal piled high at the far end.

Coal carts lined the wall to our left. To our right were three more vaulted doorways, smaller than the first, and here the rumblings, the roar of flames, and choking heat threatened my very consciousness. It felt akin to walking into purgatory—or worse. I couldn't imagine spending more than a few minutes here, yet I knew the workers' shifts lasted a full eight hours. Streaked with sweat and coal dust, they scurried back and forth between the stored coal and the furnaces, incessantly shoveling in fuel to keep the flames licking high beneath the boilers that fed the electrical generators.

My ankle turned as I ventured a step, and I looked down to discover rail tracks that spanned the length of the space, along with a turntable that allowed the full carts to easily change direction. Those tracks disappeared into the gloom of the tunnel, a square opening at this end whose double wooden doors stood open.

"She was found in there," the footman told us. "All the way in, beneath the bulkhead on Dixon."

"Has anyone discovered why the bulkhead hadn't been locked?" Derrick asked him.

"No, sir. It's a mystery, that's for certain. Could be someone unlocked it in preparation of tomorrow's delivery, but no one's owning up to it."

I walked to the mouth of the tunnel. "May we?"

"You want to go in?" His eyes opened wide in disbelief. "But those clothes. Surely you don't want to ruin them."

"We'll take our chances." Although the bricked, vaulted expanse more than accommodated my height, I ducked and took a tentative step through the opening, as if testing the integrity of the stone flooring. Derrick followed me, and we proceeded, single file, guided by dull orange spots of electric lighting. I was reminded of the chilly, dank tunnels that ran beneath Fort Adams at the mouth of Newport Harbor. My stomach clenched at the memory of being lost in one of them. Thank goodness we hadn't long to go, a few dozen yards, yet it seemed like forever.

A coal cart sat at the very end, beneath the bulkhead. My feet dragged once it came into sight, my steps continuing to slow the closer I got. Finally, Derrick's hand closed over my shoulder, bringing me to a halt, and he eased in front of me. We continued until the cart sat directly in front of us. Derrick gripped the edge and peered inside. After drawing in a slow, deep breath, I did likewise.

"Oh, Ines," I whispered upon seeing the heap of maid's uniform and the dark, lustrous hair that had come loose from its pins. That was what she had been reduced to: a heap, crammed into the cart like so much refuse. Then, small, pale hands took shape in my vision, and finally her lovely face, half covered by her streaming hair. I couldn't help reaching in, stretched to my very limit, to sweep some of that hair out of the way. I knew I shouldn't touch her before the police came, but the cruelty of her death rendered me unable to resist that small act of compassion, that small effort to comfort someone beyond comforting.

My action uncovered her neck, revealing bruises at her throat.

The ache in my heart rose to grip my throat and burn my eyes. "Why didn't she come with me to Gull Manor? Why didn't I insist? Why did I leave her here?"

"Emma, don't do that. It's not your fault." Derrick turned me to him and grasped my upper arms. "It was her choice. You offered Gull Manor, but she chose to stay here."

"I know, but—"

He shook his head. "No. You did all you could short of tying her up and carrying her to Gull Manor yourself."

"I should have."

I inhaled the sobs that pushed against my throat. Now was not the time for them. Yes, perhaps I could have done more for this young woman, could have prevented this— somehow—but what had happened to her couldn't be undone. I could only discover what, exactly, *had* happened. All I knew for certain was that the time to suspect foul play had come.

"Please tell me neither of you touched the body." Jesse Whyte, police detective and a longtime friend of my family, scowled at Derrick and me with the full force of his constabulary authority. Yet I knew that he was only following protocol, and that his irritation with us was professional and not personal.

"Of course we didn't touch anything," Derrick snapped when I hesitated. "Give us some credit."

I bit my lip at the lie. From the tunnel came the squeaking of the cart's wheels as two workers pushed it along the tracks toward the coal room. I tried unsuccessfully to block out that forlorn sound.

"Don't act as though it shouldn't even be in question," Jesse scolded. "I know you both. When you believe you're justified, you'll take any liberty that comes into your heads."

"That's not fair," Derrick started to say, but he was interrupted by Jesse's partner, Detective Gifford Myers, a man younger than Jesse with less experience but far more swagger.

"Then what are the pair of you doing down here? Why didn't you wait upstairs with the rest of your sort?" He said "your sort" as though it were an insult, something to be ashamed of.

"I knew her," I told them, raising my chin in indignation. "I met her the day I came to cover the strike. I've been worried about her ever since. Rightly so, it seems."

"You knew it was her in that cart before you saw her?" Detective Myers challenged.

"Yes, as a matter of fact."

"How?"

"One of the house staff told us. Out by the bulkhead."

"Ah." He showed me a triumphant smile. "You were already interfering by that point."

Derrick bristled. "We came because we were concerned—"

"You came," Detective Myers said with stiff-lipped irritation, "because you're a pair of busybody reporters who can't keep their noses out of police business. Whyte and I ought to take you in. A night in a cell would keep you well out of our way. In fact, since you're married now, we'd only need to tie up one cell."

"That's enough, Myers. We're not taking them in." Jesse exhaled audibly and turned to Derrick and me. "Look, if you say you didn't touch anything, I believe you. Let us do our jobs, and then you can tell me everything you learned the day of the strike and anything since."

Chapter 4

Derrick and I did as we were told, though it cost me an effort to leave the subbasement without an argument. Upstairs, we joined Mr. and Mrs. Berwind in the Chinese breakfast room, so named for its black-and-gold lacquered wall panels depicting traditional Chinese gardens and architecture. Another couple and a woman sat at the square table with them, while a dark-haired gentleman meandered about the room, shifting curtains to gaze outside, running his fingertips along the tops of the furniture. They had been served tea, but I noticed brandy snifters and cordial glasses on the table as well. Fatigue dragged at the faces around the table. They greeted us with quizzical looks.

"Detective Whyte will be up as soon as he and his partner complete their examination of the . . ." Derrick paused, his gaze lighting on each of the three ladies. "The scene."

"What happened down there?" one of them asked in a tight voice. "The police haven't told us anything." She looked to be in her thirties. Though pretty, her features were fleshy, her figure plump, and she wore her light brown hair in a loose topknot with tendrils curling about her cheeks. "Was it very horrible? I understand someone . . . died."

I felt Mrs. Berwind's probing gaze burning into me. I hadn't forgotten my promise to inform her of any details I could find. "Yes, a young maid. A girl from Portugal who refused to strike. Her name was Ines."

Herminie Berwind met my eye and gave a nod. A third woman peered at us, her face blanched, a corner of her lip raw where she had obviously chewed it. With wheat blond hair and a pale complexion, she looked as if she might disappear into thin air with nothing left but a wisp of vapor. She ran her fingertips along a fringe of bangs that had recently seen a too-hot crimping iron. "How did she die?"

"Before we get to that," Mrs. Berwind intervened, "let me introduce everyone." She gestured to the plump woman and the dark-haired man who had drifted across the room to stand behind her chair. "Derrick and Emmaline Andrews, this is Rex and Silvie Morton."

"Oh, yes. I'm sorry we hadn't had a chance to meet earlier," I said, and extended my hand to Mrs. Morton. We briefly shook, her grip tenuous and half-hearted. "I understand that you arranged tonight's entertainment, Mrs. Morton, that you sponsored the musicians all the way from London."

While Mrs. Morton nodded and smiled faintly, her husband winced at my comment, his nearly black eyes narrowing as he gazed speculatively down at me, his mouth pulling to a smirk. Rex Morton looked to be of similar age to his wife, robust for a man in his thirties, though without the sportsman's build of so many gentlemen of the Four Hundred. He was too slender to be called athletic, his figure almost reedy. With his black hair slicked straight back from a high forehead and his mustache trimmed to a thread above his lip, he appeared snakelike to me. I won't say I took an instant dislike to him, but something in his bearing made me sorry for his wife.

"And this is Charles and Kay Gilchrist." Mrs. Berwind gestured at the other couple at the table.

"Pleased to meet you all," Derrick and I said as one.

The Gilchrists were a mismatched pair, or should have been, but of course disparity in ages was nothing unusual among the Four Hundred. Kay Gilchrist could be no more than twenty-two or so—younger, even, than I. On the other hand, Charles Gilchrist looked older than Edward Berwind. Nonetheless, I detected the sportsman in him, for although his wizened features and graying hair revealed his age, his physique retained the proportions of a man who enjoyed rigorous physical activity.

I admit I found this group an odd assortment and wondered why they, in particular, had been invited to stay at The Elms. As for the rest of the guests, they had apparently been allowed to go home, as the rooms farther along the first floor were silent.

The footman on duty brought two more chairs to the table. After Derrick and I had taken our seats, the conversation dwindled from little to nothing. I had never answered Mrs. Gilchrist about how Ines had died, and she didn't ask me again. Nor did anyone else. It seemed all were content to await the official word from Jesse and Gifford Myers. I asked the Mortons and Gilchrists how long they would be in Newport but was met with ambiguous replies. It came as a relief, then, when Jesse walked in from the adjoining dining room.

"Mr. and Mrs. Berwind, I'm sorry to tell you your chambermaid, Ines Varella, is dead."

Mr. Berwind surged to his feet and held up a hand to silence Jesse. The action startled me. After all, I had already told them who had died. It was to his wife he spoke. "My dear, why don't you and the ladies go into the drawing room. Such unpleasantness is not for your ears."

"No, Ned, I wish to hear." Mrs. Berwind spoke softly, but with determination. Her husband's expression turned stony; hers became equally so. A standoff.

"Mr. Berwind," I said quickly, "whatever happened below, the news of it shall soon be all over town, and everyone will know. Including your wife."

He turned an accusatory glance at me, as if to blame me for all journalism. Then he relented and nodded. "True, very true. All right, Minnie, stay if you will. You ladies, too, if that is what you wish."

Mrs. Morton nodded vigorously. Kay Gilchrist hesitated before giving a single, tentative nod.

"Go ahead, Detective, tell us." Mr. Berwind pinched his lips together.

Jesse continued in a quiet voice, as if to soften the impact of his report. "Her body was discovered in a coal cart below the bulkhead of the tunnel on Dixon Street. It appears she's been strangled."

"Good gracious, how violent." Mrs. Berwind's hand went to her throat. Her husband raised an *I-told-you* eyebrow at her but she ignored it. "Do you know this for certain? It couldn't have been an accident?"

Jesse shook his head. "There are bruises on her neck, and the bulkhead appears to have been forced open. The coroner will perform a thorough examination in the morning, but his conclusions so far point to strangulation. By the looks of it, the perpetrator wore gloves."

"How do you know that?" Rex Morton looked skeptical.

"The killer's fingers left marks, but they're indistinct, almost blurred. That indicates gloves were worn."

"My coal workers wear gloves," Mr. Berwind murmured, as though thinking aloud.

"So do the gardeners," his wife put in.

"Yes, but generally speaking," he replied, "my gardeners do not have anything to do with the coal tunnel."

"Footmen wear gloves as well. And we're talking about a maid here." Charles Gilchrist reached for his brandy snifter.

Mr. Berwind angled his head. "What are you getting at, Charles?"

"I'm only suggesting that you cannot rule out your coalmen or anyone else who works on the estate." His gaze shifted to the footman standing at attention beside the doorway into the upper pantry. The young man fisted his white-gloved hands as if to hide them. "Why, that fellow there is wearing gloves."

So were many of the gentlemen guests, I thought. Derrick himself had worn driving gloves on the way here earlier.

"Oh, but we *can* rule out all the house staff who were working tonight." Mrs. Berwind looked suddenly optimistic, as though she had solved a difficult puzzle. "There was so much to do for the musicale, none of the kitchen staff or the footmen could have slipped away. So, you see, none of them could have done it. But my question, more than who did it, is why? Why strangle a chambermaid? Especially that one. She was a quiet girl. Did her work quickly and efficiently. No trouble atall, according to the new housekeeper."

No trouble. The memory of Ines telling me she didn't want any trouble sent a shiver across my shoulders. She had refused to strike and had stayed on despite overt threats from the parlor maid, Bridget Whalen, and the more subtle threats made by Orville Brown in the *Aquidneck Island Advocate*. She hadn't wanted trouble. Now she lay strangled.

Mr. Berwind scowled. "Perhaps the detective will enlighten us as to who would want to disturb the peace in our home in such a brutal manner."

"We don't yet know, I'm afraid, sir."

"I thought not." Mr. Berwind sighed heavily, as if to show his vast disappointment in Jesse and the rest of the police force. A man obviously used to immediate results.

"The men working in or near the furnaces have been questioned, and no one has admitted to seeing or hearing anything unusual," Jesse said.

"Of course not," Mr. Berwind snapped in return. "Why would they? She was found near the street."

Jesse let the silence stretch as his gaze traveled from the Berwinds to me and back again. "She was a chambermaid. Why would she have been on Dixon Street at all at that time of night? Why not in her room? Or in town, enjoying an evening with friends?"

"She had no friends," I murmured. I hadn't meant to be heard, but when the others stared at me, waiting, I elaborated: "She told me she had no friends or family here in America. She was all on her own, which is why she didn't wish to join the strike. She didn't want to risk losing her position here."

"A smart girl," Charles Gilchrist observed.

Was she? I kept this thought to myself.

"Either way," Jesse said, "it doesn't explain why she ended up in the coal tunnel. Could she have gone to that vicinity to meet someone?"

"Meet . . . whom?" Mrs. Berwind held up her hands.

"A beau, perhaps," Silvie Morton suggested.

I didn't think so. Ines had seemed so alone to me, so very solitary and vulnerable. I couldn't envision her sneaking out into the night for an assignation, especially so close to the house, for that could have gotten her dismissed as surely as if she'd joined the strike.

"That's probably it," her husband, Rex, agreed. The black thread of his mustache contorted along with his upper lip as he skewed his mouth to one side. "Got herself in trouble with a man, made demands, and was strangled for her pains."

"Rex." Silvie Morton looked mortified. "You mustn't say things like that. It's wrong to speak ill of the dead."

"She was just a chambermaid, my dear."

"Quite right." Charles Gilchrist reached for the decanter at the center of the table and poured more brandy into his snifter. "It's unfortunate, but it's my experience that people like those make their own beds. There's no reason for us to mourn over the fact that they must then lie in them. Literally."

"Charles, how unkind of you." Mrs. Gilchrist appeared close to tears. She had begun worrying her lip again, so much that I feared she'd draw blood.

And I . . .

I wished to shake these men, slap sense into them. Ines had been a sweet, frightened girl attempting to do the right thing, to work hard and get by and perhaps, little by little, better her life. She'd never have the chance now. I didn't know how she ended up in that tunnel, what had lured her into that part of the property, but she certainly didn't deserve to be judged based on nothing but the conjectures of men who felt no sympathy for those below their own class.

"Excuse me." My thoughts broke off. Gifford Myers stood silhouetted in the dining room doorway, jotting something in his notebook. "There's been a new development, Whyte."

Jesse pivoted on his heel to face him. "What?"

"One of the menial laborers is missing. Came in earlier for his shift. The butler tells me he's the sort who does heavy lifting, carrying things in and out of the storerooms, helping the gardeners clear away the trimmings, that sort of thing. Anyway, he hasn't been seen for about an hour now, and no one saw him leave."

"Who is this individual?" Mr. Berwind demanded. "No one walks off the job here and gets away with it."

I shook my head at how beyond the point that observation was. Derrick caught my eye and held it, silently communicating a calming message.

Detective Myers consulted his notebook. "One Rudolfo Medeiros."

I had looked away from Derrick, but now we exchanged another glance. Was it only a coincidence that, like Ines, this man happened to be Portuguese? *Had* she been completely forthcoming when she'd said she had no one in this country?

"I've never heard of him," Mrs. Berwind said, interrupting my thoughts.

"No, but you wouldn't have, my dear." Her husband spared her a tender look. "It's for the butler to hire the menial workers. There's no reason for us to have encountered him."

"Is he new here?" I asked. "Was he a recent replacement for someone else?"

Mr. Berwind considered. "I don't believe we had to let go either of our men-of-all-work. They're not strictly house servants, you see, not considered part of the domestic staff. The kind of work they do hardly brings them into the house, and never beyond the basement."

Detective Myers closed his notebook. "According to the butler, he lives in a boardinghouse in town. On Holland Street just off Lower Thames."

"We'll send a uniformed pair there to look for him," said Jesse. "We'll also need to spread the word along the wharves and the train depot to be on the lookout for this man. Hopefully, it's not too late. Did we get a description?"

His partner met this question with a blank look. "He looks like any other foreign worker: muscular, dark, olive-skinned, not very clean."

I surged to my feet, words of rebuke ready to tumble from my lips. I swallowed them down. Justice for Ines required so much more than mere words and a display of temper.

Before Jesse left the breakfast room, he secured the Berwinds' permission to search through Ines's room. He asked me to join him and explained to the others, "Mrs. Andrews has excellent powers of observation, and this being a woman's room . . ."

Mr. Berwind waved his reasoning away. "Perfectly understandable, Detective. Mrs. Andrews, is this an imposition for you?"

I took an eager step toward Jesse. "Not at all."

Derrick and I shared a nod before Jesse and I left. We went through the butler's upper pantry onto a tiled landing and took the service staircase all the way up to the third floor. The housekeeper met us there and showed us down the hall to Ines's room. She eyed me curiously. Or, rather, she eyed my attire inquisitively, no doubt wondering why someone who was obviously one of the Berwinds' guests should accompany the police on such an errand.

"Did she share?" Jesse asked her.

The woman shook off her curiosity. "No, not presently. When the previous staff left, Ines's roommate at the time went with them. She's had this room to herself ever since, but soon more female staff will be hired, so that will change." She frowned. "No, I suppose in Ines's case, it won't matter, will it?" The woman compressed her lips.

"Did you get on well with her?" I asked.

"I didn't know her long, obviously, but she seemed a good worker."

That was what Mrs. Berwind had said. So impersonal. "Anything else? Was she pleasant? Did she help out even when it wasn't her task to do so?"

The woman considered a moment. "She kept rather to herself. I credited it to her being Portuguese, while most of the maids here are Irish. Although, her English was certainly good. I suppose she was shy, perhaps."

"Perhaps." I'd generally gotten the same impression. Shy and fearful of making a mistake.

"This is—was—her room." The housekeeper turned the key and opened the door.

Jesse observed, "The rooms are kept locked."

"Of course. Servants come and go. We can't require that they trust one another with their private belongings," the woman said severely, as though she were speaking to one of her underlings. In the next instant she seemed taken aback by her own tone. She cleared her throat and said, "Well then, I'll—uh—leave you to it."

Jesse thanked her and he and I entered the room. Our search didn't take long.

"There's nothing here," I pointed out after only a couple of minutes.

Jesse opened each drawer of the tall bureau. "Not a thing," he confirmed, and shut the bottom drawer with a thud. His gaze traveled the room, devoid of belongings. "The closet's empty too. She'd left, Emma. There can be no mistake about it."

"I don't understand. She'd been so adamant about *not* losing her employment here." I thought about what the men downstairs had implied, that Ines had gotten into trouble with a man. I didn't wish to believe it. Besides, I'd learned from prior experience that men, whether police or otherwise, tended to jump to that conclusion with any mystery involving a young woman.

"There's the worker who has also disappeared," Jesse reminded me. "Perhaps . . ." Rather than speak the words, he merely raised his eyebrows and waited for me to agree.

I shook my head. "I don't know. . . . I hope he's found soon. That would answer so many questions."

"Yes, I think it might. Come. We won't find out anything else here. I'm going to start interviewing the staff. All of them, including the footmen and maids. They might not know who killed her or why, but perhaps they can shed some light on Miss Varella herself."

I nodded absently, then stated the obvious. "They hadn't known her long. Only a few days, really. It's the former staff you need to speak with." I preceded Jesse into the hallway.

"I understand some of them have already left Newport, but others must still be here," he said.

"I'm hoping one in particular can be found."

"Who is that?"

"The former head parlor maid. Her name is Bridget Whalen."

"I'm determined to find her and speak with her," I told Derrick the next morning. We had stayed the night at Gull Manor, and this morning a smiling Nanny had made us buttermilk griddle cakes with wild blackberries. We dug in with relish. Despite having grown up with French chefs and eating in the finest restaurants in this country and Europe, Derrick seemed to like nothing better than Nanny's simple New England cooking. He certainly made short work of this morning's breakfast.

I, on the other hand, ate more slowly, although with no less enjoyment. It was my contemplations that slowed me down, and the fact that I'd risen much earlier than necessary. With plenty of time yet before we were needed at the *Messenger*, we could enjoy the morning at a leisurely pace.

Still, I tried not to make eye contact too often with Nanny, as her knowing and gleeful looks left me uncomfortable. The awkwardness of being here with Derrick seemed as though it would never wear off. I didn't fully understand it, certainly didn't wish it to continue, but Gull Manor, after being *my* home for so long, simply didn't feel like *our* home. And I certainly didn't need Nanny—or Katie, for that matter—looking at us as though they knew what had transpired between us during the night.

In fact, we'd both slept soundly, despite the evening's upsets.

It hadn't been until about an hour before dawn that my speculations concerning Ines and her murder had driven me from between the bedcovers. As soon as I'd stirred, so too had Derrick. As quiet as I might be, he had an intuitive sense when it came to me. He seemed always to know whether I slept or not, or whether troubles unsettled my mind.

"I offered Bridget a place at Gull Manor the morning of the strike, just as I did with Ines. She turned me down rather vehemently, but she also disclosed, perhaps without quite meaning to, that she had family on the island. I'm guessing either Newport or Middletown. It shouldn't be too difficult to find where the Whalens live."

My prediction proved correct. It did take several hours, especially since the records on the former staff of The Elms had been disposed of after they were fired. I'd gotten the idea to search through our own records at the *Messenger* in hopes of finding a Whalen family among our subscribers. They were not on our list, but my next notion took me to the offices of my former place of employment, the *Newport Observer.* I didn't ask to see their subscription list, for I knew such a request would be denied, and for good reason. The owner, Mr. Milford, could have been held liable for giving out the personal information of a customer. However . . .

"Donald!" I cried out as I crossed Spring Street and hurried up the side street that ran alongside the *Observer*'s building several blocks north of the *Messenger*. I held my hat securely on my head and picked up the pace before the newsboy sped away on his bicycle. "Can I speak to you?"

The boy in question looked about him. Upon spotting me, he broke out in a grin. "Hiya, Miss Cross! What are you doing here? You coming back to work for Mr. Milford?"

I came to a halt, panting to catch my breath. "No, Donald, I'm afraid not. But I have a question for you. Would you happen to have a Whalen residence on your route?" I gestured to the basket of rolled newspapers hanging from his handlebars.

"Whalen . . . no, sorry."

My hope deflated. But at that same moment, the side door of the building opened and another newsboy stepped out, a leather bag slung crossways from his shoulder to hip.

"Hey, Tommy, you got a Whalen house on your route?" Donald blurted of his own accord.

Tommy adjusted the brim of his flat cap. "Sure do. Why?"

I took over before Donald could intercede again. "Can you tell me where they live, please?"

The boy frowned, bringing attention to a smudge above his eyes. "Why ya wanna know?"

I resisted the temptation to pull off a glove and wipe the dirt off his brow. "There's someone there I need to speak with. Someone who needs my help." I nearly cringed at the lie, although I told myself that I had been sincere in my offer of Gull Manor to Bridget, and that if she were in need of assistance now, I'd gladly render it if I could.

As long as she hadn't murdered Ines Varella.

As it turned out, I had to retrace my steps down Spring Street, and then keep going until I crossed Washington Square.

I kept walking north. According to Tommy, the Whalens lived just beyond the Common Burying Ground. I'd known that if the Whalens lived in proximity to Newport, even if they were a poor family, they would probably subscribe to one of the local newspapers, which meant one of the newsies would know of them. It was one luxury most Newporters availed themselves of so they could keep track of everyone in town.

Burnside Avenue lay opposite the southeast entrance to the cemetery. To call it an avenue was perhaps to assign it more than its due, as the street was so narrow it could not have accommodated two carriages passing each other in opposite directions. The houses stood close together, similar in style and size to the colonials where I had grown up on the Point, but showing sure signs of wear accompanied by a lack of means to remedy matters. I felt no disdain for the fact, for I had until recently been in similar circumstances, at times forced to choose between replenishing our larder or paying for necessary house repairs.

My heart sank when I came to the house Tommy had indicated. It was smaller than the others, a single main story with perhaps a room or two jammed beneath the eaves. The width facing the street allowed for only three narrow windows, with the entrance around the side. I went up the dirt walkway and knocked.

To my surprise, Bridget Whalen answered. She did not appear to recognize me, for she squinted against the sunlight and demanded in her brogue, "Aye? What would you be wanting?"

"Miss Whalen, I'm Emma Cross. We met a week ago at The Elms."

The door started to close.

"Wait." I shoved an arm out and gripped the latch. "Miss

MURDER AT THE ELMS   57

Whalen, please. I just want to ask you a couple of questions."

"Why? What could you possibly want with me?"

Her contempt for me was puzzling. "I fear we started off on the wrong foot, and I'm not sure why. I believed your cause was just, even if I wasn't certain a strike would achieve the results you desired."

"Well, it seems you were right on that count." She attempted to close the door again, but I thrust myself across the threshold.

"Please. Is there somewhere we can talk? Just for a few minutes." I stole a glance over her shoulder into the room, a parlor with scant furnishings but packed with boxes, sacks, and piles of clothing. I immediately had the impression of a large family crammed into too-small quarters. "Are you alone here? Perhaps we could walk."

"I'm alone. The rest of the family is at work, school, or my gran's. But you can't come in."

"Bridget, do you know Ines Varella is dead? Murdered last night during the Berwinds' musicale?"

Had I shocked her? She merely shrugged. "I heard. It's in the papers. Serves her right, doesn't it?" Her eyes narrowed on me. "Have you got it into your head I did it?"

"No," I quickly assured her. "But I am trying to find out who did. And I thought you—and some of the other former staff—might help me learn more about Ines."

"Why you?"

It was a fair question and one I'd been compelled to answer many times in the past. "I'm helping the police. And I'm doing it because I care. Ines had no one. Perhaps there's no one else in the entire world who cares that she's gone."

She exhaled a breath through her nose and rolled her eyes. Walking away from the door for a moment, she returned with a battered straw bonnet and tied its fraying ribbon beneath her chin. "We'll walk. But only for a few minutes. I've chores to do or my folks'll toss me out. We'll walk in the cemetery. But let's get one thing straight. You seem to think Ines was some kind of saint. She wasn't. Far from it."

Chapter 5

Bridget and I picked our way along the path between the jagged rows of headstones, many of them so old and worn their etchings were barely visible. I thought of those souls who could not now be remembered, their names lost to history. Some stones stood close together, their sides touching, grave after grave of young siblings lost to disease and hunger in the early days of the Rhode Island colony.

Where would Ines come to rest? In a pauper's grave, unmarked and just as unremembered?

"Why do you say she wasn't a saint?" I asked Bridget once we'd gone a short distance. "No one is perfect, certainly, but—"

"I read she was found in the coal tunnel," she said abruptly. She lifted her skirts clear of the tufts of grass at the side of the path.

"That's right."

"It wasn't her first time out there." Without pausing her stride, she turned to look at me, raised her brows significantly, and faced forward again.

"Then tell me why she went out there, if you know."

"Sure, I know. She was always sneaking out. Meetin' someone."

The missing Rudolfo? "Who did she meet?"

Bridget shrugged. "Don't know, don't care. But there was someone on the grounds she found mighty interesting. Interesting enough for her to leave half her chores undone some days. The housekeeper, Mrs. Sherman, warned her she'd be gettin' the sack if she didn't mind her ways. *Hmph.* Turned out the rest of us got the sack while saintly Ines got to stay."

"But not for long," I reminded her.

Bridget darted another glance at me, and I thought I detected a smidgeon of shame in her countenance. Softly, she said, "True. Not for long."

The graveyard stretched away with a gentle downward slope to where it bordered on Farewell Street. I glanced across the way at a pair of women who appeared to be tidying a fenced plot with several graves in it. It reminded me that not everyone here had been forgotten; the ancestors of many of those first Newporters continued to live here.

"You did threaten her, Bridget," I said. "I was there."

"I didn't kill her," she retorted in a near shout. The women across the way stopped what they were doing, straightened, and looked over at us. Bridget blew out a breath. "Yes, I threatened her. She betrayed us. But I didn't mean it. I was angry. Everyone says things when they're angry."

"Yes, that's true."

She continued staring at me, as though waiting for me to say more. When I didn't, she scowled. "You said you didn't think I killed her."

I hesitated, then said, "Honestly, I don't know. I'm not sure that you could have done it, that you could have lured Ines outside that night, although I do know a housemaid possesses the strength to subdue another person, especially a woman. I intend to find out who did do it, that much I promise you." We had paused in our walk, and now I started us going again. "Tell me what you know about her."

She shrugged. "Not much. None of us had been workin' together very long, only since a few weeks before the house opened. But I didn't like her, even before the strike came up."

"Why not?"

Bridget made a noise of disgust in her throat. "Because she was mean, that's why."

That brought me to another halt. "Mean? Ines? She seemed so docile. So . . ."

"Saintly? Hah. An act, one she put on only when it suited her. Other times, she complained, demanded favors of the other servants, and, like I said, she'd go off without finishin' her work and expect the rest of us to cover for her."

This utterly contradicted the nature of the young woman I'd met. Could she have been that good an actress? Right now, it was Bridget's word against everything Ines had said to me. And Ines was no longer able to defend herself.

I changed the subject. "There is a man who does menial work on the property. Rudolfo Medeiros. I understand that, not being a house servant, he wasn't involved in the strike. Did you know him?"

"Barely. As a parlor maid I didn't come into contact with him. I had seen him in passing, traded nods in greeting. That's all."

"He never worked upstairs in the house? Moving furniture, that sort of thing?"

"Never. The Berwinds hired professionals to place the furniture. The Manuel Brothers, in town. Someone like Rudy Medeiros only works outside and below stairs." Her eyebrows lifted again. "He'd work in the coal rooms, sometimes."

I took her point. A possible suspect.

She brushed back loose strands from her face. "Why do you ask about him?"

"He's been missing since last night. Arrived for work on time but left early. No one saw him leave."

Bridget let go a laugh. "That's it, then. She must have gone out to meet him, they fought, he killed her and ran off."

"That's possible. But until we find this Rudy, we can't know for certain. The police are looking for him."

"Good. I hope they find him quick, so the rest of us can get on with our lives and not have people thinkin' we're murderers." She cast me a sideways glance filled with resentment.

"Bridget, I meant what I said that day. Should you need help, you can come to me at Gull Manor."

She was shaking her head before I'd completed the offer. "I've got a family. And I'd best be getting back and seeing to the laundry and all before anyone realizes I've gone out. Got to earn my keep. My mam and da made that plain enough."

She retreated briskly down the path, making it clear I wasn't invited to follow and leaving me to contemplate her claims about Ines's character. It made me wonder how many of the deceased surrounding me went to their graves with unanswered questions hanging over their souls.

On my way back to the *Messenger*, I stopped at the police station on Marlborough Street, hoping to tell Jesse about my conversation with Bridget. He wasn't in, so I continued on my way, the shop windows and traffic along Spring Street blurring at the corners of my eyes as Bridget's assertions echoed in my mind. Could I have been so wrong about Ines? So fooled? What did that say about her? Or about me and my powers of observation? Had I been too hasty in reaching my own conclusions?

Derrick met me in the front office, practically blocking

my way as I stepped inside. "Don't take your hat off. We're wanted at The Elms."

Any plans I'd had to go through the pile of Associated Press articles on my desk, sent by wire, would have to wait. I let Derrick guide me outside and into the carriage.

"Is there new information about Ines or this Rudolfo Medeiros?" I asked as he steered the carriage up the side street to Bellevue Avenue. Once on the avenue, we headed south toward the cottages.

"Not exactly. Jesse was vague. All he really said is that there have been developments and he'd appreciate our being there to smooth things over."

"Smooth things over . . ." I rolled this around in my thoughts. "That could only mean he has to deal with the Berwinds or their guests, or he's already tried and they're proving uncooperative. Do you think he suspects one of them?"

"We'll know soon enough." Despite his assurance, we inched slowly along the carriage- and pedestrian-choked street as we passed the Newport Casino. People were flocking there for the tennis match to be held later that morning. The walkways and upper porches overlooking the courts would be lined with spectators. It wasn't merely the sport that drew attention, I knew, but the competitors themselves, our summer cottagers such as the Astors, Oelrichs, Wilsons, and my Vanderbilt cousins. There would be ladies playing today as well, and spectators would be as interested in what they wore on the court as on the dance floor.

We finally squeezed our way through and emerged onto the shaded thoroughfare that Bellevue Avenue became as soon as it left town behind. At The Elms, a footman awaited us outside the center front door, took our outer wraps and Derrick's hat, and led us immediately to Mr. Berwind's library at the far end of the long gallery. Deep reds and dark woodwork defined this as a men-only domain, even before Mr. Berwind glanced up from his heavily carved desk with a look that implied I was trespassing. He did not, however, ask me to leave.

Jesse sat opposite him across the desk, and now he came to his feet. "Derrick, Emma, I'm glad you're here. We've made a discovery."

"Is that what you call it?" asked a voice behind me. "I call it a disaster."

I hadn't realized there were others in the room. Behind Mr. Berwind's desk, two side chairs sat against the wall between the front-facing windows. Shrouded half in shadow were two of the Berwinds' houseguests, the snakelike Rex and round-figured Silvie Morton.

Mr. Morton sat low in his chair, his torso curved inward and his legs thrust out in front of him. His elbows rested on the arms of the chair and his head sagged onto his hands. Even his hair had fallen out of place, with thick, pomaded strands falling over his brow so that he no longer reminded me of a snake. Beside him, his wife leaned to rub his back. She had been whispering something to him, but now looked up with beseeching eyes.

"Mr. and Mrs. Morton, what has happened?" A sudden fear sent me whirling about to face Jesse and Mr. Berwind. "There hasn't been another—"

Jesse cut my question off. "No, not another murder. As you know, I began questioning the servants last night. I returned today to finish up, and one of the footmen told me something highly interesting."

Mr. Morton groaned and spoke without raising his head from his hands. "*Interesting*. You have a way with words, Detective. What that footman told you is catastrophic."

"Now, Rex, don't speak to the detective like that," his wife whispered. "It will be found. We'll get it back."

Mr. Morton shook his head.

I clasped my hands at my waist in a show of patience I didn't feel. "What will be found?"

"Tell us what this footman had to say," Derrick urged Jesse. He stared in turn at each solemn face, squinting slightly to make them out. I've always wondered why so many gentleman's libraries were so dark, between the somber furnishings, the heavily draped windows, and sparse lighting beyond the desk.

Jesse remained standing rather than retake his seat. "Apparently, he came upon Ines Varella in the Mortons' guest room the evening of the musicale, at a time she shouldn't have been there. She mumbled something about fresh linens, but this footman, well aware of the schedule, knew she wasn't being truthful. When he confronted her about it and asked what she was really doing, she told him to mind his business or he'd get hurt."

"And the young beggar didn't think to report it," Mr. Morton said, his words muffled in his hands. "You need to fire that one, Ned."

"I'm looking into it." Mr. Berwind fingered one side of his abundant mustache and addressed Derrick and me. "My footman said he had the distinct feeling that this chit would make good on her threat, that she had someone willing to fight her battle for her."

"He also said," Jesse put in, "that he nonetheless warned her she'd better go about her own business. Once she'd left, he took a good look around the room and didn't see anything that seemed disturbed or rummaged through. And she had left a pile of fresh linens on the dresser top."

Mr. Morton swore under his breath. "He still should have reported it."

"Be that as it may," Jesse went on, "as soon as I learned about this, I informed the Mortons, who went up to their room to check on things themselves." He picked up an ob-long velvet box from Mr. Berwind's desk. Rex Morton let out another groan. His wife murmured something and put more vigor into rubbing his back. "They're traveling with a safe, and apparently something has been taken."

"Something . . ." Rex Morton nearly doubled over. "It's not just *something*. Not just *anything*."

"Rex, please," his wife said, "you're not helping."

"I'm not sure I understand." Derrick leaned against a cor-ner of the desk. "Assuming Miss Varella stole this . . . piece of jewelry, I'm guessing . . . out of your safe, the question is how? Could this maid have been a safecracker? It's not likely."

"No." The word dragged from Mr. Morton's lips as though with his dying breath. "It wasn't the first time she'd been in the room when she shouldn't have. The day we ar-rived . . . I was crouching before the safe, entering the com-bination. I thought I was alone, had closed the door. I should have locked it. . . ." He shook his head, his expres-sion self-chiding. "Suddenly I heard a noise, the faintest creaking of a floorboard, and when I looked around, there she was, standing several feet away, with yet another stack of linens in her arms. I jumped and she jumped. She made ex-cuses that she didn't think anyone was in the room, hadn't seen me there, and she was so sorry." He scrunched his fea-tures and mimicked in a high, nasal voice, " 'So sorry, sir. I did not know you were here. I will go.' And she scurried from the room like a startled mouse."

"Neither Rex nor I thought much of it at the time," his wife added.

"No, but I realize now how *stupid* I was to trust her. No, not a safecracker, but she could certainly see well enough to read a combination at several paces and over a man's shoul-der. Stupid, so *stupid*." He formed a fist and brought it down on his thigh, once, twice and again, until Mrs. Morton stopped him by grasping his wrist.

I reached for the box in Jesse's hands, released the clasp, and opened the lid. "I assume this item was a necklace, by the shape of the box." Odd, I thought, that the thief, whether Ines or someone else, had taken the time to take the piece out of the box, rather than run with the entire package and sort it out later. "Mr. Morton, you did have this necklace insured, didn't you?"

Rex Morton's face turned crimson. He collapsed in a fit of coughing and nearly tumbled out of his chair. For an instant I feared he was suffering an apoplexy or heart attack. Only his wife's quick action in gripping him with both arms kept him from falling. She met my gaze, her own brimming with fear and bafflement and tears. "No, he hadn't insured it. If it's not found, it shall be a complete loss."

Silvie Morton plied her husband with brandy while pressing a cold compress to his brow, the latter brought by a footman, the former poured by Ned Berwind. While the man recovered what he could of his composure, Jesse gestured for Derrick and me to follow him out of the library. He led us several yards down the hall, to the wide alcove beside the north staircase, identical to one on the south side, with windows looking out over the front drive and Bellevue Avenue.

"We found Miss Varella's belongings," he said before we could ask any questions. "They were wrapped in a bundle and tossed beneath some hedges on the other side of Dixon about twenty yards from the tunnel entrance."

"No necklace?" Derrick asked, his tone implying he already knew the answer.

Jesse shook his head.

"Well, that certainly confirms her intentions of leaving The Elms and not coming back," I said. "But I'm confused.

What can Derrick and I do in this situation? I'm not sure why you called for us."

"I need to know more about this necklace and Rex Morton isn't talking." Jesse glanced down the hall toward the library, then back at us. "Every time I've asked, he's pulled a stunt like the one just now, making me think he's about to expire permanently."

"He's obviously distraught." A bird outside the window began singing a shrill song, momentarily distracting me. I turned my attention back to Jesse. "What about his wife?"

Jesse pursed his lips in a moue of frustration. "She either doesn't know anything about this necklace, which I find hard to believe, or she's helping her husband cover something up."

"Like what?" Derrick also sent a glance down the hall. There were voices coming from the conservatory, its open doorway close to that of the library. "Morton certainly seems to want this necklace back. Why would either of them be reticent about helping you find it?"

"That's what I'd like you and Emma to help me find out. They won't confide in me, for whatever reason. And while they might be persuaded to open up to the Berwinds, the Berwinds are unlikely to enlighten me without the Mortons' consent." He sent critical looks at both of us. "You two, on the other hand . . ."

"So how do we go about it?" I spread my hands wide. "Divide and conquer?"

"Yes," Derrick agreed. "Emma will take Silvie aside, and I'll get Rex alone somewhere. But we can't make any promises."

"See what you can do." Jesse started back to the library but stopped and turned to us again. "Don't come back in with me. I'll finish up with the Mortons, see if I can learn anything more, and leave the rest to you. Be subtle."

Derrick rolled his eyes and clucked his tongue in derision. I said, "You're not dealing with amateurs, you know."

Derrick and I decided we might be more effective if we left The Elms for a while and returned later. Then, our questions might not be interpreted as an obvious scheme to collect information for Jesse.

Along the way, I cleared up some questions I had about the Mortons, or Mr. Morton in particular. "What does he do?"

"He's a financier," Derrick replied. "Steel, coal, precious metals, corporate and municipal bonds . . ." He trailed off, indicating that Rex Morton traded in whatever promised to be lucrative at any particular time.

"Risky."

"All financial trading is risky. That's why there's such potential to reap a fortune, both for himself and for his clients."

I glanced at his profile. "Or lose one."

He nodded.

"Do financiers typically trade in costly jewelry?"

"No, they don't, at least not for their clients. This was personal, for Rex himself. The question is why."

We entered town and soon turned onto Spring Street. I was glad to return to the office for a few hours and work on those waiting news stories. I also reviewed what I had already reported about Ines's murder. The circumstances had become much more complicated with the addition of this missing necklace. Could she have read the combination over Rex Morton's shoulder? Or . . . could he be using Ines's death to cover the fact that he, himself, had somehow lost the piece? Although, if he had done so, it would have made much more sense if he'd had the necklace insured. I realized he hadn't given us a description of it. It must be terribly valuable for him to make himself so sick over it.

The sun was slanting long over the island when we finally

retraced our route down Bellevue Avenue to The Elms. It was teatime, and as luck would have it the men had decided to stay up on the terrace while the women had gone down to the sunken garden at the western end of the property. Mr. Berwind gestured for me to go on down, while Derrick joined the men. A footman accompanied me with a chair, while a maid followed with another place setting.

As I descended the stone steps into the garden, I saw the three women around a garden table, complete with linen tablecloth and napkins, bone china, and gleaming silver flatware that caught the sun's coppery rays. Two tiered trays of delicacies took up the center of the table, and off to the side, another table held reserve teapots. A second footman stood ready to serve. The women each wore a wide-brimmed hat decorated with colorful silken flowers, ribbons, and feathers, tilted just so to accommodate her coiffure. My straw boater paled in comparison.

"Mrs. Andrews, how fortuitous," Mrs. Berwind called to me with a wave. "So glad you're in time to join us."

"I hope I'm not intruding," I called in reply. I didn't speed my steps but continued toward them at a sedate pace befitting a lady. Such were the details I had learned to be mindful of since marrying Derrick. I didn't fret overmuch about being accepted in society, but for his sake neither did I wish to be ostracized. The Berwinds and most of their guests had been accommodating and friendly enough at the musicale, no doubt owing to the fact that the Berwinds and many of their circle were new money—even newer than my Vanderbilt relatives. Of course, no one was newer money than me, but these people didn't seem to hold it against me.

After sitting, being served a cup of tea, and selecting a delicate triangle of a sandwich from one of the trays, I ventured to touch my fingertips to Silvie Morton's hand. "How are you holding up? I was glad to see Mr. Morton on the terrace with the other gentlemen. May I take that as a good sign?"

"Only temporarily." Her slender eyebrows drew inward. "I'm afraid my husband is beside himself. It was all I could do to calm him down earlier. You saw him, Mrs. Andrews." She shook her head, at the same time fussing with ribbon trailing from the back of her hat, which the breeze had blown over her shoulder. "He's never been so overwrought before, and I'm at a loss to understand it."

"You mustn't worry, Silvie," Mrs. Berwind said decisively. "This matter shall be cleared up in no time. All will be well."

"But can we assume that?" Mrs. Gilchrist, so much younger than either Mrs. Morton or Mrs. Berwind, looked suddenly apologetic for speaking up. Her bangs weren't quite so crimped as last night, although they retained the frazzle of having been overheated by the crimping iron. She plucked a miniature tart from her plate but didn't eat it. Rather, she waved it in the air as she spoke. "I'm sorry, Silvie, but with this chambermaid having died, how will we ever learn what she did with your necklace?"

"Kay, you shouldn't say such things," Mrs. Berwind admonished gently, causing the much younger woman to redden and tuck her chin. "We'll learn what happened in due course. That detective seems determined to get to the bottom of things, and, well"—she flicked a glance across the table at me—"Mrs. Andrews has experience in solving even the most vexing quandaries."

Silvie Morton turned to me, her eyes wide. "Do you indeed?"

"I've . . . helped the police a time or two."

"Don't be modest, Mrs. Andrews. Senator Wetmore's wife Edith, Mamie Fish, and your own relative, Alva Belmont, have told me all about you." Mrs. Berwind leaned forward to take the other two women into her confidence. "Before she married, our Mrs. Andrews proved herself to be quite the sleuth, very much in the vein of Mr. Doyle's Sherlock Holmes. Have you read those stories?"

Before the discussion could diverge into an assessment of detective stories, I said, "How could Miss Varella have known about the necklace in your husband's safe, Mrs. Morton?"

"I wish I knew." She heaved a long sigh. "Especially since *I* didn't know it was there."

"Where *did* you think it was?" Kay Gilchrist asked in all seriousness.

Mrs. Morton stared blankly at her a moment before explaining, "I didn't know the necklace *existed*. Rex never told me about it. The first I learned of it was when he ran upstairs to check the safe, dumped everything out all over the floor, found that empty velvet box, and began swearing at the top of his lungs. Oh, dear, how he swore." She pressed her fingertips to her temples.

Mrs. Berwind patted her shoulder. "Don't think about that now, Silvie dear."

"I simply don't understand the secrecy," Mrs. Morton lamented. "He doesn't typically keep things from me."

"Why then, it must have been a gift for you," Kay Gilchrist suggested brightly.

"I don't think so." Mrs. Morton pinged the edge of her teacup with a fingernail. "The way he's behaving suggests losing this necklace could all but ruin us. I think he intended to sell it. Probably at a great profit."

Yes, that made perfect sense. "Do you know when and where he made the purchase?"

"I don't know for certain, but my guess is while we were in London. He's been acting tetchy ever since. No, since before that, really." She paused to consider, one finger absently toying with the brooch at her throat. "He began behaving strangely before we ever left New York."

"Strange how?" I asked her.

"Jittery. Impatient. Short tempered."

"Rex, short tempered?" Mrs. Berwind pursed her lips. "I can hardly fathom it. He's always such an amiable gentleman."

I could hardly fathom *that*. But perhaps I had met a Rex Morton who was already suffering from the nervous dyspepsia his wife described.

"In fact," Silvie Morton went on as if her friend hadn't spoken, "the trip to London was entirely abrupt. We hadn't planned to go. One morning Rex simply announced to me that he'd booked our passage on the White Star Line's *Oceanic* for the following week. You can imagine my vexation at having so little time to prepare for such a voyage."

"Oh, indeed. Rather horrid of him, I'd say," Kay Gilchrist ventured, then hid her face by sipping her tea.

This earned her another glare of admonishment from Mrs. Berwind.

"Do you think the trip was for the purpose of purchasing this necklace?" I asked, earning my own reproving glance from beneath Mrs. Berwind's lashes.

"Perhaps we should stop grilling Silvie about this," our hostess said. "It's distressing enough without our harping on the details."

"No, no." Mrs. Morton stared down at her plate as if her miniature lemon torte could help her sort out her confusion. "I want to understand. I *need* to, Herminie. Rex won't tell me anything. But already Mrs. Andrews has helped me see the situation more clearly." She raised her chin, her eyes holding a new determination. "Yes, I believe we went to London specifically for this necklace. And I believe his secretary, Mr. Johnston, knew all about it. The two of them had been closeted in Rex's study back home the whole day before Rex told me we'd be leaving. And the man had brought telegrams. I saw them peeking out of his coat pocket when he arrived."

"Where is this man now?" I tried to sound calm and not let my excitement show. If this secretary was here in Newport, he could possibly shed light on the necklace and why Rex Morton was being so reticent about it, even to his wife. Could there be a link between Mr. Morton and Ines—a personal one that involved this necklace?

"Still in New York, I suppose," she replied with a shrug.

"Of course." That might make questioning him more difficult, but not impossible. "And Ines Varella—Mrs. Berwind, had you checked her references?"

"I didn't directly, but the housekeeper—my former housekeeper—most certainly did. The girl came with a letter of reference from a family in New York."

"Are you aware of any particular reason she left her former employment?"

Mrs. Berwind made a careless gesture with her hand. "One supposes she heard The Elms was to be the grandest and most modern house in America. Who wouldn't wish to work here?"

Servants moved around all the time, looking for higher wages and better working conditions. Yet I could think of a good number of servants who hadn't wished to work at The Elms once they realized the bargain they had made: good wages and comfortable accommodations, but at the expense of no personal time.

I turned to Mrs. Morton. "How do you suppose Ines might have learned about the necklace, assuming it was she who stole it?"

"Who else could it have been?" Kay Gilchrist once again selected a petit four from the tray but put off popping it into her mouth. "It's so mysterious, isn't it? I mean, how could a common chambermaid come by that sort of information? It's not as if she had been in London and witnessed your husband making the purchase." Her eyebrows surged and her green eyes opened wide. "Could she? You don't suppose . . . ?"

"Nonsense, Kay." Mrs. Berwind only just succeeded in suppressing a huff of frustration. "Ines was here while Silvie and Rex were in London, She was helping to ready the house."

"Oh . . . yes." Mrs. Gilchrist slumped back against her chair as though someone had let all the air out of her. "But then . . . how?"

How indeed. Unless Rex Morton had told her, or his secretary had, but if that had been the case, why?

Chapter 6

"He's not talking," Derrick told me after we left The Elms. We headed in our carriage to Gull Manor, and although I would have preferred spending the next several nights on the Point, I said nothing as we drove along. My qualms about sharing my house with him continued to niggle at me, and I still couldn't say if it was the house itself or the knowing eyes of Nanny and Katie, who couldn't seem to repress their delight that he and I were now husband and wife—with all that that entailed.

Good heavens.

I sighed at the thought of Rex Morton's silence. "He added nothing to what was said in front of Jesse?"

"Not a blessed thing. He won't even describe the necklace to us. I'm afraid I'm to be little help, if at all."

"How does he expect the police to find and return it if they don't know what it looks like?"

"He claims they'll know it when they see it, the piece is so astonishing." The carriage wheels struck a bump in the road and I steadied myself with a hand on his forearm. "He seems . . . afraid. That's the best way I can describe it."

"That's understandable. He obviously spent a great deal of money on this necklace."

"Yes, but why?" His lips skewed to one side as he concentrated on dusty Bellevue Avenue for several moments. "Why spend so much money on something that could potentially ruin him if he lost it? And then not bother to insure it?"

I wondered that myself. "Aren't the Mortons obscenely wealthy?"

"Until today I'd thought so. The Morton family made its fortune a generation ago in finance and in coal and steel investment. As far as I know, Rex has increased the family holdings to an impressive degree."

"Rather like Great-Uncle William Henry," I mused. William Henry Vanderbilt had been the first Cornelius Vanderbilt's son. His father had put little faith in his abilities, had called him a blatherskite, yet William Henry Vanderbilt had more than doubled the family fortune he had inherited.

Not that my branch of the family had seen a dime of it.

"There is also this missing handyman," Derrick reminded me, banishing my thoughts of my ancestors.

"Rudolfo, yes. Who were he and Ines really, and had they been working together?"

"And did he kill her and take the necklace?" Derrick finished for me.

"I can't think where else it could be." I smoothed a sleeve with my gloved hand. "This is all so contrary to my initial impression of Ines. I wish I had at least caught a glimpse of Rudolfo."

"An elusive character, that one. Ines came with references, but he did not, apparently. All a laborer really needs to recommend him are muscles and decent health."

"Ines's references could have been forged," I suggested. "Which would raise serious questions about her character. How I wish . . ." I trailed off wistfully.

"What?" He turned his head to raise a quizzical eyebrow

at me. "Wish she had been the woman you believed her to be?"

I nodded sadly. "Yes. She still could be, and for now I'm going to give her the benefit of the doubt." Despite my optimistic tone, my confidence in Ines's integrity dwindled with each new development. The same could be said for Rex Morton.

In the morning, Derrick and I took care of pending business at the *Messenger* before walking down to Thames Street. So far, the police had discovered no sign of Rudolfo Medeiros, and they feared he might have made it off the island the night of Ines's murder. That being the case, he might never be found.

However, that wouldn't stop me from trying, nor Derrick from accompanying me to ensure no harm came to me. Besides, Jesse's men had already inquired at the ticket booths along the main wharves, as well as the train depot. No one fitting Rudolfo's description had turned up on the night of Ines's death or in the days since. But that didn't mean he hadn't stolen a boat and rowed himself to Jamestown and beyond.

"It's unnecessary for you to come along, you know," I told Derrick as we approached Long Wharf just west of Washington Square. "It's broad daylight and most of the men I intend speaking with know who I am. They know I'm a Newporter."

"That doesn't make you invincible," he insisted while looking doggedly straight ahead toward our destination.

I felt a twinge of annoyance immediately followed by a rush of affection. How could a man's actions be so infuriating and endearing at the same time? Flicking a glance at his profile, I slipped my arm through his, both resigned to let him tag along yet unwilling to give him the satisfaction of an easy capitulation on my part. "Some of them might not be willing to open up with you in tow, you know. You might prove more of a hindrance than a help." With an impish grin, I couldn't help adding, "Just as with Rex Morton."

"Oh, yes, rub *that* in." He pushed out a laugh that told me he wasn't the least bothered by my teasing. "The man is scared silent. I doubt you'd have any better results than I."

"We'll see," I murmured, still smiling.

Upon reaching Long Wharf, billows of dust from beneath the wheels of countless carriages, carts, and wagons swirled around us. The shrill whistles and chugs from the adjoining train depot made me want to plug my ears. We proceeded carefully, so as not to be jostled by the nonstop streams of pedestrians advancing in both directions.

"Where to first?" Derrick asked. "Angus?"

Angus MacPhearson was an old friend of mine and my brother Brady's who had grown up on the Point with us. Nowadays he rowed a skiff back and forth between the wharf and the vessels anchored in the harbor, and occasionally conveyed passengers to other parts of the island.

Angus had proved a vital source of information in the past, but I shook my head. "Not yet. I think the taverns are the better place to start."

"I wish you wouldn't."

"Why not? I've been to them all before."

He looked aghast. "All?"

"Most," I conceded. "Always in the effort to find a suspect. You know that."

He blew out a breath. "Perhaps, but that doesn't mean I like it."

"It isn't necessary that you do." I scanned the line of businesses flanking the north side of the wharf. Circling seagulls squawked above the rooftops, on the alert for scraps of any kind. "Shall we start with the Red Mariner?"

"What exactly are you intending to ask? And of whom? There won't be any patrons this time of day."

I chuckled. "Oh yes, there will be. But it's the owners of these establishments I hope to speak with."

Without having answered his first question, I led the way in through the first door along the way. The Red Mariner was much like any other tavern on Long Wharf or Thames Street in that it boasted a dim interior, rustic furnishings, and a sticky floor despite the presence of a bucket and mop leaning against the bar. The tables were unoccupied except for one up front in the corner near the window, where two men sat leaning over tankards of ale. They barely looked up at us as we walked in.

"Charming place," Derrick murmured.

"Don't be a snob. Actually, it smells rather good in here." I raised my face for an appreciative sniff. Yes, there were the usual unpleasant scents lingering in the air: stale beer and stronger spirits, perspiration, and a prevailing hint of mustiness emanating from the damp, shadowy corners. However, the aromas of stewing beef, frying bacon, and roasting potatoes wafted from the kitchen, making one almost forget the other odors vying for attention.

I walked up to the bar and called out, "Hello? Is anyone here?"

A man in shirtsleeves and a soiled apron ambled out from the kitchen. "We're not serving yet unless you're here for a pint or a shot."

"Neither, thank you." I pulled myself up taller to meet his considerable height and look him evenly in the eye. Despite my claim to Derrick, this man was unknown to me and must have taken over from the previous owner who had been here the last time I visited. "I don't believe we've met, but I am Mrs. Andrews and this is my husband, Mr. Andrews."

He seemed unimpressed. "Uh-huh."

"Are you the owner?" I inquired.

"Uh-huh."

Goodness. I couldn't help wondering if the man's vocabulary extended further than that. "We're looking for someone." Before he could bestow another *Uh-huh* on me, I hurried on. "He would have been Portuguese, large and muscular, and might have seemed somewhat in a hurry. Possibly even desperate." I gave him the description Jesse had managed to obtain from the Berwinds' new butler and a few of the other laborers. Even with those details, however, I might have been describing scores of young men on Aquidneck Island.

"Cops have already been here asking." He started to turn away.

"And what did you tell them?"

"Not that it's any of your business, but I told 'em I ain't seen him."

"Are you quite sure? It's vitally important."

He narrowed his eyes and peered at Derrick. His head slanted at a slight angle.

Derrick nodded. "You might as well answer my wife to her satisfaction or she won't leave you alone."

"Can't say I saw someone if I didn't." After a quick look over his shoulder at the sounds of activity in the kitchen, he leaned an elbow on the bar top. "What you want with him? He steal something from you?"

His guess, so close to the possible truth, startled me, but I quickly recovered. "Not from us, no, but he's suspected of stealing from someone else." Then I added for dramatic effect, "And of murder," hoping it might alarm the fellow and goad his memory.

"Huh."

So much for alarming him.

"Perhaps you might ask some of your patrons later," I suggested.

"Maybe." The word carried an implied *maybe not.*

Just so our efforts there weren't entirely in vain, we asked the two men at the table the same question. They replied with shakes of their heads.

We made our way outside, back into the glaring sunshine, obscuring dust, and confusion of unceasing activity. We tried a couple more dockside taverns, to no avail. In one, a man I've known most of my life treated me like a stranger.

"Have you seen someone of that description?" I asked Ben Bradley, who swabbed a mop back and forth over the remnants of the previous night's revelry at an establishment called The Sailor's Knot.

"Sorry, Mrs. Andrews, I haven't." He hadn't looked up from his task since we walked in. Not even to inquire after my health.

"Mrs. Andrews?" I raised my brows at him. "Really, Ben? Did I not patch you and Brady up after that fight you had with those older boys when you were in the fifth grade, and then *not* tell my parents or yours about it?"

"I suppose you did, Mrs. Andrews." He slid two chairs aside to mop under a table.

"Perhaps we should go and leave your friend to his work," Derrick murmured in my ear.

I ignored him. "How are your parents, Ben?"

"Well, thank you."

I frowned, not understanding. "May I pass along your regards to Brady?"

He turned his mop in a new direction. "Brady's probably forgotten who I am by now, Mrs. Andrews. What with his new acquaintances and all."

It dawned on me what the problem might be. When Brady and I had lived on the Point, we were the same as all the other children. From modest families who worked hard and managed as well as they could. Despite my father being a descendent of the first Cornelius Vanderbilt, he was the great-grandson of one of the Commodore's daughters, and her inheritance had run out long before my father had been born.

Now, I realized, some of my old friends and playmates would view us differently: me, the wife of a wealthy, Providence newspaper heir; Brady, an executive of the New York Central Railroad. We no longer belonged, at least in the eyes of some of our old neighbors, Ben apparently one of them.

With sadness pressing against my throat, I bade Ben good day and good health, and Derrick and I left the tavern. Ben's "Same to you, Mrs. Andrews, Mr. Andrews" felt like a shard of ice at my nape.

We hadn't gone far when Derrick took my arm and brought us to a halt in the shade of a bait and tackle shop. "This isn't going to work. We can't stop at every tavern along every wharf in Newport. Besides, either no one has seen or heard of this man, or they aren't willing to talk to us."

"I know." I blinked my sadness away. Then I frowned and tried to think of a strategy that would yield results. "But it makes sense, doesn't it, that the first place Rudolfo would go after committing murder and theft would be a place where he could indulge in some strong spirits to dull the shock of what he'd done? Especially if he hadn't *planned* to murder Ines. Unless, of course, the man is an absolute monster and felt no remorse at all for his actions."

"People like that exist."

"Yes, I know."

From the corner of my eye, I saw the door of the first pub swing open. The owner stepped out and looked right and left. He spotted us and shuffled over, dodging people in his way.

In my eagerness, I nearly ran to meet him halfway. "Did you remember something?"

"No, but you might want to try the pub at the end of

Lower Thames Street. Way down, near the corner of Lee Street."

"Why there?" Derrick asked.

"It's where a lot of Portuguese go of an evening."

My pulse picked up speed. "And the name of this place?"

"Don't know. Follow the voices. When you hear fellas talking Portuguese, you'll know you're there."

I felt no fear walking down Lower Thames Street, even though Derrick and I had returned to the *Messenger* for several hours and didn't venture to the south end of town until dusk approached. Still, he insisted on walking close beside me, my arm tucked firmly in his, his body tensed with readiness. I, on the other hand, glanced about for people I knew. In this area, they would mostly be men, leaving after a long day's work at the Newport Illuminating Company, the Newport Gas Light Company, or the many stores, warehouses, repair shops, shipyards, and manufacturers inhabiting this part of town. In fact, I waved at several, and returned the evening greetings of several more. Each time, I hid my smiles when Derrick braced to protect me.

"Please don't become wretchedly possessive or protective," I said with a chuckle. "These are friends and acquaintances."

"I know, and I'm sorry. It's taking some getting used to being with you when you're doing things you used to do alone. Then, I didn't know about them, not in any great detail, so it wasn't nearly as worrisome."

"But you're with me now. Surely you don't think we'll be accosted at the end of the workday when all these people wish to do is go home to their suppers."

The setting sun slipped between a pair of harbor-front warehouses and caught the aristocratic lines of his profile. "It makes me think of the risks you've taken over the years."

"There's no use in fretting about that now." I slowed our steps and tilted my head.

"What are you doing?"

"Listening. For Portuguese."

Except for occasional snippets from workers wending their way home, we didn't hear much of the language until we'd gone nearly to the edge of the business district, where Thames Street left the waterfront behind and entered a residential area. There, small wood-framed houses lined both sides of the street, with grocers and dry goods shops here and there. We passed the doorway of a narrow two-story building with a grimy window overlooking the street. We peered in as best we could. There were a good two dozen men packed inside, ranged along the bar to one side, crowded around small wooden tables, or simply standing wherever there was room. Even through the glass, we heard their laughter and shouting, which gave way to the occasional round of roars. I pricked my ears, unable to make out any distinct words.

"Does that sound like Portuguese to you?"

Derrick leaned closer to the window. "I hear the language quite a bit in Providence. And yes, I believe it does."

I read the sign above the door: GUS'S. Not a name I would have expected. "I'm guessing this is the place, then. Shall we?"

The protest was written in every nook and cranny of Derrick's features. But he merely breathed in and out audibly and opened the door for me.

The silence spread almost immediately through the room. It began with the patrons sitting at the front tables catching sight of me and nudging each other with dubious expressions. Their stares made me feel exposed and on display. Their scrutiny extended to Derrick as well, with no less wariness. The wisdom of coming here suddenly became very much in doubt.

A particularly large man, both in height and in bulk, took it upon himself to express what they were all thinking. After scraping his chair back against the rough floorboards, he pushed to his feet and shuffled in our direction. A mocking smile flitted across his lips. "*Peço desculpa, senhor e senhora*"— he didn't look at all like he desired our pardon as his gaze dipped to our feet and slowly returned to our faces—"but surely you must be lost. You don't belong in here."

It wasn't a friendly observation, for that last statement came with a warning growl in his accented voice.

"We're sorry to disturb you," I offered, then paused as I felt Derrick's posture become more rigid than a moment before. "We mean no harm."

Chuckles made the round of the room. The bartender leaned on his elbows over the bar, his attention riveted on us. He seemed amused.

"We're looking for someone," Derrick said as he took a step forward. "Rudolfo Medeiros. Rudy. He lived not too far from here."

The large fellow rubbed the back of a hand against the dark bristle on his chin, raising a scritchy sound. "What you want him for?"

I opened my mouth to reply but Derrick's hand brushed mine to silence me. "He's gone missing," he said, "from his work at The Elms. Do any of you know him?"

A murmur of conversations buzzed around us, some in English, others in broken English, others still entirely in Portuguese. Their self-appointed spokesman continued to hold us pinned with his smoky-eyed gaze. "The problem is, we don't know you. We don't know if Rudy would want us to tell you anything. So maybe it is better if we don't."

I couldn't help myself. "Please, it's important."

A silence stretched for several moments, followed by murmurs of speculation, but deeper in tone this time. A tone that raised the hairs on my nape. Derrick stood very still, only his eyes moving as he darted his gaze around the room, then back to the tall fellow.

That man pursed his lips, then said, "Many things are important to us. No one cares. What is important to you might not be so important to us."

I was beginning to think we should simply leave, but Derrick didn't budge. Nor did he respond at all to the questioning look I tried to send him. He said, "Can you at least tell us if he's been here in the past day or two?"

A chair somewhere behind me shrieked against the floor as it was shoved back. I flinched at the sound, then again at the slow thud of footsteps. Goose bumps erupted on my arms as a man circled me too closely, his arm nearly brushing against mine. I glanced again at Derrick, who only turned his head toward the newcomer, a wiry man with thin features set in a dusky complexion.

"You would not like it if we intruded on your fancy clubs. You would not like us there with our rough clothes and our halting English."

I wanted to refute that, to assure him we were not those kinds of people, but I thought perhaps in this instance I should continue to let Derrick handle these men. Still, I expected him to protest that claim, but he didn't.

"You're right," he said, "we are intruders here. If you can't tell us anything about Mr. Medeiros, we'll go and leave you in peace."

He offered me the crook of his arm and I slipped my hand into it. Without hurrying, we turned and walked to the door. My senses stood at attention, and my body tensed with readiness. Would we be allowed to leave unmolested? Would someone attempt to stop us before we reached the door? Would someone follow us outside?

A hand came down on Derrick's wrist before he pressed the door latch. "He was here the other night."

My pulse jolted. As the man released Derrick's sleeve, I

regarded his balding pate, his weathered features, the yellow cast of his skin. I glanced down at his hands. They were roughened, soiled, and gnarled. A workman's hands, yet he seemed too old to be laboring like the younger men here.

"How many nights ago?" I asked him. "Do you remember?"

A chorus of complaints drowned out his answer. Several of the men seated near us came to their feet, their features twisting in anger. One of them called out, "Traitor! Don't tell them anything."

"Rudy owes me money," he retorted defiantly, his accent suddenly thicker. "I need it back." He turned back to Derrick and me. "Two nights ago? Three?"

"And how did he seem to you?" Derrick asked him.

"Seem?"

"Was he agitated? Nervous? In a hurry?"

"A hurry, yes. I tell him I want my money. He pushed me away, went to the bar and downed a drink in one gulp."

"Then what?" Derrick prompted him.

"Then he took out his watch, looked at the time, and ran out of here." He moistened his dry lips with the tip of his tongue. "Funny thing, that watch. Too good for him. Too costly. Gold, I think. I shouldn't have lent him money."

"Is there anything else you could tell us about him?" As Derrick asked this, I felt the tension in the room steadily rise, as if each moment wound a spring tighter until it might snap.

I feared these men would snap if we didn't leave soon. Despite the complaint of the elderly man before us, they didn't like us lingering. As their spokesman had said, we were intruders.

"There is a woman," the old man said.

"Yes, we know," I murmured, and didn't add that she had died. "Do you know anywhere on the island he might go, other than to his boardinghouse?" Jesse had had a man watching the house and Rudolfo hadn't turned up there.

"No. You find him. Get my money back."

"We'll certainly try." Derrick leaned closer to him and held out his hand. "Mr. . . . ?"

"Hermeto. Joaquim Hermeto." He took Derrick's offered hand and shook it.

We didn't waste another moment but took our immediate leave. Derrick hurried me along the sidewalk. "Don't look back. Just keep going."

It was on my lips to protest that they weren't going to follow us, but in truth I wasn't overly confident. We did hear a door open, but as Derrick had instructed, neither of us peered over our shoulders. No footsteps hurried after us as we blended into the general foot traffic, then turned a corner to return to Spring Street.

Chapter 7

We spent the next two nights at Derrick's flat on the Point. Our flat. I could hear the pout in Nanny's voice when I telephoned, but she didn't make a fuss. How could she, when I told her work concerns made it necessary for us to stay in town?

How strange it felt, though, to sit in the parlor, a room that had once been my parents' bedroom. Their dressing room had been converted into a tiny kitchen, and my old bedroom now served as Derrick's and my bedroom. When my family had lived here, our parlor and kitchen had been on the first floor, along with a dining room and small study, and my brother Brady's room was, and still is, in the attic, with a sink and a small stove to cook on. He still used it whenever he came to Newport. The rooms on the first floor had been converted into two small flats, rented to two elderly women.

But whereas my parents had owned the house in those days, Derrick had bought it from them several years ago. It had infuriated me, his sneaking in and purchasing the house right out from under me, though at the time I couldn't have raised the money to buy it myself. Not without appealing to my Vanderbilt relatives, and that was something I had done in the past only sparingly, and only in emergencies. But any resentment I had harbored had long since faded. Derrick had wished to create a permanent link to me, his way of letting me know he wasn't about to walk out of my life even when I stubbornly suggested he should.

He had made significant changes in the décor, having the old wallpaper removed, the walls freshly painted, and the furnishings changed to reflect his taste. Gone were the florals my mother favored, replaced with deep solid tones of blue and red, from the Oriental rug to the leather sofa to the upholstered armchairs. He encouraged me to make further changes to the rooms, but so far I hadn't. It simply didn't feel like mine, and no amount of redecorating would change that. This small colonial on Walnut Street near the train tracks might have been my home while growing up, but now it felt nearly as awkward to be here as it did to be at Gull Manor. I tried to hide it, but Derrick had come to know me too well.

"You're jumpy," he observed that first night, after we'd eaten the light supper we had brought home from town.

"I'm perfectly fine," I quipped in return and stared down at the book in my lap. The curtains fluttered in the open windows. The evening breeze smelled of rain.

"What are you reading?"

"What?" I flipped the cover closed over my index finger to read the title: *Jane Eyre*. I couldn't help feeling a bit like Jane myself. I couldn't claim to have suffered as Jane did in the story, nor did I suspect Derrick to be harboring some devastating secret like a mad wife in the attic. But I did know something about coming into an unexpected inheritance that brought Jane—and me—on a more equal level financially with the man she loved.

The book had been sitting on a side table, unread for several days, though I could practically recite it by heart, I'd read it so many times in the past. Tonight, I'd pulled it onto my lap to make myself look busy and at the same time relaxed, but I hadn't read a word. I hadn't even realized what book I'd been pretending to read until Derrick asked me what it was.

I looked up to see him smiling knowingly at me. Then he strolled to the sofa and settled beside me. "What's wrong, Emma?"

"Nothing." I released a breath. "No, that's not true. Ines is what's wrong. Wanting to find her killer. And wanting to understand who she was."

He lifted my hand in his, turned it and stroked my palm with his thumb. "I think there's something else. Something to do with us."

"No!" I shifted on the cushions to face him fully. "Never. You mustn't think it."

"You're certain you're not"—he flicked a glance down, then quickly up again—"regretting anything?"

I shook my head and leaned in to kiss him. I melted my lips against his slowly, lingeringly, letting him feel the full, deep measure of the love I felt for him. When I spoke, it was with our foreheads pressed together and my lips moving against his. "I don't regret anything to do with us. I never will."

When we eased away I saw he believed me, saw the relief and something more in his eyes. Lust. Love. And always his patience—the same patience he had shown me during the years I hadn't known what I wanted. Or had known, deep down, but struggled to acknowledge.

He relaxed against the back of the sofa and pulled me against his side. "What is it, then?"

"I don't know, exactly. It's me. Something I need to come to terms with." That much was true. I had been single far longer than most women, had lived independently in my small, all-female household, and I had been the head of that household. Now, I felt at odds with my new role as wife, and with deciding exactly how to relinquish some of what had once been solely mine without also losing my sense of autonomy, which had been so important to me until now.

"Is there anything I can do?" He lifted my hand again, brought it to his lips, and kissed my fingertips.

"I don't think so. It'll be all right, I promise." I would make it all right, one way or another. We retired soon after, and whatever qualms were plaguing me evaporated, temporarily, in the heat of our joined bodies.

It was on the morning of the second day we spent on the Point that Jesse telephoned from the police station with startling news.

"He's been found, Emma. Rudolfo Medeiros is on Goat Island. He's dead."

Jesse hastily gave me the details and told me that Derrick and I could meet him at the crime scene. Thus far, we hadn't run the full story in the *Messenger.* We had reported only on the mysterious circumstances of Ines Varello's death and that an unnamed worker had gone missing from The Elms. There had been no mention yet of the stolen necklace, in the *Messenger* or any other paper. With this new development, more of the story would need to come out.

Especially if a clue to the missing necklace was found on Rudolfo's body.

To meet Jesse, we set out on foot across the Point to Long

Wharf, where we found Angus waiting to row us out to tiny Goat Island in the bay. It was a short trip, quite swimmable if one were wearing the proper attire. At different times a goat pasture, a colonial fort, and now a torpedo-manufacturing plant, the twenty-acre island housed numerous buildings used in the making and storing of the weapons. A small lighthouse sat at its northern tip. Even now, men and women were arriving via small boats from the main island to start their workday. Jesse met us at one of the docks and helped me out of the skiff.

We thanked Angus, and Derrick paid him. Then we followed Jesse between buildings and along paths to the bay-facing side of the island. Along the rocks lining the water's edge, several police officers were examining the area. A police vessel sat anchored close by.

A man I recognized as Newport's coroner crouched beside a body lying faceup among the weeds. He stood as Derrick and I approached. Another man, hovering several yards away, struck me as familiar. I stared into his face and realized why I knew him. It was Mr. Boreman, the former butler from The Elms.

Jesse spoke to one of the uniformed officers. "Do we have a positive ID?"

Mr. Boreman, dressed in dark trousers and formal morning coat, came several steps closer. His clothing told me he'd secured another position as butler and I silently rejoiced for him. With a bob of his Adam's apple, he cleared his throat. "We do, Detective Whyte. It's him. It's Rudolfo Medeiros."

"No doubts?" Jesse pressed.

"None, sir."

Jesse turned to the coroner, effectively giving Mr. Boreman permission to back away to a more comfortable distance from the body. "Any conclusions? Did he drown?"

I immediately imagined an inebriated Rudolfo Medeiros stumbling along the water's edge until he had fallen in, later to wash up here.

The coroner rubbed the back of his neck and shook his head. "No, he doesn't appear to have aspirated much water, at least not that I can tell from an initial examination. I'll of course need to do a thorough autopsy back at the hospital, but I'd say he died before he hit the water."

I glanced down at the body and winced. I had seen a corpse washed up before, and the details here were similar: the flesh as white as a fish's belly, the face bloated, the eyes open and milky. I forced myself to take another look, not at the body this time, but at Rudolfo Medeiros—at the man he had been. Young, sturdily built, and, even with the effects of drowning, handsome in a rugged way. His eyes were dark, nearly black, rimmed with equally black lashes, and his mouth, had it not been drained of color, would have been lush and sensuous.

I looked away, overcome with the waste of such a death, and of a life that seemed not to have been well lived.

"What's your guess as to the manner of death?" Jesse asked the coroner.

"Strangulation." The decisiveness of the man's reply made it clear an autopsy would merely be a formality. He stooped beside the body again and gestured us all closer. "See these marks on the neck?"

Jesse crouched to look closer. "They're nearly identical to those found on Ines Varella's neck."

"Someone who wore gloves," I murmured, and the coroner nodded.

"Exactly."

At that moment, I noticed Mr. Boreman's fingers clenching to fists—inside his gloves. But of course, all butlers wore gloves, as did footmen.

"It's quite possible whoever murdered Miss Varella also murdered Rudolfo," Jesse concluded.

Derrick shoved his hands into his trouser pockets and stared down at the body. "Any sign of the necklace?"

"None," the coroner replied. "He had nothing in his pockets."

"No, of course not," Derrick said grimly. "Whoever did this took everything Rudy had on him."

I nodded, my gaze returning to the dead man's face. We had thought he killed Ines and stole the necklace. But now . . . "Suddenly the list of murder suspects is wide open."

That afternoon saw me back at The Elms for another interview with the Berwinds. Derrick remained at the *Messenger* to conduct business, but Jesse had requested I join him. We were once again escorted into the Chinese breakfast room, where we found Ned and Minnie Berwind waiting for us.

Jesse conducted most of the interview, but I noticed whenever the Berwinds seemed uncomfortable with one question or another, they looked to me as if my very presence helped alleviate the experience for them. Indeed, I understood that to be the very reason Jesse had me come along. After years of dealing with members of the Four Hundred, he had learned their tendencies and idiosyncrasies, one of them being a disinclination to cooperate with the police. Just as discussing money was considered crass, engaging in police business was looked upon as unpleasant business to be avoided at all costs. Especially if the crime involved them or their property.

"As Mrs. Andrews can tell you," Mrs. Berwind replied to Jesse's inquiry concerning the intermission during the musicale, "most of the guests were on the terrace and the walkways directly below it. A few did wander, of course, as people are wont to do. Some of the men—and their wives, one assumes—drifted out onto the lawn to smoke. No one of good manners would do so in the mixed company of the terrace or, heaven forbid, in the house."

"One also assumes a guest or two might have gone inside to use the . . . uh . . . facilities," Mr. Berwind offered.

"I don't suppose there is any way to account for each and every guest, is there?" Jesse looked up from his notebook, his expression one of hope. "Where were the Mortons and the Gilchrists, for example? I only ask because they are staying here and, I assume, have the liberty of the house. They might have seen something that night without realizing it."

While Mr. and Mrs. Berwind mulled this over, I held my breath. I found both couples of particular interest, not only because of the Mortons' stolen necklace, but also because, unlike the majority of the other guests that night, those four were not summer Newporters. I already had questions about why Rex Morton had brought his necklace to Newport, instead of securing it in a vault in New York when they arrived home from England.

"I'm afraid you'd have to ask them what they did during the intermission." Mr. Berwind ran his fingers over his mustache. "Though one loathes subjecting them to further unpleasantness."

"Mr. Berwind, need I remind you that two people connected to this house are dead?" Jesse's tone neither threatened nor pressed his authority. He waited patiently, at least outwardly, for an answer.

"We damned well haven't forgotten, Whyte," Ned Berwind snapped. His wife gasped, reminding her husband of his manners. He reached across the table to take her hand. "Forgive me, my dear. And you too, Mrs. Andrews. This is unsettling business all around. I forgot myself for a moment."

"Are the Mortons and the Gilchrists here presently?" Jesse asked.

"They are," Mr. Berwind replied, though his reluctance was plain.

"Then I'd like to speak with them." Jesse tapped his notebook. "Individually. I'll start with the ladies. Mrs. Andrews will be present to ensure their comfort."

The Berwinds came to their feet, but both hesitated. Mrs. Berwind drew a breath. "Mrs. Andrews, have we your word that whatever is said between our guests and the detective will not make its way into your newspaper?"

"Whatever is said in an official capacity will not stray farther than these walls," I assured her.

"I went upstairs to our guest room." Silvie Morton sat stiffly upright in her chair, her hands resting on the table before her. "During the first half of the performance I'd noticed a bit of lace on my dress had come loose. I buzzed for my maid and also had her smooth my hair. The weather, you know. The damp ocean air can wreak havoc on one's coiffure."

Jesse nodded as if he often encountered the same problem, prompting me to suppress a chuckle. "Did she come right away?"

"Oh, yes. Riverton never keeps me waiting."

"And how long was she with you?"

"For about twenty minutes, perhaps longer. Then I dismissed her and returned downstairs. It was then I saw all the commotion and realized something was dreadfully wrong."

"While you were moving through the house, did you ever see Miss Varella?" Jesse asked.

Mrs. Morton's brows drew together. "No, I did not."

"Are you quite sure?" I put in. "Would you have known it was her if you had seen her?"

"No, probably not, but I didn't see any maids on my way up or down the stairs. Only my own maid, Riverton, and she doesn't dress as a housemaid, you know."

Jesse made a notation on the fresh page he had started for Mrs. Morton's replies, her name at the top. "Did you see anyone else?"

"No, I don't believe so. . . ." She left off, her brows tightening again. "Well . . . there were footmen moving about on the first floor."

"What were they doing?" Jesse wanted to know.

"Doing? They were doing whatever it is footmen do. I didn't pay any attention. Why should I?"

Jesse made a notation. "Did you see any other guests inside?"

"I suppose. . . . Yes. There were others lingering about. Mostly in the long gallery."

"And where was your husband?"

Her frown lines deepened and her lips flattened. "Outside. Somewhere. Probably on the lawn, smoking. I don't know. I didn't see him again until after the to-do, and in light of what happened I didn't think to ask him where he'd been."

"You mean Miss Varella's death?" Jesse clarified.

"Of course I mean Miss Varella's death," she retorted, then dragged a breath through her upturned nose. "Forgive me. This is all so upsetting, what with the discovery that the necklace was missing." She scoffed, her disgust evident. "The discovery that the necklace existed at all, I should say. And you're no closer to discovering where it went?"

"No, ma'am, I'm afraid not." Jesse paused, letting the silence fill the room until even I began to grow uncomfortable. My nape began to itch. Mrs. Morton rubbed her hands over her plump forearms, back and forth as if she'd taken a chill. Then Jesse asked, "How did your husband seem to you once you and he were reunited that evening? Was he agitated? Disheveled?"

"Disheveled? Rex? Why would you ask . . ." She trailed off, her pupils growing larger. She sank back against her chair. "Oh, I see. You think . . . Do you actually believe . . . Rex . . . ?"

"No, ma'am. I merely asked you how he seemed."

"He seemed his normal self, Detective. He obviously drank a little too much, but then he always does at social affairs. Like any other man." She sat up taller again, defiant. "There was nothing out of the ordinary."

"Thank you, ma'am. That will be all for now." He stood as Mrs. Morton did. Before she reached the door, he called to her, "Please send your maid down. I have a question or two I'd like to ask her as well."

She stared hard in return, then nodded. Some five minutes later, there came a soft knock at the door. A young woman in dun brown serge entered the room.

"You called for me, sir?"

"You are Miss Riverton?" Jesse asked, and flipped to a fresh page in his notebook.

"Yes, Evelina Riverton, sir."

"Please take a seat." He gestured at the chair Mrs. Morton had vacated. "This is Miss Cross. She is here only to ensure that you are at your ease speaking with a man." His eyebrows went up, his mistake in calling me Miss Cross obviously occurring to him. "Mrs. Andrews, I mean."

"That's all right. I'm still Miss Cross in a professional capacity." I turned to Miss Riverton. "I work for the *Newport Messenger*, but rest assured I am only here, as Detective Whyte indicated, to ensure propriety."

"Thank you, ma'am." She folded her hands in her lap and waited. She sat as calmly as could be, appearing not alarmed in the least to have been summoned by a policeman.

Jesse began by asking, "Did you know the chambermaid who died the night of the musicale?"

"*Hmph.* Yes. Oh, only barely, sir, as we haven't been here but a few days, but I'd had the *pleasure* of her acquaintance." The sarcastic emphasis she placed on the word *pleasure* implied anything but.

"You didn't like her?" Jesse asked.

"I didn't." She gave a shrug. "She was abrupt and rude. Bossy. Didn't know her place. She pretended around the housekeeper and the butler, and if the Berwinds were anywhere within hearing, but when they weren't . . ." She shook her head. "I know it's wrong to speak ill of the dead, but in this case, I can't help it. Quite a shrew, that one."

My gaze met Jesse's. Miss Riverton had just confirmed what Bridget Whalen had told me about Ines's character. "Can you give us an example?"

"Well, the very first morning when I was unpacking Mrs. Morton, Ines comes into the room and orders me out because she has to change the linens. I said, 'You go ahead and do what you must, and I'll stay out of your way.' Well, she plunks her hands on her hips and tells me under no uncertain terms that she doesn't work to an audience, and I'd best make myself scarce or she'd find ways to make my life difficult."

"Goodness," I murmured. "Did you report it?"

"No, I didn't. No one likes to hear about spats between the servants. Reporting it would only bring me under scrutiny as well as her. I value my job with Mrs. Morton too much to risk losing it."

"Were there other incidents like that one?" Jesse asked.

"There were little things every day. Mean little comments in passing, and sometimes I'd find some of Mrs. Morton's toiletries out of place. Ines claimed she didn't touch them, but I knew better. And once I could have sworn I smelled Mrs. Morton's Le Parfum Idéal by Maison Houbigant on her. Have you any idea how much a four-ounce bottle of that costs? More than I make in a month, I can tell you that."

Jesse nodded, scribbling in his book. "Now, the night of the musicale, did you spend time with Mrs. Morton in her room during the intermission?"

"Indeed I did, sir. Mrs. Morton rang for me to come fix her hair and a bit of trim on her dress that was dangling. I came down right away with my sewing kit."

"And this all took how long?"

"Not ten minutes, sir."

Jesse flicked a gaze to me. Silvie Morton had seemed quite certain she had spent at least twenty minutes with her maid. "Are you sure that was about how long you were in the room with her?"

Miss Riverton shifted on her seat, peeking at us from beneath her brows. "Yes, sir, I'm quite sure."

"Where were you before and after?" Jesse asked next.

"In my room, sir. On the third floor. I'm sharing with Mrs. Gilchrist's maid, Nell, so she can vouch for me."

"And when you left Mrs. Morton, she was still in her room?"

"She was, sir."

"Do you remember what time she sent for you?"

"Yes, I do, sir. It was ten minutes to ten. I know that because I consulted my timepiece"—she patted the locket pinned to her bodice—"when she buzzed for me."

"Thank you, Miss Riverton." Jesse jotted a few final notations in his notebook.

As soon as the door closed behind her, I said to Jesse, "The intermission started at nine thirty. That means Silvie Morton couldn't have gone straight up to her room and buzzed Miss Riverton. That leaves twenty minutes of her time unaccounted for."

Jesse skewed his lips to one side and nodded. "So then, what did she do between the time she left the ballroom and called for her maid?"

I leaned back in my chair, pondering. "Yes, and why *had* her hair needed tending and her dress repairing?"

Chapter 8

Jesse next called Kay Gilchrist, who stole in through the partially open door like a schoolgirl summoned to the principal's office. She hesitated just over the threshold until Jesse cordially bade her to come and take a seat.

Her bottom lip disappeared between her teeth and the furrows scoring her brow threatened to leave permanent marks despite her youth. Once she'd settled, I reached across the table and gave her hand a reassuring squeeze.

"I'm glad you're here, Mrs. Andrews." She spoke in a whisper, her gaze darting to Jesse and then back to me. The spot on her lip threatened to bleed. "Thank you. I don't think I could do this otherwise."

"You're very welcome," I said with a smile, "but this won't be difficult at all. Will it, Detective Whyte?"

"Not a bit, ma'am," he replied gently. He turned a page in his notebook to another fresh sheet and wrote her name at the top. "I'm only going to ask you a few questions about the night the maid died, and about some of your impressions since arriving at The Elms."

"My impressions?" Her gaze shifted back and forth again. "I don't understand."

"Don't worry," I said. "Just answer the detective's questions as well as you can."

"All right." With her right hand, she fidgeted with the tiny pearl buttons on her left sleeve.

"Now then, Mrs. Gilchrist." Jesse held his pencil at the ready. "On the night of the musicale, where were you during the intermission?"

"I went upstairs."

"To your room, ma'am?"

"Uh, yes, I mean . . . that is . . . No. First, I used the . . . uh . . . uh . . ." She blushed fiercely and her voice dropped in volume. "The guest lavatory. Then I went into our bedroom."

"That's fine," I whispered to her. "Did you happen to summon your maid?"

"Nell? No, I . . . uh . . . managed on my own."

"And on your way upstairs or back down, did you see anyone else?" Jesse asked.

"Only downstairs in the gallery, and a few in the drawing room as I made my way back outside."

Jesse made a notation. "Do you know who Miss Varella was? Would you have recognized her?"

"I would, indeed. She made up our room every morning and evening, and sometimes I would see her in passing as I was going up or down."

"Had you ever spoken to her?" Jesse wished to know.

"Well . . . only to say good day. My husband doesn't like me to speak with the lower servants. He says it isn't proper. But really, to utterly ignore them seems terribly unkind to me. They *are* human beings, aren't they?"

I found myself grinning in appreciation and approval;

Mrs. Gilchrist had just won my esteem, going from a timid ghost of a woman to one of compassion and conviction. I reached again to pat her hand. "You are absolutely right, Mrs. Gilchrist."

"Only, please don't mention it to my husband."

"No, there shouldn't be any need to, Mrs. Gilchrist." Jesse set his pencil down and leaned slightly over the table toward her as if to encourage her confidence. "While you were upstairs, did you see or hear anyone else on the floor?"

"Not a peep."

"Is your room near the Mortons'?" he asked.

"Right next door."

"And you saw neither Mrs. Morton nor her lady's maid?" Jesse asked for clarification.

"No, neither."

Jesse nodded and recorded her answer. "What time did you go up? Was it as soon as the intermission began, or did you linger downstairs a while?"

"No, I went straight up. I wanted to be sure I'd be back downstairs before the music started again. I didn't wish to miss a note."

"All right, Mrs. Gilchrist, thank you very much." Jesse closed his notebook and came to his feet. "That will be all for now."

Mrs. Gilchrist stood up uncertainly. "Did I do all right?"

I stood as well. "You did just fine."

As she left the room, Jesse traded a knowing glance with me. "That's two people contradicting Mrs. Morton," he said. "Two people with no reason to lie."

"Exactly," I agreed. "It was Silvie Morton who was lying."

"Could she also have been lying about the necklace—about not knowing it existed?"

I didn't bother to reply. It was a question neither of us could answer—yet.

* * *

With no good reason to be present while Jesse questioned the two husbands, I rejoined the Berwinds and the two wives, along with Derrick, who had recently arrived. We gathered in the conservatory on the side of the house opposite the Chinese breakfast room. It was a large room of marble and glass with a red marble fountain taking up nearly the whole of the back wall, its water streaming soothingly from its bronze figures of seahorses, dolphins, tritons, and sea nymphs. Red marble planters on either side held a profusion of short, bushy ferns, while white marble statues depicting mytholog-ical figures stood along the sides of the room at intervals.

The French doors on the two outside walls had been thrown open to the sun-drenched afternoon air, and the Berwinds and their guests sat grouped on lushly upholstered wicker chairs and a settee in the middle of the room. Cordials and brandy had been served, and as I entered the room, a foot-man appeared as if by magic and offered me a crystal glass of sherry on a silver tray.

Kay Gilchrist shifted over a bit beside Mrs. Berwind to make room for me on the settee. She once again seemed re-lieved to see me. "I'm glad you've come." She took my hand as I settled in beside her. "I thought perhaps you'd help the detective interview our husbands." She shot a glance at Silvie Morton, sitting in a chair across from us.

"Detective Whyte will take it from here," I told her. Der-rick also sat opposite us, looking too large for the delicate garden chair, yet he managed to maintain a posture of appar-ent ease. Our gazes met; questions flashed in his eyes.

"Whyte seems a capable man," Ned Berwind observed. "Efficient. One hopes he makes short work of this matter."

"I don't see the need for him to upset Rex any further," Mrs. Morton said with a moue of impatience. "He is, after all, a victim in all of this. That woman stole something of great value. Besides, Rex was on the lawn at the time of the murder, and I've already answered the detective's questions. We shouldn't be subjected to any more unpleasantness."

True, but the murder occurred just beyond the lawn, so Mr. Morton's being outside certainly didn't rule him out. And Mrs. Morton was clearly hiding something.

"But, Silvie," Mrs. Gilchrist said, "by questioning Rex, Detective Whyte might find your necklace that much sooner. And then all of this will be over."

Would it? Finding the necklace would not make Ines and Rudolfo any less dead.

"It isn't *my* necklace," Mrs. Morton muttered under her breath.

"What's that, dear?" Mrs. Berwind inquired, and Mrs. Morton merely waved the matter away.

Just because my role as Jesse's co-interviewer had ended didn't mean I planned to sit quietly and do nothing. I raised my glass to my lips and sipped the sweet, velvety sherry, then caught Mrs. Berwind's eye.

"Ma'am," I began, but she cut me off.

"Please, after everything that's happened and your help with the police, shan't we dispense with formalities?" She glanced at her husband, who nodded his concurrence. "I'm Minnie to my friends."

"Yes, we should all dispense with formalities," Kay Gilchrist agreed with a relieved expression. "May we call you Emmaline?"

"Emma, please," I said, as my full name always seemed overly fussy to me. "Minnie," I continued, "were you aware of any difficulties between Ines and the other servants, either before or after the strike?"

"Not at all." She appealed to her husband. "Ned, had you

had any reports of problems among the servants? Other than their discontent with life at The Elms, that is."

"No, my dear, I'd heard not a whisper of trouble between any of them." He brought his snifter beneath his nose, inhaled, and then gulped a portion. "Ungrateful baggages that they were."

"And no conflict among the new staff and Ines?" I pressed.

"What are you implying, my dear?" Ned Berwind spoke politely, but a steeliness claimed his facial muscles. "That we don't run a tight ship? That our servants are out of control?"

"Not in the least," I assured him. "But perhaps this particular woman, Ines, had a tendency to breed discord among her coworkers."

"*Hmph.*" He offered no further comment.

"Look, Ned. Obviously, this woman had a serious run-in with someone," Derrick calmly pointed out. "Someone *murdered* her."

Ned Berwind's face flooded with waves of ruddy color. "Don't be crass, Andrews."

"Murder *is* crass, Ned," he rejoined quietly. "And a lot of other things besides."

Ned cast a gaze around at the rest of us. "Not in front of the ladies."

"That's enough, both of you." Minnie came to her feet. "Ladies, join me for a stroll on the terrace? We'll bring our drinks."

Charles Gilchrist came striding into the room. That magical footman followed him in, offering him a snifter of brandy. Charles took one look and waved it away with a succinct, "Whiskey."

The footman sent a subtle glance at his employer, who nodded just as subtly. Charles threw himself into the seat vacated by Silvie. The ladies were halfway across the room to the nearest French door when Minnie stopped and turned. "Mrs. Andrews? Are you coming?"

She wasn't granting me a choice in the matter. With great reluctance I hauled myself to my feet and crossed the room. Minnie all but slipped an arm around me to ensure I made it out of the house. Did she suspect that all I wished to do was remain behind and hear how Charles Gilchrist's interview had gone? To ask if he and Rex Morton had been questioned together or separately? Yet, I knew that had I stayed in the room the discussion would have been stilted, heavily edited for my benefit so as not to shock a lady's delicate sensibilities.

Derrick would tell me everything later, as would Jesse. With no other graceful option, I joined the ladies on the terrace, feeling all the more thwarted when Minnie closed the door behind us. The other doors into the room were too far away from where the men sat for their voices to be clearly overheard. Besides, the ladies fell to discussing their charitable endeavors, and I couldn't waste an opportunity to remind them of St. Nicholas Orphanage in Providence and their summer donation drive.

After leaving The Elms, Derrick and I returned to our flat on the Point, and Jesse joined us there once he had written up his report at the police station. I brewed a strong pot of tea and set out a tray of Nanny's shortbread cookies. I added a bottle of brandy for the men as well, though I took my tea with nothing stronger than a spot of honey bottled on a farm in Portsmouth at the other end of Aquidneck Island.

Jesse waved the brandy away, but then on second thought reached for it before Derrick could set it on the low table by the sofa. "I'm off duty, after all."

"No need to justify," I told him as he poured in a trickle. "And thank you for detouring here before going home."

He waved my thanks away. "Emma, if I could hire you for the force, I would. As it is, you and Derrick can tell me your impressions of the Mortons and the Gilchrists. Sometimes these people elude me. Their motives, their intentions. They say one thing, but their eyes tell a different story." He reached into his coat pocket. "But here, I thought you might want a look at this."

He handed me an envelope that had been previously unsealed. I slid the page out and scanned a few lines, then started over, reading more carefully. "Ines's letter of reference from New York."

Jesse nodded. "Mrs. Berwind's housekeeper was able to find it in the former housekeeper's files. On face value, it looks authentic."

Derrick studied it over my shoulder. "Who can say, though? These are easy to forge, and if no one bothered to check with the family . . ." He shrugged.

"Someone most certainly will do so now," Jesse said.

"Written by the lady of the house, it seems." I held the letter closer to the lamp on the table beside me. The neat, feminine handwriting spoke of careful lessons in penmanship. "Says all the usual things, gives Ines's progression in the household from kitchen maid to underparlor maid to chambermaid. Whoever wrote this put some thought into it."

"Yes, but whether it's all true remains to be seen." Jesse reached for the letter and envelope. I gave them one last perusal before handing them back.

Derrick held his cup and saucer balanced on his thigh. "So then, what did Morton and Gilchrist tell you when you questioned them?"

"Mr. Morton repeated what his wife said, that he was out on the lawn smoking. One wonders if they collaborated beforehand."

"Highly likely," Derrick said.

"And Mr. Gilchrist?" I prompted.

"Claims he drifted into the library, looking for a book he and Mr. Berwind had discussed earlier that day."

"What book?" I asked, then realized it probably didn't matter.

Jesse's expression told me that perhaps it *did* matter. "That's the thing. He seemed to think for a few seconds before answering. Then he said it was *The Tree of Knowledge* by Henry James."

"Did you ask Ned if they'd discussed the book?" Derrick asked.

Jesse shook his head. "Not yet. But I asked Mr. Gilchrist what he did with it. Did he take it up to his room? He said he flipped through it and put it back on the shelf for another time."

I frowned in puzzlement. "Why would he bother looking for a book during a social event, especially if he wasn't going to take it up to his room?"

"I asked him that very question," Jesse said after a sip of his tea. "He made the excuse that he wasn't in the mood for chitchat during the intermission. Going to look for the book was merely a way to avoid having to make unwanted conversation."

"I can't say I blame him for that." Derrick chuckled, then sobered. "But the fact that he had to think about the title of the book before he answered you implies he was making it up as he went along. As for the book itself, I suspect he was trying to remember a title he knew Ned had in his library, and one they might well have discussed at one time or another. I'm guessing if you went looking for it, you'd probably find it, although not necessarily where he claimed it was."

"Good point," Jesse said. "Now I wish I had asked him exactly which shelf it was on."

"You still can, of course, although he might be clever enough to actually find it beforehand." Derrick reached over to pluck a shortbread cookie off the tray.

"I don't know." I paused, considering the reasons Charles Gilchrist might have lied about the book. Perhaps he really did wish to avoid having to make conversation during the intermission. Or perhaps he and his wife had argued. Perhaps they argued often, which would account for her jittery behavior. She'd already indicated that she feared his disapproval. But their problems seemed to be between themselves, whereas Rex Morton most certainly did have a reason to wish ill on Ines, if she had stolen his necklace. "If anyone had a reason to go after Ines, it's Rex Morton. Jesse, I believe your attention is best focused on him for now. And perhaps his wife as well."

"You think she was lying about knowing about the necklace?" he asked me, his voice laced with uncertainty.

"We both know she was lying about something, or at least hiding something." I had already filled Derrick in on her interview on our way home. "In the meantime, it might be a good idea to ask some of the servants if they happened to see Silvie Morton anywhere in the house where she oughtn't to have been that night. I'll go back tomorrow."

"A good plan," Jesse agreed with a nod. "How will you manage it?"

"By using the pretext of following up on Ines's murder for another article in the *Messenger*. That will get me below stairs. In fact, I might be able to avoid the Berwinds and their guests altogether."

"First thing in the morning would be the best time to go, then," Derrick said. "Before anyone above stairs is up."

I smiled at him. "Yes, and that will allow me to still work a full day at the *Messenger*."

"I wasn't complaining." He raised his hands in protest.

"I know, but I wouldn't blame you if you did."

He reached out his hand to me, and I wrapped my own around it. "If I've learned anything in these past few years," he said, "it's that you're fully capable of handling this and the paper, too. And that once you've set your feet on a certain path, there is no diverting you until you've reached your destination."

"Don't I know it," Jesse mumbled begrudgingly, but I knew not to take it personally. We went back many years, he and I, to when I was a tomboy running after my elder brother, trying and often succeeding in keeping up with him and his friends. He slapped his thighs and came to his feet. "It's time I went home. It's been a long day."

"You don't have to run off." Yet I stood as well.

"No, my housekeeper will have a nice supper waiting for me, and then I can kick these shoes off and put my feet up." Before he made his way to the door, he pointed a finger at me. "And *you*, remember it's questions only tomorrow, and you're to report back to me as soon as you arrive in town."

I saluted him. "Yes, sir."

"Thank you for seeing me, Mrs. Rogan." As planned, having parked my buggy along Bellevue Court, I had entered the kitchen area of The Elms through the wisteria-covered servants' entrance. The cold-preparation room and main kitchen bustled with activity as the staff made the initial preparations for the day's meals. Mrs. Rogan, the housekeeper, led me through to her parlor. Like the former housekeeper, she was in her middle years, her features plain but for her dark eyes and heavy brows, which lent her an exotic look.

She bade me sit in an armchair of pale green brocade. She sat opposite me and folded her sturdy hands in her lap.

"What is it I can help you with, Miss Cross? Or should I call you Mrs. Andrews?"

I smiled. "I'm here on behalf of the *Messenger*. Miss Cross will do."

She tilted her head, raising both her chin and her eyebrows, clearly in judgment. "Your husband doesn't mind?"

I merely smiled again and shook my head. "Now then, Mrs. Rogan, we at the *Messenger* are still attempting to piece together the events of the night of the musicale."

"You were here that night. You witnessed what happened."

"Yes. But I only witnessed things from upstairs. And Ines Varella wasn't murdered upstairs."

"No. Nor downstairs either," she rightly pointed out. Her hands tightened their grip on each other. "Poor thing. Most unfortunate. But what is it you think we saw down here? We were all much too busy making sure the evening ran smoothly. There might not have been a formal dinner served, but we were responsible for providing ceaseless champagne and hors d'oeuvres to the guests. Along with anything else they might need."

"Was Ines helping in any way?"

"No, none of the upstairs maids were needed that night. Their job came much earlier in the day, ensuring all the rooms were perfect."

"Did any of the guests come down here?"

Her eyes narrowed fractionally. "Why on earth would a guest come below stairs?"

"It's only a question, Mrs. Rogan. Perhaps to make a special request of the chef or ask for a certain wine. Perhaps to check on something that had gone to the laundry." That last came to me suddenly. Could whoever had murdered Ines have deposited clothing with the evidence of it directly in the laundry room?

I waited for her reply, several seconds in coming. When it did, it carried distinct disdain. Whether she aimed the sentiment at me personally or merely at the suggestion I'd made, I didn't know. "Outlandish. No. I didn't see anyone down here who didn't belong."

"You're quite sure?"

She came to her feet. "Miss Cross, I don't understand the purpose of these questions. I thought you wanted to talk about Ines. As it is, you are wasting my time and your own."

"I'm very sorry, Mrs. Rogan." I slowly rose to standing. "Perhaps if I was more specific. Did Mrs. Morton come down for any reason that night? Or at any time since she arrived?"

"Mrs. Morton?" Her gaze darted away, then came quickly back to mine.

"Yes. Silvie Morton, who is staying here. Surely you know who I mean. Or have you ever encountered her anywhere in the house that seemed odd to you?"

"Certainly not."

"What about *Mr.* Morton?"

Mrs. Rogan gathered her dignity and swung open the parlor door. "I've work to do, Miss Cross. The Berwinds and their guests will be awake soon. Good day."

"Good day, Mrs. Rogan. Thank you for your time." I strode past her but didn't turn toward the kitchen and the way outside. Instead, I wandered in the opposite direction.

"Miss Cross, where do you think you're going?" she called after me. "I must insist you leave the premises."

I turned fully around to face her, my cordial smile in place. "It's quite all right, Mrs. Rogan. You can clear my being here with Mrs. Berwind. It's she, really, who would like the answers to these questions."

Pivoting, I continued along the corridor and into the laundry room. My claim concerning Mrs. Berwind was a calculated risk—a half lie, to be honest—but I didn't think Mrs. Rogan would rise to the challenge. To do that would only raise further questions, this time about the housekeeper's own activities, and everything about our little chat convinced me she did not wish to bring attention to herself.

Why? And what did her reticence have to do with Silvie Morton?

Chapter 9

I asked similar questions of the laundry maids. Had they seen anyone from above stairs come down? Had any of the guests made inquiries or special requests concerning their laundry? The latter seemed to befuddle them more than the former.

"Why, they'd have sent their valet or maid to ask any questions," one of the assistants assured me. "A guest would never come down to speak to us. Never!"

My inquiries ended there. Although I wished to poke around down in the subbasement, I guessed I would be escorted out the moment a worker spotted me. With the furnaces and coal rooms housed there, it would be deemed far too dangerous to allow access to anyone but an experienced worker.

With a sigh of frustration, I left the house, but I didn't quite leave the property. Instead, I turned the corner onto Dixon Street and walked down to the entrance of the coal tunnel. Had another delivery been made earlier this morning? The bulkhead doors now seemed securely locked. It had been mere curiosity, really, that had sent me there. But the figure I spied crouching among the foliage farther along the side of the road propelled me with renewed purpose.

"Mr. Morton, good morning."

He surged to his feet, and I glimpsed his moment of indecision; he must have been debating whether to pretend he hadn't heard me and walk off at a brisk pace or stand and face me. Luckily for me, the latter won out.

He dragged his hat from his head. "Good morning, Mrs. Andrews. Um . . . whatever are you doing here?"

"I could ask you the same thing." I stopped and peered up at him from beneath the brim of my own hat. His hair had been freshly pomaded, his mustache trimmed to its perfect line. Yet he still managed to look disheveled. Sleep, I decided, or the lack of it, had left his face slack, his eyes puffy and bloodshot. "I'm surprised to see anyone up this early."

"Yes, well."

When nothing more seemed forthcoming, I said, "I came to ask a few more questions about Miss Varella's death. For the *Messenger*."

"Ah, of course." He drew a breath, still looking indecisive, wary. He glanced at the ground around us.

"Oh, I just realized." I showed him a look of sympathetic understanding. "You're searching for your necklace, aren't you? Hoping the police missed it when they investigated the area."

He looked about to deny it. Then his shoulders sagged. "Yes, Mrs. Andrews, I am. I keep hoping. . . ."

"I'm sure the police did a thorough search." I, too, glanced around. "But these hedges and trees can hide so much. I suppose it must be impossible to peek between every flower stem and tuft of grass."

"Exactly. So perhaps . . ." He compressed his lips.

I looked up at the elms forming canopies above our heads. "Have you considered that Miss Varella could have tossed it up into a tree when she realized someone had come to confront her?"

His eyes went wide as his head tilted upward. "No, I hadn't. But that's a capital suggestion, to search through the branches." Another breath escaped him. "But how?"

I didn't answer him. I searched his weary features, his defeated posture. "Mr. Morton, obviously this is no ordinary necklace. What is it? Why all the secrecy?" I didn't say "from your wife," but the implication hung in the air between us.

He hesitated for so long I didn't think he would reply. Just as I concluded I had overplayed my hand, he said, "I bought the piece from a London auction as a silent bidder. My London solicitor represented me. I didn't want word getting out it was me."

"Yes, but why?"

"Mrs. Andrews, need I remind you the necklace has been stolen. My anonymity was supposed to prevent anyone from knowing I had it in my possession as we traveled back to the States. How it was discovered, I'll never know."

One possibility seemed obvious to me. "Are you sure you can trust your solicitor?"

Once again, he hesitated. Then, "Yes, absolutely."

"Him, but not your wife," I couldn't prevent myself from observing.

"A man isn't obligated to tell his wife everything, Mrs. Andrews. It might serve you well to remember that, now that you are married."

I didn't think it wise to insist that Derrick would never keep important information from me, nor sneak about without my knowledge.

As these thoughts ran through my mind, he went on in an

offended tone, "I might also remind you I am the victim in this matter, not the perpetrator."

My shoulders squared. "Ines Varella is the victim. She may or may not have stolen your necklace, but either way, she has been murdered." His nostrils flared, and I feared he would walk off. When he didn't, I braved another question, or, rather, a rewording of one I had already asked. "Mr. Morton, all members of the Four Hundred own costly jewelry. Many pieces once belonged to European royalty. What made this necklace so important as to prompt such a carefully planned crime?"

He spun away, reaching out to press his palm against a tree trunk. His head fell forward against his chest while his shoulders collapsed around his ears. Without lifting his head or looking at me, he said, "It belonged to Marie Antoinette, a gift from the king, her husband. Its centerpiece is a ten-carat diamond of the first water. There are larger gems, certainly, but a stone of such clarity is exceedingly rare and, indeed, almost miraculous. The other diamonds surrounding it are virtually worthless in comparison."

My breath caught. "Goodness."

Still hunched over, he managed to lift his head toward me. "It is essential I get it back. *Essential*."

"Yes, I understand. Of course. It must have set you back a great deal. And it was uninsured. I understand why you must have it back."

"No, Mrs. Andrews. No, you do not." At that he walked away, slapping his hat on his head. As he strode along the street, he kicked at the flower beds, at the carefully molded shrubbery that lined the perimeter of The Elms property, still searching for his missing necklace but showing little hope of finding it.

*   *   *

"Nanny telephoned," Derrick told me when I arrived at the *Messenger.* "She's hoping we'll come for dinner." He turned in his office chair, draping an arm around the high wooden back. "I think she misses us badly when we're not there."

I slipped off my gloves and ran a finger under the starched white collar of my shirtwaist. The day had grown hot. It had rained last night, but rather than cool the air, it had only released a swell of humidity. "I know she does. Yes, I'll let her know we'll be there."

"And stay the night?"

"Yes, that too."

He studied me several moments, his gaze boring into me. To escape his speculations, I went over to Stanley Sheppard, presiding over a stack of papers on his desk at the other side of the room. Our offices on Spring Street were rather cramped, and this front space overlooking the street served as our administrative office for both Derrick and our editor-in-chief. Their desks faced the wide windows that gave generous views onto the street, with its constant daytime onslaught of vehicles, pedestrians, trolleys, and dust.

"Anything new come in over the wires yet?" I asked him.

"Already in your basket." Mr. Sheppard, a bachelor in his forties with thinning hair, light brown eyes, and a young man's energy tempered by an older man's good judgment, gave me a good morning waggle of his eyebrows. "Learn anything more about the Varella murder?"

It didn't surprise me that he used such a businesslike term for Ines's death. He hadn't known her. He wasn't a cruel or unkind man, but an efficient one, and just then he spoke to me with the efficiency of an astute newspaperman.

"No, and yes."

My answer brought Derrick to his feet and over to join us. "I was about to ask you the same question."

I set my handbag on the desk. "To begin with, neither Mrs. Rogan, the housekeeper, nor any of the women working in the laundry admitted to seeing either Silvie or Rex Morton below stairs at any time, much less the night of the musicale. I believe the latter but not the former."

That caught the interest of both men. Derrick said, "You think Mrs. Rogan was lying? About seeing which one?"

"I'm not sure, but I do believe she was hiding something." I pulled the pin from my straw boater, took the hat off, and laid it beside my handbag. I gave the sides of my hair a pat. "The main question, though, is why. Did one or both of the Mortons bribe or threaten her to keep quiet?"

"So really, you haven't learned much," Mr. Sheppard commented, "except that the Berwinds' housekeeper doesn't like to answer questions about the guests. That's really not unusual in these situations. Especially given how apt the Berwinds are to fire their servants."

Derrick nodded, holding a forefinger against his chin. "That's very true. I can imagine the servants not wanting to take any chances."

"Fair enough, but I still believe, quite firmly, that Mrs. Rogan has something to hide. But that's not all. When I left the house, I decided to take a walk down Dixon Street to the entrance to the coal tunnel." I ignored Derrick's murmured, "Of course you did." "And whom do you think I saw?"

Mr. Sheppard held up his callused hands, but the answer dawned in Derrick's features immediately. "Rex?"

I nodded, showing him half a smile. "He was searching for his necklace."

"Poor idiot." Derrick gave a shake of his head.

"He's hoping it became lost in the struggle when Ines's killer struck. It was truly pitiable, seeing that desperate man scratching among the weeds. On his hands and knees."

"Good grief." A breath whooshed from between Mr. Sheppard's lips. "What kind of necklace is this, to drive a man to his knees, especially after the police had already searched the area?"

"A diamond of the first water, apparently. According to Rex Morton, it once belonged to Marie Antoinette. He told me the main stone was so valuable as to render the rest relatively worthless. And there's more." I leaned closer to him. "When I told him I now understood how much was at stake, he insisted I didn't."

Derrick and Mr. Sheppard exchanged looks of incredulity. Derrick leaned against the wall at his back. "I don't suppose he confided how he came by such a treasure?"

"Not entirely," I replied. "Only that it came from a London auction, and that he was represented anonymously by his solicitor there."

The men exchanged another glance, this one brimming with mutual knowledge. Mr. Sheppard voiced what they were both thinking. "Black-market auction. Mostly stolen goods."

"Stolen?" I honestly hadn't thought of that. I had naively assumed the purchase had been legitimate. This meant that if the police reached the same conclusion, the necklace, if found, would not be returned to Rex Morton.

What would he do then?

"One thing is certain," Derrick said. "We can't expect this necklace to turn up in a Newport jewelry store or pawn shop, or around the neck of a society matron. Given the secrecy under which Rex made the purchase, whoever has it must know its value and will likely smuggle it off the island. Probably to New York, to yet another black-market auction. Or to his private vault."

"I don't understand." Absently I turned my wedding ring this way and that on my finger. "What good is having something like this if one's wife can't wear it, and in fact no one else can ever know you have it?"

Derrick showed me the kind of smile one uses to reassure a child who must be told a sobering fact. "There are men in this world who wish to own things simply for the sake of having them. It's greed, pure and simple, and I suppose proof of their power. It's also a kind of insurance. The bottom can fall out of a country's monetary system but a diamond of the first water will never lose its value, even if one must resort again to the black market."

That evening, Nanny greeted us outside, her arms open to embrace us both as we alighted from the carriage. She kissed my cheeks and rocked me back and forth as she squeezed the breath from my lungs.

"You act as if we've been away for months, not a couple of days," I chided amiably as we went into the house.

Nanny gave a happy shrug. "Can I help it if I miss my lamb when she's not here?"

Patch came running down the hall from the kitchen, his ears flapping and his tail wagging wildly. In his jubilance, he sprang up into the air, but came down on all fours before trotting over to greet us. It had taken months to break him of the habit of jumping up on people in his happiness to see them. Derrick and I both paid our respects with vigorous rubs and scratches and pats.

Nanny laughed at our pup's antics. "This one misses you too. He doesn't understand that you're just a few miles away in town."

As we had planned, we spent the night at Gull Manor. It was some time after we'd retired that I suddenly woke, blinked in the silver glow of moonlight nudging its way through the curtains, and sat up in bed.

"London!"

Beside me, Derrick stirred and shoved at his pillow. Then, groggily, he opened one eye. "What?"

I gazed down at his sleep-warmed features. "London. Derrick, that's where Rex bought the necklace. And that's where the musicians at the Berwinds' musicale came from. Silvie Morton sponsored their way to America."

"Er . . . um . . ." With a yawn, he pushed higher in the bed and leaned against the headboard. "All right. And . . . ?"

"Don't you see? They could have followed the Mortons here because they knew about the necklace and planned to steal it. Or at least one of them did."

"But how could they have known about it?"

"Musicians are rather like servants, hovering in the background at social affairs and generally able to move unseen among society. They're in a unique position to overhear things."

"Perhaps." The shadows couldn't quite conceal his doubts. "But to come all the way to America? Why not steal the necklace in London?"

"Because they wouldn't have had the chance. Here, they were all brought together under the same roof—the Mortons, the musicians, and the necklace—here at The Elms."

He took this in while rubbing the sleep from his eyes. "Where does Ines come in?"

That gave me pause. "I'm not sure. But if Rex's solicitor is also involved, he could have helped arrange things. Even planting Ines at The Elms to help with the actual theft."

"There are a lot of *ifs* in this theory." He reached his arm around me and drew me close. "I still don't understand how a woman of Ines's background came to know about and steal that necklace out of a locked safe."

"I don't know. But we need to learn more about these musicians and how Silvie Morton came to sponsor them."

"It's something she does," he reminded me.

"Yes, I realize that, but why *these* musicians? Who approached whom? We need to find out."

"I have no doubt you will in due time." He kissed my forehead. "How about getting some sleep first?"

Just after dawn, Derrick and I padded down to the morning room to find that Nanny and Katie had breakfast ready, a lovely assortment of eggs, meats, baked goods, and fruit laid out buffet style on the sideboard.

"You two were up early and busy," I called into the adjoining kitchen. "Honestly, you needn't have gone to so much trouble."

While Derrick concurred with a vigorous nod, he nonetheless went straight to the sideboard and enthusiastically began loading up a plate.

Nanny came out a moment later with a pot of coffee and set it on the table. She smiled in approval as Derrick returned from the sideboard.

"Juice?" she offered.

"Yes, thank you," he replied, and she turned to go back into the kitchen, where the sound of running water could be heard.

The savory aromas had their effect on my appetite and I also chose a bit of everything. Derrick held my chair for me when I returned to the table, and then Nanny came in with a pitcher of orange juice. How our lives had changed, even in such small ways, since I'd gained my inheritance from my uncle Cornelius.

"Nanny, really," I said with a hint of good-natured reproof, "I don't want you working so hard. Derrick and I would be fine with scrambled eggs and toast."

"Pish." She waved her hand as if to swat me away.

At the same time, Derrick nudged my foot under the table. When I glanced at him, he gave me a flat-lipped look and shook his head slightly—an admonishment for me to allow Nanny to do for us as she liked. It was true, I had to admit, that she never looked so happy as when she did special things for us. In fact, Derrick's and my marriage had returned some of the old spring to her step, despite her advanced years and the extra pounds that now padded her figure.

Katie soon joined us, looking equally gratified by her morning labors. She filled a plate and sat with us at the table—something that would shock members of the Four Hundred. But Katie was much more than my maid-of-all-work. She had become family and I would not draw a line between us.

"Well," I said, duly chastised, "thank you, both of you. It's all quite wonderful."

At my elbow sat a shallow stack of morning papers and I quickly flipped through to see what had been delivered. The *Messenger* was among them, along with the newspaper I'd initially worked for, the *Observer.* There was also the *Daily News*, and . . .

"The *Aquidneck Island Advocate*? Really, Nanny?" It was the newspaper run by Orville Brown, who had encouraged the Berwinds' servants to strike without a thought to the risks involved.

Nanny only shrugged, but a blush engulfed Katie's fair complexion. "It's mine, Miss Emma. I subscribed to it. I don't agree with half of what Mr. Brown says, but I'm interested in what the workers on the island want. What they're facing . . ." She trailed off. "I'm sorry. I'll cancel it, if you want."

I held up a hand. "No, no. You're quite right, actually. It's good to see all sides of a matter. As long as you realize

Mr. Brown's encouragement of violence and other extreme measures is not only ill advised, but often ineffectual."

"I wouldn't let his opinions influence me, Miss Emma. I only read the paper for the facts."

Did Mr. Brown report the facts without a hefty dose of his own opinions thrown in? I doubted it, but I also doubted that our sweet, sensible Katie would be led astray. While we continued with breakfast, I halfheartedly slid the *Advocate* from between the other papers with the intention of turning the pages to see what Orville Brown might be ranting about this week. I didn't make it past the front page.

There, emblazoned halfway down in thick, bold letters, was Ines's name, along with the headline: JUSTICE IS SERVED.

All week there had been articles written about the murder in Newport's various newspapers. With the theft of the necklace not yet common knowledge, most of the papers had painted Ines as a victim. But not this article. As I perused the report, my hackles rose and my pulse pounded in my temples.

"Listen to this." I smacked the page hard, immediately capturing the attention of the others. Nanny frowned. Katie flinched with trepidation. "Miss Varella, in believing herself better than her peers, destroyed any chance The Elms's servants had to prevail in their demands. Is her death murder, then, or aptly applied justice for her traitorous views and failure to condemn social inequality?"

Derrick's fork dangled in midair until he slowly lowered it to his plate. "What?"

"Social inequality?" Katie looked thoroughly baffled. "For not wanting to risk losing her position?"

"That awful man." Nanny clucked her tongue. "How he stretches the truth to sell newspapers. Katie, you *should* cancel your subscription, this very day."

"I think I will," she agreed.

"He's a downright danger." I pushed the newspaper aside. "He'll incite violence, even murder, yet I'm sure he'd be the last to take responsibility when it happens."

Derrick pressed his napkin to his lips. "Cowardly, men like him. The biggest problem with him is that much of what he presents is true, and many of his ideals are just. But he wraps them in sensationalism and tries to entice people to react."

I went still as a numbing thought slithered up my spine. At Derrick's prompting, I said, "Are we certain he's only leading other people to violence, and not himself as well?"

Chapter 10

After discussing the matter with Jesse, he and Derrick agreed to keep an eye on Orville Brown's activities in the coming days. More than that, Jesse deemed it a good idea to interview the man. We had all assumed Ines's death to be connected to the theft of the necklace, but could Orville Brown, with his inverted sense of justice, have committed the deed in a fit of uncontrolled rage toward someone he considered a traitor to her class? Then what of the necklace? Perhaps, as Rex Morton hoped, it was hidden somewhere on The Elms property.

I had told Jesse about my encounter with Rex and his disclosure about how he had acquired the necklace in London. Jesse very much doubted Rex Morton's claim of being a victim. More and more, Ines's murder seemed to involve many perpetrators, in one way or another.

But speaking of the Mortons, I arranged to visit The Elms—and Silvie—again later that afternoon. After arriving at the *Messenger*, I penned a note to Mrs. Berwind inquiring after her state of mind and well-being, then sent it off with one of our newsboys whose delivery route took him along Bellevue Avenue. As I had anticipated, she sent a reply with one of her footmen, an invitation to join her and the other two ladies for luncheon.

"The men are playing golf," she told me when I arrived, "so we women may enjoy one another's company and speak freely."

Yes, I had been hoping that might be the case. As I relinquished my boater and gloves, I did, however, apologize for my working-day clothing.

"Not a bit, Emma, not a bit. I must say I admire your industry. And lucky you, I say."

Was she placating me? I thanked her, and once again she dismissed my sentiments as unnecessary. "I'm not from old money, you see, so my standards are different from those of many other wives you might meet. My father was a diplomat, so while I had the advantage of living abroad and in good style, there were no millions at our disposal. And of course, Ned is *certainly* not from old money. Why, every cent we have he made himself, something I greatly admire."

"As do I, Mrs. Berwind."

"Didn't we agree you would call me Minnie?"

"Yes, we did, Minnie." I hurried to keep up as she briskly led me to the drawing room, where Silvie Morton and Kay Gilchrist awaited us. As we greeted each other, Minnie pressed the buzzer beside the hearth. Then she simply stood there, her gaze fixed on the wall. I wondered what on earth she could be doing, but when the footman arrived, I understood.

As she turned to him, Minnie gestured at what revealed itself to be a timer set in the wall above the buzzer. "Very good, Fergus. That was less than twenty seconds. A marked improvement over last time."

The footman bobbed his head. "Thank you, ma'am."

"Please let Carver know we're ready for luncheon."

She timed her servants, I realized with a shock. How could she be tolerant of my working, claim herself to be different from other society wives, yet be so exacting when it came to her staff?

The Berwinds' dining room might not have been as large as the one at The Breakers, but it was every bit as ornate. I often thought the Four Hundred saved the most sumptuous décor for their dining rooms, where they held the captive attention of those sitting around the table. After all, in a ballroom one's attention is on one's partner and the steps of the dance, and making sure the pair of you don't collide with your neighbors. But in the dining room, one's gaze is free to roam in between choosing which fork is intended for which course.

Whereas the adjoining ballroom and the drawing room beyond it were light and airy, the dining room boasted more somber hues of rich dark paneling, deep green accents, and brilliant gilding that surrounded the massive Baroque murals depicting scenes from Venetian history. We took our seats at the end of the table closest to the rose and ebony-hued marble fireplace, Silvie Morton and I on one side, Minnie and Kay Gilchrist opposite us. It seemed fortuitous to me that I'd joined them, as I made an even number at the table.

Over braised veal and stuffed cucumbers, we discussed the usual topics when women are together, which easily allowed me to guide the conversation to the subject of music, and then the musicians we'd heard here on that fateful night. Their faces tightened at first, then relaxed as I showed no inclination to discuss the murder.

I turned a smiling face to Silvie. "Have the musicians gone on to New York yet?"

"I don't know, really." She speared a cucumber and dragged it through the white wine sauce on her plate. I noticed how pale she looked, how drawn, as if she hadn't been sleeping well. "I don't think so."

"Didn't you say they were performing in town first, at the Casino?" Kay supplied eagerly. Though always pale herself, she seemed animated and much more relaxed today than usual.

"Yes, I do believe that was their plan." Silvie sipped her wine. "And one or two other recitals, now that you mention it."

I lifted my wine as well. "They're really quite talented. You were inspired to sponsor their way to America."

"They were wonderful," Kay agreed, craning forward over her plate. "A pity the night was cut short." Her mouth formed an O and she raised her fingertips to her lips. "I *am* sorry to bring that up."

After a pause, Minnie smiled. "Never mind. It's quite all right, Kay." Then she said to Silvie, "Emma is right, you *were* inspired. Where did you find them?"

"At the home of friends in London." Silvie's enthusiasm didn't at all match that of her two friends. She seemed so listless I half expected her to lean an elbow on the table and rest her chin in her hand.

Nonetheless, I said, "And you approached them with the idea of performing in America? Your husband must have been keen on the idea as well."

"Rex? Hardly . . ." She stared down at her plate before raising her gaze with an apologetic look. "Music doesn't interest Rex terribly much. But actually, I didn't approach them. They approached me. Or their first violinist did. He speaks for the rest of them. I suppose my reputation as a patron of the musical arts preceded me, and this ensemble has been eager to play in America."

While the other three discussed the merits of these musicians, I mulled over the fact that they had sought out Silvie

Morton, not the other way around. That could mean they had more than music on their minds at the time. I also made a mental note of Silvie's implied reluctance on her husband's part. I seemed to remember his expressing just such sentiments the night of the musicale, with a less than enthusiastic look when the subject came up. It seemed he would have been happier *not* paying the passage for several musicians to cross the Atlantic, not to mention housing them once they arrived. But that made me wonder. At that time, he had the necklace in his possession and was counting on the profits from selling it here in America. Then why balk at his wife's project? Was he a skinflint by nature, or had his financial woes begun before the theft?

After lunch, Minnie suggested we retire to the conservatory for tea and a round of bridge. I would have preferred to return to the *Messenger*, but etiquette dictated I not rush off immediately after luncheon. I made the most of our trek through the house to the garden room by maneuvering myself to Silvie's side.

As we lagged a few steps behind the other two, I asked her, "I wonder, did you speak to the musicians during the intermission?"

"Why do you ask that?"

"I'm interested to know how well you got to know them, and whether they sought your advice on their American debut."

"They did, but as for getting to know them . . ." She turned her face in my direction, her gaze searching and uncertain. "What are you getting at, Emma?"

I decided to be direct with her. "Could any of the ensemble members have known about your husband's necklace?"

"Are you implying—" Her mouth fell open as she continued to regard me. "I can't see how any of them could have. Do you think one of them . . . ?"

"It's merely a thought I had after you said they sought you out for your patronage, rather than the other way around."

"Dear heavens." She came to a swishing halt in front of the first set of French doors in the drawing room, overlooking the north curve of the terrace. If I had noticed her paleness in the subdued light of the dining room, here, with the sunlight streaming through the glass, I detected the ravages of constant worry and sleeplessness. "Have I been had? Used like a pawn to swindle my husband?"

"It's only a possibility, one the police should look into."

"Why haven't they already? What are they waiting for? Any day now those musicians might leave Newport, and then what? Emma, I don't know the full significance of this necklace or what effect the theft of it will have on our finances. I only know I have never seen my husband so utterly devastated. And that tells me we are in trouble. Perhaps terrible, *terrible* trouble."

Back in town, I enlisted one of our newsboys to deliver a message to the address Silvie had given me before I left The Elms. In it I requested an interview with the five musicians from England, and I admit I worded my missive in a way that would have led them to believe my interest lay solely with their talents. Within the hour, I received a reply: they would be delighted to speak with me later that afternoon. Did I feel a slight frisson of guilt? Perhaps.

I busied myself meanwhile with several articles, one of which covered the latest meeting of the city council. As I went down the list of their proposed ordinances and budgets, I heard Derrick whistling as he entered the building. He appeared in my doorway moments later.

"I have news."

The set of his features told me this news would be of particular interest to me. I set down my pen. "What?"

"Jesse told me they've tracked down the family who supposedly supplied Ines with her references."

"Supposedly?" I guessed what was coming.

"They've never heard of her."

"There can be no mistake?"

"None whatsoever. They were quite adamant, not to mention offended at having been named fraudulently."

I sat back and sighed. "Then who is she?" I didn't expect an answer, nor did I receive one. Not then, anyway.

Later, he and I set out together to the inn where the musicians were staying, walking up Spring Street to Pelham and finding the Federal-style house just up the street from the United Congregational Church, a brownstone building with two ornate towers and Byzantine-style stained-glass windows. The woman who answered the door seemed to be expecting us. She led us into a formal parlor where all five musicians sat waiting for us, as if they were the audience and we the entertainment.

They seemed younger than I remembered, or perhaps it had been their talent that had led me to believe they must be older to have such expertise. The harpist I remembered simply for the fact of her being a woman, the only woman of the group. She looked almost girlish to me now, in her simple yellow day dress and her blond hair swept back into a braid coiled at her nape. I wondered that her parents had agreed to let her travel so far from home.

They all stood as the introductions were made. Then one of the men, the one I remembered as being the first violinist, stepped forward to shake our hands. He towered over Derrick by several inches but was of so slight a figure I didn't doubt a winter gale would knock him off his feet.

"We didn't expect two of you." He spoke in a cultured English accent with no hint of accusation in his voice. Quite the contrary, he looked uncommonly pleased. His next words confirmed that impression. "We're honored that you've taken an interest in our little group. This being our first foray into the Americas, we are hoping for as much exposure as possible."

"Yes, of course. And you are?" I slid my notebook and pencil from my handbag. Before he answered, he gestured for us to make ourselves comfortable on the main sofa after signaling for two of his fellow musicians to vacate its velvet cushions.

"David Swinford," he replied, folding his length into an armchair opposite us and sitting forward. His clasped hands dangled between his knees. "I'm first violinist and the leader of the group."

I caught the others subtly rolling their eyes.

Derrick said, "We were at The Elms the night you played there. Your talents are well known to us."

Mr. Swinford's dark, abundant eyebrows shot inward. "But you only heard half of our performance. We were saving the best for last, but . . . well." He turned his palms upward.

"Really, David, don't make it sound as though we were somehow cheated out of our performance." The blonde shook her head and smoothed her skirts with swift, impatient motions. "That poor woman." She turned to me. "Did you know her?"

"Know a servant?" Mr. Swinford made a moue of distaste.

"I had only recently met her, but yes, I knew her." I emphasized the words, with a significant look at the first violinist. Readying my pencil again, I asked the woman, "And your name, may I ask?"

"Dorothy Everson."

Soon I had all their names recorded, along with which part of England they were from. Most hailed from London or just outside it, although the violist and youngest of the group, a Jonathan Wiles, came from faraway Edinburgh. I enjoyed his accent and was annoyed when Mr. Swinford kept speaking over him.

We asked them the usual questions: how they had come by their musical training; how long they'd been playing professionally; how they came to form the ensemble. David Swinford took most of the credit for their success, his boasting being the cause of several more rounds of eye-rolling. I found it necessary to cough lightly to cover my inclination to chuckle.

I let Derrick ask most of the questions, but now that we'd gotten them out of the way, I brought up the Mortons.

"I understand Rex and Silvie Morton sponsored your way to America." I paused to gauge their reactions to hearing those names. Their faces remained impassive as they nodded, although the harpist, Miss Everson, frowned.

"I can't say Mr. Morton had much to do with it, although one does assume the money that brought us here was his. But it was Mrs. Morton who spoke with us and made all the arrangements."

"Mrs. Morton is a renowned patroness and a woman of impeccable taste," Mr. Swinford confirmed with a twitch of his upper lip. "We aren't the first musicians she has sponsored, nor will we be the last." The others nodded their concurrence.

"So then, her reputation as a patroness preceded her," I said. When no one responded to that, I clarified, "You had all heard of her before."

"Oh my, yes," Miss Everson said with a sigh. "You cannot imagine our excitement when we learned she would be attending our recital at the Cheswicks' townhome in Mayfair. Goodness, such an opportunity. We've all dreamed about coming to America and playing in New York."

The Scottish Mr. Wiles leaned across the space between their chairs to touch her hand. "Our dream is about to come true, Dotty."

"I suppose she broached the subject with you?" I held my breath as I awaited the answer. Silvie had already told me they had approached her—or, rather, Mr. Swinford had. Would he lie about it?

"Actually," Miss Everson said, "we went to her. Or David did."

"That's right." He pulled himself up, sitting tall with an air of authority that nearly made *me* roll my eyes. "As the leader and spokesman of our group, it was my place to speak with Mrs. Morton about our hopes of playing in America. It is delicate business, you understand, engaging the goodwill of a lady of means."

I exchanged a glance with Derrick. "I can imagine. Why Mrs. Morton, though? I assume there are many such American patronesses roaming the theaters and music rooms of London."

The others chuckled while Mr. Swinford recoiled. " 'Roaming'? Miss Cross, how tawdry you make it sound." He shifted his gaze to Derrick. "Sir, is this the sort of operation you run? One of crude sensationalism? If so, we do not wish our names to be associated with your newspaper."

As Derrick assured him the *Messenger* employed the utmost discretion in presenting the facts of any story, and I hastened to apologize for my choice of words, Miss Everson tsked.

"David, come down off your high horse." For the first time, I detected a bit of London's East End in her speech, if only the barest hint. "Miss Cross has a point. Why *did* you pick Mrs. Morton over, say, Lady Randolph Churchill; Mrs. Belmont; or even Mrs. Belmont's daughter, the Duchess of

Marlborough? They were all there that night and any of them would have been willing to listen to our plans."

My pulse jumped at hearing that Aunt Alva had been at the Mayfair gathering that night. Was she back in Newport yet? Could she shed any light on Rex and Silvie Morton's activities in England?

"Yes, our readers would be keen to know what it was about Mrs. Morton that made her a likely prospect in your eyes," Derrick said, breaking into my thoughts. "For sponsoring your way here, I mean," he added, lest Mr. Swinford take offense again at any impropriety suggested by the choice of words spoken, this time *likely prospect*. But I had the sense that Derrick meant those words and their perceived meaning, implying that Silvie Morton might well have been a mark singled out because of her husband's necklace.

Mr. Swinford seemed flustered, his eyes darting as he cleared his throat and stumbled over his first few words. "Well . . . you see . . . she seemed such an amiable lady . . . and since she herself was returning to the Americas shortly . . . Lady Marlborough had no such plans, nor did Lady Randolph, and Mrs. Belmont was planning an extended stay in England. . . ."

"And you wanted a patroness who would be here with you, to help expand your opportunities," I finished for him, hoping they didn't perceive my disappointment that Aunt Alva was still out of the country.

He thrust his forefinger in my direction. "Exactly. To expand our opportunities. Among the grand ladies in attendance at the Cheswicks' that night, only Mrs. Morton had imminent plans to return home. And when one considers her connections in New York . . . well." As he left off, his eyes gleamed and a high color suffused his face.

Suddenly, I understood. Mr. Swinford was smitten with Silvie Morton. Adored her from afar, I was sure. I glanced again at Derrick, who encouraged me with a slight nod. "Can you tell us more about the Mortons? I assume you traveled here on the same ship?"

"We did," Miss Everson spoke up, "on the Red Star Line's SS *Zeeland*. What a lovely vessel. I haven't the words to describe her. Except to say I've never known such luxury, and we were down in second class, so you can imagine what first class was like. Still, such food, such accommodations. I nearly wished we could remain on board permanently and play our music for the passengers."

"Don't be ridiculous, Dot." Mr. Swinford sniffed. "There is neither fame nor money in shipboard performances."

I ignored his irritation. "Then you must have gotten to know the Mortons somewhat."

This comment was met with blank faces. In his brogue, Mr. Wiles said, "Not in the least. We saw nary hide nor hair of 'em the entire voyage. Indeed, we didn't encounter them again until we played at The Elms. Our communications have all been through correspondence sent back and forth by messenger."

"Yes, I'm afraid they rather see us as servants," Miss Everson said with a look of regret. "Not the Mortons in particular, you understand, but most people of their class. We are useful to them, we entertain them, but we are not to be on familiar terms with them."

Although this came as no surprise to me, I did my best to hide my disappointment as I gathered up my handbag and gloves. "Then I don't suppose you know anything about an item they were bringing back to this country, something Mr. Morton purchased from a London auction?"

This abrupt question came as a last resort, my final hope for learning something significant from these musicians, who so far had little to add to our knowledge of the Mortons or their necklace. That hope sank as I regarded their blank faces, their utter lack of reaction or any sign they might have an inkling of what I was talking about. They offered only shrugs, faint shakes of their heads.

Mr. Swinford smiled. "Miss Cross, I can assure you that we musicians don't make enough money to ever take an interest in auctions. Unless, of course, there is a rare Stradivarius on offer, and then our attention is purely academic."

Chapter 11

My dear Mrs. Andrews . . . I read, though with difficulty as those words had been struck through and a new salutation began just below it:

> *My dear Emma,*
> *There has been a development here at The Elms*
> *and I am growing frightened. Can you meet with*
> *me here today?*
> *Sincerely,*
> *Silvie Morton*

That message had been delivered to Gull Manor, where, luckily, Derrick and I had once again spent the night. Otherwise, I might not have gotten it until much later in the day. We seemed to be spending so much time at The Elms, I was beginning to think he and I should simply take up residence there. The Berwinds' footman waited for my reply. I sent it with him, and soon after, we detoured to The Elms on our way into town.

Silvie awaited me in the Chinese breakfast room with Minnie. I saw no sign of Kay and assumed she hadn't yet arisen from bed. Derrick continued outside onto the rear lawn, where Ned Berwind and his two male guests, Rex and Charles, were enjoying some target shooting. The first several reports of their guns made me flinch until I grew accustomed to the sound.

Silvie, on the other hand, recoiled with every sharp blast. Her hands shook and her teacup rattled each time she set it down. She did so now, compressed her lips, and drew in a deep breath. "Emma, I asked you here because I'm hoping that with your knowledge of everyone here in Newport, you might help us identify someone."

My gaze darted to Minnie, who gave a shrug. To Silvie I said, "I will if I can, certainly. Can you describe this person?"

"That's just it. We have very little description." Her fingers wrapped around her teacup. "We know only that he appears well to do, as his clothing appeared of fine quality—quite fine, the footman said. His hair is dark but graying, and his age looked to be about my own and Rex's."

"That's very general," I said. "It could be any one of hundreds of men in Newport. Is there anything else at all? What made you suspicious of him?"

Minnie reached over and patted Silvie's shoulder. "Let me, dear." When Silvie nodded, Minnie said to me, "Yesterday afternoon, one of our footmen reported spotting a man lingering on the sidewalk outside the front fence. He said this fellow kept looking up at the house and walking back and forth. At one point, he turned the corner and walked down Bellevue Court. When the footman went out to ask if he could be of assistance, this individual thanked him, tipped his hat, and walked off as if his behavior hadn't been odd."

"Could he have been a reporter?" I suggested. "Someone interested in what happened to Ines?" Even as I asked these questions, I recalled a similar incident the previous summer, when a strange man showed up in Newport and threatened several gentlemen of the Four Hundred, my cousin Neily included. His argument against them had been justified, if his methods less than conventional. Could this be a similar situation?

"That's exactly what I thought," Minnie said, "but then . . ." She studied Silvie's features, which had gone tight and pale.

"But when Rex heard about it from Ned," Silvie said with a tremor in her voice, "he began acting even more erratically than he had been."

"Erratically? How so?"

"It isn't so much what he did," his wife replied, "as what he didn't do. He didn't move for the longest time. Was almost catatonic, staring without blinking, trembling and silent . . . I didn't know what to do, whether to call a doctor or . . ." She released her hold on her teacup and pressed her palms to her cheeks.

"Did anyone tell the police about this man?" I asked.

Silvie pinched her lips together and allowed Minnie to reply. "We did. And all they said was they can't arrest or even detain someone for walking on the sidewalk. Now, if he'd so much as placed a toe on the grounds it would be a different story, but he didn't."

"Whom did you speak with?"

"The chief himself came to speak with us." Minnie fingered the edge of her saucer. "He tried to be accommodating. Said he'd have a patrolman come by several times a day, but he couldn't do more than that."

I'd be sure to let Jesse know about this, although I didn't say anything to that effect to the women. I didn't wish to raise their hopes that anything could be done at this point.

"It must have to do with the necklace, with the theft." Mrs. Morton hugged her arms around herself. "Only that wretched piece of jewelry could put Rex in such a state."

Another shot sent its charge through me like a jolt of lightning. "If Rex is as upset as all that, should he be outside shooting? Handling guns?"

Minnie waved my concerns aside. "It's all right. Ned managed to calm him down. Told him he's among friends and perfectly safe here. Gave him a bracing snifter of brandy and told him to get hold of himself. Seemed to do the trick."

"Is that true?" I asked Silvie, wondering why Ned considered brandy and shooting a sound combination. "Do you think he's better now?"

"I don't think he'll shoot any of the others." She stared down into her tea. "We needn't worry about *that*."

The emphasis she put on that last word prompted me to ask, "Are you afraid he'll harm himself?"

"I don't know. . . . No, I don't think so."

"That's hardly reassuring," I pointed out. Minnie caught my eye and shook her head, a request that I let the matter drop. I raised another. "I spoke to the musicians yesterday. They spoke of you in the highest terms and are most grateful for what you've done for them. But as for your husband's necklace and the auction where he bought it, they seemed to have no knowledge."

She raised her gaze to me. "Would they have admitted it if they had?"

"Perhaps not, but I do more than listen when I ask questions. I watch for clues. A rise in color, a stutter, perspiration, and the like. They remained unruffled throughout except for the first violinist, but I don't believe his moments of discomfiture had anything to do with the theft of the necklace. Rather, they had to do with his admiration of you."

"Goodness," she murmured, then seemed to shake off the notion. Women like her—wealthy, cultured, often neglected by their husbands—found themselves warding off unwanted attention on a regular basis.

"Silvie, I must ask you something, and you probably won't like it." I considered asking her to move to another room where we might have privacy, but this being Minnie Berwind's home, I decided the woman had a right to hear what came next. "It's about the night of the musicale."

Silvie braced herself. "Go on."

"Did you go anywhere else besides your room during the intermission?"

She hesitated a long moment. Finally, she angled her gaze away. "You've already asked where I went that night."

"I'm asking again."

Minnie came to her feet. "Perhaps we shouldn't pressure Silvie right now. It's been a trying time for her."

"No, Minnie, it's all right." Silvie drained her teacup. "I did move about the house more than I wished to admit."

"Where did you go?"

"Really, Emma, it's none of our business." Minnie spoke at the same time Silvie said, "I'd rather not say. But how did you know? Did my maid tell tales?"

"She merely related the facts with no inkling that they didn't match what you'd told the police." I folded my arms on the table and leaned forward. "Please don't blame her for telling the truth. It wasn't a betrayal. She simply had no reason to say she had been with you for more than the few minutes it took to smooth your hair and sew the trim on your gown."

"Yes, of course." Silvie studied her hands. "She cannot be faulted for telling the truth."

"Silvie, perhaps you've said enough," Minnie warned. She tossed a stern look my way.

Silvie ignored her. "I had nothing to do with the maid's death, that much I promise you. My errand that night had nothing whatsoever to do with her. I hope you'll believe me, but if not, I cannot help you."

She pressed her lips firmly together after that, and I knew she had finished saying her piece. Whatever Silvie Morton was hiding—and she left me in no doubt that she was, indeed, hiding something—obviously frightened her even more than being accused of murder.

What on earth could that something be?

The following morning brought fair weather clouds and a springlike freshness to the air. Derrick and I dressed casually, he in a tweed jacket and matching trousers tucked into thick socks in imitation of knickerbockers, and me in a cotton sweater, pleated skirt, and low-heeled boots. We used my carriage and horse, Maestro, for the short trip to the Newport Country Club, housed in a sprawling Beaux Arts structure perched on a wide swell of land overlooking Brenton Point and the Atlantic Ocean.

An invitation from Charles Gilchrist had arrived the evening before, asking us to join him and his wife, the Mortons, and the Berwinds for a morning round of golf—to ease the tensions of the past week, as he'd put it. When Derrick and I arrived at the clubhouse and entered between its imposing columns, the rest of the group had already assembled in the main hall. Charles saw us and waved us over, and I realized there were more people there than we had expected.

"You remember the Lehrs, don't you?" Minnie Berwind asked as she gestured to the smartly dressed couple, he in a pale flannel suit and she in a cream linen skirt with a short crimson jacket that hugged her figure perfectly. "They were here so we've asked them to join us."

Derrick and I greeted the extra guests as well as the others and accepted cups of coffee from the waiters milling among the golfers waiting to take to the course. A lively conversation was struck up about recent tournaments in which some of the gentlemen present had participated.

While the others compared their experiences, I noticed Kay Gilchrist was uncommonly quiet, even for her. As she stood to my immediate left, I could easily converse with her while her husband described a course in Scotland he'd played on the previous spring. "Do you share your husband's enthusiasm for the sport?"

"No, I barely play at all, actually," she said shyly, her color rising to a delicate pink. "I'm returning to The Elms as soon as you all go out."

"I told you that would leave us with an uneven number," her husband grumbled half under his breath. "My apologies, everyone, for Kay's stubbornness. I suppose we'll have to join up with someone playing singly."

"I'm sorry, Charles." Kay worried her lip with her teeth. "But I'd be no use to any of you. You know how dreadfully I play."

"Kay," I said before her husband could comment again, "why don't you stay?" I offered her an inviting smile but tried not to look too eager. This might be a good opportunity to learn more about the night of the musicale, and whether her husband's claim of searching for Henry James's *The Tree of Knowledge* had been sincere or merely a ruse. "I'm not the best golfer by any means. I'd be delighted to stay behind. That would even out the number of players, while you and I enjoyed a bit of brunch and became better acquainted."

Her face lit up, but before she could summon a reply, Elizabeth Lehr surprised us both, not to mention the others standing around us. "I'll stay as well. I'm really not so keen on playing today."

"But, my dear," her husband said with undue urgency after a brief hesitation, "surely you wish to play. The weather is superb, and besides, without you, we'll again be an uneven number. As Charles just pointed out, we might have to allow a stranger to join our jolly crew."

The woman's aristocratic features fell as she considered this. Then her expression smoothed. "There are no strangers in Newport. Everyone knows everyone."

"Come now, Bessie." Her husband placed his hand over hers. "If you don't come with us, I shall be wretched."

Minnie was quick to break the silence and Mrs. Lehr's indecision. "Why don't all we ladies stay behind?" She turned to her friend. "Silvie, what do you think?"

"Well, I . . ."

"Ladies, please." Charles Gilchrist set his cup and saucer on the tray of a passing footman. "This outing was intended to clear our minds of the recent unpleasantness." He darted a glance in my direction, almost implying, silently, that I was somehow at fault for that unpleasantness. "We mustn't start dropping out one by one. Now, it's true Kay's swing is nothing to boast about. Emma will stay behind and keep her company. As for the rest of us"—he thrust a finger in the general direction of the course—"to the links!"

It was with relief that I took a seat beside Kay at a small table in the dining room by one of the large windows that looked over a section of the course. We watched as the others filed outside, where caddies had already assembled with their clubs. Our friends teamed up in groups of four and headed for the first tee.

We ordered tea and a tiered tray of delicacies, both savory and sweet. I expected to have to extract information from

Kay practically by force, but it wasn't long before she surprised me by chattering away, mostly about her children.

"Little Charles is four now, though I find it hard to believe. Seems he came into our world only yesterday. He's already proving himself to be a future sportsman. Loves his pony. And my husband got him the sweetest little golf clubs for his birthday. Charles Junior adores chasing the balls around the lawn."

I smiled and nodded, adding in sounds of admiration when I deemed them appropriate. In the meantime, based on Kay's youthful appearance and the fact that her son had reached four years of age, I judged her to have been still in her teens when she married the much older Charles.

"Lilah seems determined to keep up with her brother, and it's utterly hilarious to watch her toddle around after him. She often tumbles, being only a year and a half, but does she cry?" After a sip of tea, she shook her head vigorously. "Not in the least. She merely pulls herself up and toddles some more. Charles Junior considers leading her on a merry chase great fun."

"I'm sure he does," I replied politely. "Are they at home in New York now?"

"They are, and my goodness, I miss them. I wanted to bring them, but Charles insisted it would be too much of an imposition on the Berwinds. I suppose he's right, especially with their not having had children themselves."

I thought to contradict this assumption. True, the Berwinds were a childless couple, but I happened to have heard, from others, that they enjoyed the company of their nieces and nephews and often welcomed them to their home in New York. Most of the Four Hundred here in Newport hadn't added many guest rooms to their cottages because it was assumed everyone had their own home nearby. The

Elms, however, included five guest rooms. One could only assume Ned and Minnie intended to continue the tradition of having their nieces and nephews come to stay.

But, as the Gilchrists had already made their decision and come without their children, I said nothing. I was glad for my silence, for Kay spoke again. "Charles surprised me with this trip. We haven't been to Newport in years."

I perked up at mention of her husband. "And why is that?"

"Charles simply doesn't care for the summer season here. He says it's too fussy and too crowded. He prefers Upstate New York. Says it's much more relaxing. Even Saratoga, now that most of society comes here instead."

"He may have a point," I said amiably. "What made him change his mind this year?"

"The house." When I stared blankly, she craned forward. "The Elms. He and Ned are business associates. Charles is in coal, too, although as an investor, not the head of a mining operation. When he learned Ned and Minnie were opening this house, with all of its wonders, why, he said he must see it firsthand."

"It *is* remarkable," I agreed.

"I feared we might be imposing on Minnie and Ned, especially so soon after they moved in. I told Charles as much. I said surely they wanted time to enjoy the house themselves, or to entertain guests with whom they're better acquainted."

Her expression tightened as she made this disclosure, and a fretful light entered her eyes. I felt impelled to ask, "What did he say to that?"

She pinched her lips together and frowned. "He told me to . . . mind my business." She attempted a smile, which withered before it had quite formed. "Men. You know how they are. They don't like to be told anything."

I patted her hand. Then I slid the tiered tray closer. "Have you tried the crabmeat sandwiches? They're always wonderful here."

She took a dainty triangle of a sandwich and chewed it with relish, her discomfiture apparently forgotten for the moment. But I hadn't forgotten it. Charles Gilchrist was a bully to his wife, no mistake about it. It wasn't uncommon, especially among powerful men with younger, less experienced wives, but each time I encountered it I became indignant all over again.

On the other hand, I considered two of my Vanderbilt aunts, Alice and Alva. Now, there were two women strong enough to stand up to any man, including their husbands. In Aunt Alice's case, of course, it had rarely been necessary, as Uncle Cornelius had been a true gentleman who both adored and respected his wife. Aunt Alva and her first husband, Uncle William, on the other hand, had certainly had their share of contention, and Alva had stood up for herself to the point of ending the marriage. A scandal at the time, but growing gradually more accepted as time passed.

Still, I couldn't see gentle, timid Kay Gilchrist standing up for anything—not anytime soon.

I changed the subject—slightly. "I understand your husband likes to read. Especially Henry James."

Her hand stopped before it reached for another offering on the tray. "Henry James, you say?"

"Yes, he specifically mentioned James's *The Tree of Knowledge*. Have you read it?"

"Why, no . . . ." She looked baffled. "I've never heard of it."

"Perhaps some others of James's work?"

She shook her head. "Not that I can recall. I prefer American authors, and poetry especially. Charles tends toward more physical endeavors. Golf, sailing, horses. Swimming. I rarely see him with a book in hand."

"I see." I lifted the porcelain teapot and poured us each another cup. "Did you already have plans for the summer before changing them to come to Newport?" I asked her in a casual tone.

"Mm, yes," she said after swallowing a sip of tea. "We were already packing last week to go to our summer home in Tarrytown. We've an estate near the Goulds, you know. Sleepy Glen, it's called."

"I understand Tarrytown is lovely."

"It is. Very peaceful. The children are there now." A note of pain had entered her voice.

"I'm sure they're fine." I smiled again. "Chasing each other around the grounds."

She brightened at that.

"It must have been terribly chaotic for you, though, changing plans so suddenly."

"It was," she said with a nod. "But now that I've seen The Elms, I understand Charles's enthusiasm."

I considered what she had just told me. The Elms had been under construction for the past two years. The announcement about its opening and the date the Berwinds would be moving in had been made some weeks ago, along with their plans to hold the musicale. Yet until last week the Gilchrists had their sights set on Tarrytown, New York. It would seem Charles's enthusiasm had sprung up very suddenly.

A new suspicion prompted another query. "Did you and your husband go abroad this year?"

"No, I wouldn't hear of it. I simply put my foot down and refused to travel with such a young child. Nor would I leave Lilah—or Charles Junior, for that matter—for the length of time needed for European travel. It was one battle Charles let me win." She sat taller, looking proud of herself.

I felt proud of her, too. I would not have thought her capable of standing up to her husband, but perhaps Kay Gilchrist feared the wrath of no man when it came to her children's welfare.

But that still left me with a question: Had Charles Gilchrist somehow known of Rex Morton's necklace, and was that the reason he had suddenly changed their plans and hurried to Newport?

Chapter 12

Kay and I decided to return to The Elms before the others had finished golfing. We would go in my carriage, as there would be plenty of room in one of the Berwinds' carriages for Derrick. After leaving word with the maître d', she and I collected our handbags and wraps and headed outside. We didn't expect to meet up with the others, who seemed to be hurrying to reach the vehicles, trailed by the caddies.

Rex Morton led the group, with Silvie trotting to keep up a step or two behind him. "Rex, what is it? Are you ill?"

I sped my steps to intercept the group. When I reached them, Rex brushed past me. His wife did likewise but not without first angling an anxious look in my direction. They stopped near one of the Berwinds' two carriages, and the driver jumped down from his perch to open the door.

The others were calling out to Rex, asking, as his wife had, what was wrong. Derrick came up beside me. "This is the strangest thing. Everything was fine one minute, and the next I feared Morton might expire right there on the course."

I searched his gaze before shifting my sights back to the

Mortons. Rex was just then climbing into the vehicle, making a shaky job of it. The driver reached to steady him by clasping his arm. "Has he said anything?"

"Only that he had to leave." Derrick beckoned Ned Berwind over to join us. "Any idea what brought this on?"

Ned looked as mystified as the others. "Not a clue. He was talking to the group waiting behind us, and waiting to take his own shot, when suddenly he came hurrying over to me, pale as bleached linen."

"It was most perplexing," Minnie said as she and Mrs. Lehr joined us, their arms linked.

"Is he always prone to such maladies?" Mrs. Lehr's brow creased with concern.

"Is that what it was?" I asked in turn, wondering whom he had spoken with on the course.

"What else could it be but that he'd taken ill?" Standing behind the two women, Harry Lehr placed a hand on his wife's shoulder and attempted to take Minnie's place at his wife's side. Neither woman yielded to his not-too-subtle nudging.

"He seemed fine this morning." Minnie's eyebrows drew inward as she apparently attempted to recall Rex's demeanor earlier in the day. "At least, better than previously. Almost as though he had forgotten all about his stolen necklace."

Silvie, seeing her husband settled in the carriage, came over to speak with us. "I'm so terribly sorry about this. I don't know what's gotten into Rex." She held out her hands. "I don't know what to say, except that the rest of you should go back and continue your game. I'll accompany Rex to the house."

While the others protested this idea and insisted on returning to The Elms, I drew Silvie aside. "Ned mentioned that your husband spoke to someone in another group while waiting to take his shot. Do you know who it was?"

"I didn't see." She rubbed her hands up and down her arms as if to ward off a chill. "I was with Minnie, Charles, and your husband. We'd already gone on to the next tee."

"So then your husband played with Mr. and Mrs. Lehr and Ned?"

"Yes, that's right." She darted a glance over her shoulder. "Excuse me now, I really must get back to Rex."

I nodded as she hurried away. I continued to wonder about this person Rex Morton had spoken to on the course. Apparently, none of the others had seen anything, and Rex refused to explain, which made me wonder if the individual had intended to catch Rex off guard. Something to do with the Marie Antoinette necklace?

At the *Messenger* later, I decided to walk to the police station to obtain the list of recent police reports, especially burglaries, muggings, and vandalism. The *Messenger* ran them periodically as a warning to city residents to be extra watchful of crime in their areas. One burglary remained foremost in my mind, and it seemed far from being solved. How could it be if the self-described victim, Rex Morton, refused to be forthcoming about how he had obtained the necklace, where it had originated, and why it could make or break his and Silvie's future? Whomever he had spoken to on the golf course had upset him greatly. Had the individual threatened him in some way, and had it been in connection with the necklace?

Why did he continue to refuse to cooperate with anyone willing to help him?

At the station, I scurried up the steps to the street door and breezed inside. "Good morning, Scotty," I called out to the officer manning the front counter.

"Morning, Miss Cross—uh, no—Mrs. Andrews!" Officer Scott Binsford, or Scotty as I'd called him during the years we had grown up on the Point, thrust his hand out over the countertop. I grasped it and we shook. "Sorry about that. It's so hard to get used to."

"Don't worry, Scotty, I understand. It's been hard for me, too. And sometimes I do still use my maiden name. At work, for instance. It's simply easier. Besides, it's Emma. When did we become so formal?"

He nodded and grinned, no doubt recalling some of the antics we children got up to in the old neighborhood. Scotty possessed such an easygoing nature he tended to agree with just about anything that didn't defy the city ordinances. If it weren't for his imposing height and the breadth of his shoulders, he might not have been taken seriously as a policeman. We spoke for a few minutes of local matters and the acquaintances we had in common, which were considerable. Finally, I told him what I'd come for, not an unusual request since all the local papers carried such logs.

"There was a woman brought in last night," he told me with a confidential air.

I immediately took an interest. I assumed she might be a prostitute, and I wondered if she was someone I might be able to help. "Who was she?"

"A thief," Scotty went on. "Well, a pickpocket, actually. Pinched a man's purse right outside the Casino last night. Might not have been her first mark either, but so far she's not admitting to anything. Says he dropped his purse and she retrieved it from the sidewalk." He chuckled and rolled his eyes. "She hasn't a leg to stand on. Was caught red handed."

"That's a shame. She's probably desperate."

"Probably. The arresting officer said she was one of the servants recently fired from The Elms."

"Scotty, no. What is her name?"

"Whalen. Something Whalen . . ."

"Bridget?"

He nodded. "That's it. Irish girl. Not that most of them aren't, but this one—"

"Is Jesse in?" I asked him before he could go on.

"At his desk, last I saw him."

I went around the counter and through the wide doorway into the main station room. Jesse was indeed sitting at his desk, so busy he didn't look up until I stood right before him on the opposite side.

"Emma, this is a surprise." His cordial expression melted into concern. "Has something happened?"

"Why wasn't I told Bridget Whalen had been arrested?"

"I don't remember you being a member of the police force."

I scowled. "You yourself have said many times you'd hire me on if you could."

"That's true." He looked contrite. "I wasn't here when Miss Whalen was brought in. I only found out she was here this morning. Besides, I figured you'd be in for the police arrest logs."

I plunked my hands on my hips and came right to the point. "Can I see her?"

He sat back in his chair. "I suppose I could arrange it."

"Wait." I had a change of heart. "How much is her bail?"

"You want to post it for her? Her family can't."

"I'm not surprised. Yes, I want to post her bail."

Jesse folded his arms across his chest. "Fifty dollars."

My eyes opened wide. "For pickpocketing?"

Jesse held my gaze. "The thing is, while her crime last night has nothing to do with The Elms, it doesn't look good for her as far as this stolen necklace is concerned. Chief Rogers's way of thinking is she's a thief, so she might very well have stolen the necklace as well. And if she stole the necklace, she probably murdered Miss Varella." I started to protest but he held up his hand to forestall me. "He has no proof whatsoever of either, or her bail would have been set much higher."

"That makes no sense. If Bridget Whalen was in possession of something so valuable, why would she waste her time pickpocketing casinogoers?" Not expecting Jesse to answer that, I blew out a breath. "All right, I'll pay it. Before you let her walk out of here, though, I want to speak with her."

"That will be up to her, won't it?" When I nodded in reply, Jesse's face turned serious. "Are you sure, Emma? What if she did murder Ines? Do you really mean to open Gull Manor to her, and put not only yourself, but Mrs. O'Neal and Miss Dillon at risk?"

"I don't believe Bridget is a threat." My chin inched stubbornly upward of its own accord. "I've dealt with desperate women before, and they don't wish to hurt anyone. They only wish to dig themselves out of the pit they've fallen into. I only hope it's not too late for Bridget. And that she's willing to be helped."

I didn't believe anything I could have said to Bridget would have persuaded her to see me before she left Marlborough Street. Only one thing sent her in my direction once she had been released from her cell at the back of the building.

"My parents made it clear I can't go home," she said in way of greeting. "You said you'd help me. Did you mean it?"

"I'm here, aren't I?" I raised an eyebrow at her. "I paid your bail."

"I'll find a way to pay you back."

"We'll worry about that later. For now let's get you out of here and settled."

I got the list I needed for the *Messenger,* and then we walked back to the office to let Derrick and Mr. Sheppard know I would be gone for as long as it took to take Bridget to Gull Manor. I could see by Derrick's expression that he wasn't keen on the idea, but he said nothing more than, "Drive safely."

But I didn't mistake the warning glare he issued Bridget from beneath his brows. Nor did I misinterpret the blush that spread across Bridget's face in reply. We drove down Spring Street to avoid the Bellevue Avenue traffic. Even at this early hour people would be gathering at the shops and for morning tennis at the Casino. A much more residential thoroughfare, Spring Street brought us onto Coggeshall Avenue, which in turn brought us to Ocean Avenue.

"Who have we here?" Nanny met us at the front door when we arrived. She must have been gazing out the parlor window. The window seat there was a favorite perch of hers in the morning, where she would bring her tea and enjoy the quiet while Katie cleaned up after breakfast.

"Nanny, this is Bridget Whalen. Bridget, this is Mrs. O'Neal. She'll show you to a room and acquaint you with the routine, and remember, she's quite in charge around here."

Nanny smiled in amusement at that last. Yet she also caught my gaze, hers asking silent questions. She obviously remembered the name and Bridget's connection to The Elms. I nodded subtly. I needn't worry that Nanny would complain about my taking the girl in. She trusted my judgment and, besides, at Gull Manor we tended to believe people innocent until we were proven wrong. And few of the women we had helped ever proved us wrong.

Only one exception came to mind: Lavinia Andrews, my mother-in-law. She and her daughter once stayed with us after a fire on their yacht rendered them homeless while in Newport. We happily opened our doors to them in friendship and believed they accepted in the same spirit—until Mrs. Andrews had attempted to hand me money to pay for their stay. No insult the woman had ever hurled at me wounded me as much as those bills sitting in her palm. I'll never forget her sheer bafflement when I refused to accept her payment. I'd known then she would never accept me as an equal, never believe me good enough for her son.

Well.

"Telephone me at the *Messenger* if you need me," I told Nanny before I left.

"Don't you worry. We'll be just fine. Won't we, Miss Whalen?"

It was a rhetorical question. I didn't doubt Nanny would prove correct.

Chapter 13

That evening, Derrick and I returned to Gull Manor. While the rest of us ate in the morning room, which we used far more often than the formal dining room, Bridget ate alone at the kitchen table. It had been at her request, one I had seen no reason to deny. She had helped Nanny and Katie prepare dinner, although according to them she had spoken little, and only when necessary. Perhaps now she needed time to consider everything that had happened to her, and how she ended up as the guest of someone she had previously disdained. Once dinner ended, she helped with the cleaning up without being asked and took a broom to the floor. I met her at the back door when she opened it to sweep out the crumbs.

"Bridget, will you walk with me a bit?"

Her hesitation was palpable. "I suppose."

I could all but hear the unspoken, "If I must." I chose to ignore her reluctance and led the way past the kitchen garden and laundry yard, and beyond our small barn that housed Maestro and Barney. The latter had retired from pulling my carriage a couple of years ago and now spent his time munching weeds at the edges of the garden and being led on walks by Katie or me. I heard both horses as we passed, their sleepy snorts caressing my ears through the barn walls.

Patch had followed us out, but he found his own places of interest to inspect and left us to our walk. We proceeded to where the yard narrowed at the ocean's edge, with a perimeter of boulders that sent up a spray whenever the waves struck them just so. The sun had set, leaving only traces of orange in the clouds stretched languidly across the horizon. I breathed in deeply, feeling bathed from head to toe in the gentle salt breeze. Beside me, Bridget sighed.

"It's beautiful here. You're lucky, Miss Cross."

"I am, yes."

"It's what comes of marryin' a rich man."

I turned to face her. She kept her profile to me another moment before turning with a quizzical expression. "My husband didn't buy this house," I told her. "My great-aunt did, with money she inherited from her parents and increased through investments. She left it to me. So although I'm married now, Gull Manor remains my own." That wasn't quite true. Legally, the property now belonged to Derrick and me. Yet in my heart, it stubbornly continued to feel like it belonged to me alone.

"A woman who owns her own house and property?" She shook her head, a look of disbelief creeping across her features. "Well, even so, you were lucky, having a rich great-aunt and all."

"I don't deny luck has played a large part in my life. But I've also worked hard and insisted my diligence be recognized despite my sex. I refused to be told no."

She faced out over the ocean again, the breeze sweeping loose hairs back from her face. Hers was an attractive countenance, when she wasn't scowling. Her blue eyes were alert and intelligent.

And then the scowl returned. "Did you bring me out here to lecture me on the virtues of hard work? To show me the error of my ways? I ask you, how hungry have you ever been, Miss Cross? How many younger brothers and sisters of yours went to bed hungry? Yes, I stole that man's wallet, because livin' back at home, I was takin' food out of the little ones' mouths."

"I'm sorry about your family's difficulties, Bridget, and yours. No, I did not bring you out here to lecture you. Far from it. I try not to judge." I let go a chuckle. "Sometimes that is my downfall."

"Then why are we here?" Her brogue had hardened as she demanded to know my intentions.

"I wanted to talk about Ines."

Her nose wrinkled. "Why? She's dead, isn't she?"

"Yes, she's dead, but her life raises many questions. Please, what else can you tell me about her?"

"Not much. She never talked about herself, not with me. All I know is she had a habit of disappearing when she should have been working."

"You said you believed she was seeing a man who worked on the estate."

Bridget shrugged. "It's as good a guess as any."

"She said she had no family or friends in this country. Did you ever see any evidence to the contrary?"

"No, Miss Cross. As far as I know, no one ever came to the house to call on her. Not in any proper way. She had no telephone calls and no letters that I ever saw."

"It almost sounds as though she lived in a world of her own." I shook my head. Either she truly had been all alone in this country, or she kept many things hidden from her peers. "She claimed she worked for a family in New York before coming to Newport. But the family she named as her former employers never heard of her."

"I'm not surprised to add liar to Ines's list of sins. You know, she had a name she used to call the rest of us by, as it suited her. *Scooch.* It must be Portuguese, I guess. I don't know what it means, only that it wasn't a compliment." She released a humorless chuckle.

"Scooch?"

"Yes, as in 'You little scooch, you'd best stay out of my way.'"

The term seemed familiar to me, but where had I heard it before? It wasn't something one heard among Newporters. I thought back and suddenly recalled a friend of Nanny's, a housekeeper at one of the stately homes on Rhode Island Avenue, who had used that term liberally whenever a footman or maid in her charge didn't perform their tasks to her liking. She originally hailed from one of Boston's Italian neighborhoods, and when I'd asked her about the term, she told me it derived from the Italian *scocciare,* which loosely translated to a person who annoys or bothers another. She had often heard it growing up.

I laughed out loud, not from humor but from sheer relief. "Bridget, we finally have a clue as to where Ines was from."

She turned to me with yet another puzzled expression. "What do you mean?"

"*Scooch.* It's Boston slang, and you're right, it's not a compliment. Ines might not have been Italian, but she must have been from Boston, not New York."

I could hardly wait to tell Jesse this bit of information the next day. His reaction didn't disappoint me. He believed it to be a significant lead and planned to send wires to several police stations in Boston with Ines's and Rudolfo's descriptions. Derrick, too, wired a colleague at his father's newspaper, the *Providence Sun,* asking him to assign a couple of junior reporters to pore through the paper's archives for any stories about a female thief of Portuguese origin, or a Portuguese couple working scams together. The parameters were vague, and it didn't help that the couple had probably changed their names before arriving in Newport.

I attempted to put Ines and Rudolfo out of my mind and focus on other local news. A sailor, initially believed to have deserted his post, had been found washed up near the Narragansett Pier. With no sign of foul play, it was believed he had fallen overboard while on duty. A carriage had careened out of control down Broadway, sideswiping two other vehicles. No one, thankfully, had been seriously injured. And the Newport and Fall River Street Railway Line had recently acquired several eight-wheeled cars fitted out with air brakes. The new cars were capable of traveling at higher speeds while offering a smoother ride to passengers—a marvel of the modern age.

These and other news reports, some of which I covered firsthand and others that had come over the wire, kept me busy the rest of that day and the following morning. Then Derrick appeared in my office doorway.

"Fancy a trip back to The Elms?"

My hands stilled on the typewriter keys. "What now?"

"Orville Brown, apparently. We just received a tip that he's there, making trouble as usual. One of the servants telephoned."

"Does Jesse know?"

"The police have been called."

I abandoned the article in my typewriter and collected my hat and handbag. "I'm on my way."

"Shall I go with you, then?" He balanced on the balls of his feet, ready to stride out the door with me.

"This again? No, you have other work to do. I'm no good as a reporter if I need to be chaperoned everywhere I go, now am I?"

"I suppose not. . . ."

"I'll be careful." I paused long enough for a reassuring kiss, then hurried out of the office and down to Stevenson's Livery on Thames Street, where we usually kept our carriage during working hours. Maestro, my horse, seemed happy to see me and walked along at a jaunty pace, for which I thanked him. The promise of a fair morning darkened as leaden clouds moved across the island. When I arrived at The Elms, I pulled the carriage onto Bellevue Court, near the servants' driveway. A few drops of rain splattered the road and my shoulders. We kept an umbrella handy beneath the seat, but I'd hardly be able to hold it while taking notes.

I heard the voices before I entered through the gate. The police hadn't yet arrived, but they had farther to travel than I had. Orville Brown hadn't come alone. He had apparently managed to collect a hodgepodge of followers, a dozen or so men, but what they lacked in numbers they made up for in vehemence. They stood facing the entrance, where a deep recess formed a covered porch. Framed by that recess, several footmen and Mr. Carver, the butler, met their hostile gazes. Behind them, three maids peered out from the shadows, craning their necks to see. They stood near the door leading inside, as if to make a hasty retreat.

At the rear of the group, I approached a man in overalls with a stained, threadbare cotton shirt beneath. He hadn't shaved that day or probably the one before, and dark smudges cradled his bloodshot eyes. "What's going on here?" I asked him.

"What's going on?" he repeated, none too politely. I recoiled as a waft of fetid breath reached my nostrils. "We're here to protest the unlawful stealing of jobs. It ain't right. Brown here won't stand for it, and neither will we."

"What business is it of yours?" I demanded, my hands flying to my hips. "Did you work here previously?"

He hesitated, his mouth turning down at the corners. "Well, no," he admitted. "But I lost my job a while back at the Illuminating Company. They hired someone younger."

He didn't look terribly old to me, perhaps in his thirties, but his features betrayed the signs of a man often in his cups. Though I inferred that to be the cause of his unemployment, I didn't point it out to him. "Orville Brown is a trouble-maker and he's going to lead the rest of you straight into a jail cell."

He shrugged and pushed his way forward in the crowd. Orville Brown was in the middle of an oration on the evils of refusing to support a justified strike. I took out my note-book and pencil and began jotting down not only his claims, but the responses of those around him. Mr. Carver raised his arms for order, but the rabble ignored him. Mr. Brown paused to laugh at him before continuing with his diatribe.

"You're as guilty as the Berwinds, all of you!" he shouted at the assembled servants. I wished to shoo them all inside. Their presence merely encouraged his rant. Without an audi-ence, Brown and his cohorts would most likely fade away. "Had you refused to take these positions, your colleagues would have known triumph. The Berwinds would have had no choice but to yield to their demands. Either that or learn to cook and clean their own house right quick." There were a few titters of laughter. "But no, you all stepped in at the behest of a pair of greedy robber barons, and now your brethren are out of work."

"Some of them already found new positions," a footman called out.

"And some of them haven't!" Mr. Brown shouted back. "*Many* of them haven't. But that isn't the point." He turned to address his followers. "Is it, men?"

"No!" they bellowed as one. Several raised fists in the air.

Brown faced forward again and thrust out a finger. "As I

said, guilty! You and those Berwinds. I requested a meeting with Mr. Berwind to talk about justice for the working man, and he refused. That's right, refused! He doesn't want to help anyone, and these people here, these parasites, don't care about the workers they displaced."

The proceedings took an ominous turn when someone threw something, aiming for the servants. It passed my view too quickly for me to see what it was, but I cried out a warning. The servants ducked as a blur of brown and green struck the wall above the entrance and gooey shards of rotten cabbage rained down upon them. It released a putrid odor that made me and several others, on both sides of the argument, whisk our hands to our faces and back away. A brown apple followed, and then an egg.

Mr. Brown held up a fist. "That's right, men, serve them up their just deserts. They're no better than vermin, than bloodsucking—"

From beside Mr. Carver, a footman sprang forward. He hurled himself on Brown and pounded the man with his fists. Blood spurted from Brown's nose as the two fell over and tussled on the ground. Within seconds the footman's advantage of surprise wore off, and Brown fought back. The sickening thuds of fists hitting flesh and bone filled the air. Both men grunted, sputtered, and groaned.

"Stop it! Stop it this instant!" Mr. Carver's admonitions went unheeded. The other servants looked on, agape, too startled to intervene. The disgruntled crowd also stood transfixed, but only briefly. Soon, they pushed closer and shouted encouragement to their leader.

Mr. Carver strode forward. "That's enough!" he shouted in a baritone that made me flinch.

The command echoed against the house. He shoved men out of his way and approached the fighters. I sucked in a breath as he reached for a collar—I couldn't see which man it belonged to. A fist crashed into the butler's side as Mr. Brown groped to his feet. Though not an elderly man, Mr. Carver nonetheless must have been a good twenty years older than Orville Brown and the blow knocked the wind from him. He doubled over and pressed a hand to his side.

With renewed vigor, Mr. Brown threw himself on top of the footman. Suddenly, the other footmen sprang into action. They rushed forward and encircled the two men on the ground. With a collective roar, Brown's men joined in, and a brawl broke out in earnest. I backed away, horrified, praying the police would arrive. Someone struck me from behind and I went down.

I braced for a pummeling. But only raindrops pelted me as I found myself sitting on the gravel while whoever had struck me had kept going and joined the fray. Perhaps Derrick's offer to accompany me had been a good idea after all. Yet, I didn't think whoever had pushed me actually meant to hurt me. I scrambled to retrieve my notebook and pencil, which had flown from my hands.

The pounding of footsteps sounded at the foot of the driveway. "Everyone, stop what you're doing and put your hands up. You're all under arrest for disturbing the peace."

Scotty Binsford led a group of some dozen uniformed policemen up the driveway, batons in hand. The brawling men took no note of them, not until those heavy clubs began making contact with arms and shoulders. Police whistles pierced the air, bringing a portion of the fighting to an abrupt halt. Others ignored the summons and continued their assault.

I backed farther down the driveway, all the while continuing to take notes. Little by little, the police subdued the unruly crowd. Perhaps the drizzle helped dampen their enthusiasm. The half wall and hedges surrounding the circular drive also prevented most of Brown's men from slipping away, but a few managed. At first the police made no distinction between the protesting men and the footmen, but gradually they sorted out what had happened, with Mr. Carver's and my help. Regrettably, the footman who threw the first punch was arrested.

Finally, pulling the brim of my straw boater lower against the rain, I approached Scotty. "Thank goodness you came when you did. This might have gotten deadly."

Scotty gave me a smile, but his eyes showed concern. "You could have been hurt. You shouldn't have been here."

"It's my job to be where things like this happen," I told him, but said nothing about my shove to the driveway. I only now noticed the stinging scrape on my palm where it had struck the gravel to break my fall. The rest of me felt sound enough. "Do you think that footman will face severe consequences? He was provoked, in the form of rotten vegetables hurled at him and his fellow servants."

"We'll take that into consideration." Scotty wiped raindrops from his face. "You'll come by the station later and give a statement, yes?"

"I will."

Leaving Scotty and the other policemen to it, I approached the recess, where the servants the police had released had taken shelter once again. The women pressed tightly together, looking frightened.

"Why did you stay outside?" I couldn't refrain from asking. "Why didn't you simply go inside and ignore them?"

No one answered immediately. Their feet shuffled. A few coughed and darted looks at one another. The butler cleared his throat. "Is Brown right, do you think? Did we do the wrong thing in coming to work for the Berwinds? I had another position, but I moved into this one because the salary and terms were too good to pass up. But . . . was that selfish of me? Greedy?"

A rumble of reluctant agreement rose among the others.

Good heavens, Orville Brown had certainly succeeded in rattling these people. But I had no real answer for them. I didn't know what the Berwinds would have done if they hadn't found new servants to replace the old. Yet, there were simply too many people seeking employment for these positions to have gone unfilled. It would either have been these people, or others from somewhere else. Either way, the Berwinds would not have negotiated or kept on the servants who had decided to strike. Ned and Minnie had been adamant about that.

A sudden shout made me whirl about. "Where's Brown?!"

It was one of the policemen. A line of men was being herded into the police wagons, but as I scanned them, I saw no sign of Orville Brown.

"He must have slipped off!" I shouted to Scotty.

He hesitated only an instant. "After him!"

"Which way, though?" An officer turned his head toward the front of the house, then the rear lawn, back and forth more than once.

"Spread out," Scotty ordered.

But the other officers were busy securing their captives in the police wagons; if they left them now, more would escape. That left only Scotty and his colleague to chase Orville Brown.

Mr. Carver turned to his footmen. "You heard him. After that man!"

Chapter 14

Brown's men were hastily secured in the wagons. Then officers and liveried footmen scattered. Some ran onto the forecourt and onto the avenue. Others set off behind the house, taking the footpath that skirted the lawn. I hurried after them, hoping to witness Brown being taken into custody. How far could he have gotten? I tried to remember the last time I'd seen him among the others.

I peered through the drizzle and saw no sign of him. Apparently, neither did any of the others. Had he managed to scale the perimeter wall and escape onto Bellevue Court?

At a brisk pace I followed the path. My gaze adhered to the line of elms planted along the edge of the lawn, and the larger weeping beeches that dotted the property on the way down to the sunken flower garden. More of the officers had converged on this area to join the search. They apparently shared the notion that had popped into my head, that Orville Brown hid within the trailing tents of those huge beeches. As they reached each one, they swept the branches aside and stepped beneath.

Each time, however, they emerged back into the open without Brown. I kept to the side path, hurrying along, my eyes peeled for the slightest movement. As a cool wind picked up, the dripping branches played tricks with my vision, making me think I'd seen Brown when I hadn't.

Could he have reached the carriage house? A fast enough runner might have been halfway across the property before his pursuers had even stumbled onto the lawn. The trees, shrubbery, and statuary placed along the footpath might have provided him the cover he'd needed. With a hand shielding my eyes from the rain, I glanced across the wide lawn to the south side of the property, where similar conditions of trees and shrubbery existed. Could he have crossed the expanse quickly enough to disappear on that side, where another gate let onto Dixon Street?

Perhaps, but the north side made more sense, as the footpath I currently traversed ended at the carriage house. From there, he could exit onto Spring Street and then head toward the harbor, where he could disappear among the many wharves. Even if the gates were closed, they probably wouldn't be locked at this time of day. The police wagons would not be able to follow him there easily, as Bellevue Court ended before it reached Spring Street. From Spring Street, he might head for the wharf district.

A shout from the garden brought me to a halt. Officers and footmen came running from various other points on the property, all now headed in one direction. I ran as well. A stone balustrade ran along the top of the sunken garden. Two enclosed pavilions stood at either end, each with a staircase leading down. I went to the closest one and scurried down to the garden. On a gravel walkway between flower beds, the men had formed a circle. When I reached them, I nudged the shoulders blocking my view until someone stepped aside.

A man lay faceup on the ground beside a now empty pedestal. He was no one I recognized, and I wondered what he had been doing here. His features were youthful but weathered, the skin that of someone who spent his days out of doors. Then I noticed the basket lying on its side nearby. A pair of shears, a hand hoe, and a small spade lay scattered beside it. His eyes were closed, his arms and legs sprawling. His clothes were rough and dark, loose fitting, those of a workman. He might merely have stretched out for an afternoon nap, except for the blood trickling from his temple, and the scarlet smear marring the marble nymph lying beside him.

"Is he . . . ?" Despite the umbrella Ned Berwind held over his head, the shoulders of his coat were shiny with rain. He had apparently run down from the house as soon as he had noticed the activity of police and footmen across his lawn.

"I'm afraid so, sir." From his crouching position beside the body, Scotty offered Ned a sympathetic look. "It appears Brown pushed the statue over on him. It must have struck him on the temple as he went down."

Ned shook his head. "Damnedest thing. He is—was—an excellent assistant gardener, so I'm told." He regarded the broken wings on the marble statue beside the body. "Minnie will be dismayed to discover this."

"Statues can be replaced," I said calmly, though his comments had left me anything but calm. Did this young man have a family? People to support? The rain, though still a drizzle, had begun to penetrate my walking suit, and a shiver raced across my shoulders. "His name was Zachery. Zachery Mitchem, according to one of your footmen. The head gardener's first assistant."

"Yes . . . Mitchem." Ned pondered the man lying at his

feet. "I suppose I'll have to write to his family. Or, if they're local, pay them a visit. But why would anyone want to kill a gardener?"

"He was at the wrong place at the wrong time." Scotty pushed to his feet. "Brown must have come this way and, seeing he had a witness, decided to put your man here out of commission."

Ned scowled. "Blackguard. I'll see him in irons if it's the last thing I do."

I didn't doubt he would have his way. "I suppose it's possible he pushed the statue over to prevent this man from following him. He might not have meant to kill him."

"It doesn't matter. He's still guilty," Ned insisted, and I nodded my agreement.

A figure in similar clothes to those on the dead man came striding toward us from the direction of the carriage house. I realized that he must be the head gardener, that someone had alerted him to what had happened. He came down the garden steps and went still, his face turned in our direction. He drew a breath and squared his shoulders. His effort fell short; stooped as if beneath a weight, he shuffled over to where the rest of us stood.

Ned clapped him on the shoulder. "I'm very sorry about your man."

"Mitchem." His gaze met Scotty's across the gravel path. "How did this happen?"

Scotty said a parting word to another officer and stepped around the body. "It looks like he confronted a man we're after, and that man pushed the statue over on him. As you can see, it struck him squarely on the head. I'm sorry. I wish this could have been avoided. He'd still be alive if—"

I wanted to offer Scotty what reassurance I could that this wasn't his fault. I knew he blamed himself for Brown having slipped away. But there had been so much confusion, so many men to sort out. None of us had witnessed the moment Brown saw his chance and ran off.

"Yes, you police have done a shoddy job from start to finish," Ned said for all to hear.

"That isn't fair," I protested. "The police have been doing their best."

He wasn't listening to me. "Well, what do you intend doing now?"

Before Scotty could reply, several men new to the scene dashed down the garden steps: Jesse, his partner Gifford Myers, and the coroner and his assistants. Jesse led the way to the crime scene.

Before he could get a word out, Ned rounded on him. "This, Detective, is the result of your incompetence. If you had arrested Brown after the first murder, this young man would still be alive."

"Ned," I cried out, but Jesse held out a hand for silence.

"Sir, I'm sorry about your gardener, but up until now we've had no evidence linking Orville Brown to Ines Varella's death. We still don't."

"How can you say that when the man has murdered again today in this very garden?" Ned swung his arms once, encompassing our surroundings. "Once again, on my property. *My property!*" His shout echoed against the garden wall.

"Yes, I'm sorry for the inconvenience," Jesse murmured, and simply walked away to address his men. Gifford Myers and the coroner had already gone over to the body. They crouched on either side, the coroner studying the wound, Detective Myers inspecting the ground around where Zachery Mitchem lay.

"How dare he?" Ned stood watching Jesse through narrowed eyes. His expression held a thirst for retribution.

"Detective Whyte has a job to do," I reminded him.

He pivoted on his heel to face me. "Then he should do it. There was another murder as well. That Rudolfo fellow— another of my servants. They're dropping like flies, dammit."

Jesse strode back over. "Mr. Berwind, I'll thank you not to speak to Mrs. Andrews that way."

"It's all right, Jesse," I murmured, but he didn't seem to hear me.

Ned's nostrils flared, and the two of them glared at each other. Then Ned seemed to deflate. He stepped back, nodding. "Yes, you're quite right. Forgive me, Mrs. Andrews. This is unsettling business."

"No apology necessary," I assured him. Then I realized something. "With Orville Brown still on the loose, you'll want to increase the security around the house. He's proven he's not above resorting to violence, and he's still angry at you for letting your original staff go."

Ned pulled up taller and puffed out his chest. "I had no choice after they proved their disloyalty."

"Brown doesn't see it that way." I didn't either, but I let that go unsaid. "He's an irrational man with much to prove, and you must take precautions in case he decides to return and make his point."

"Good heavens!" His face paled and his eyes rounded. "Minnie could be in danger. And the others. Yes, you're right. We must take the utmost precautions. As soon as the police are through here, I'll have a word with them about posting men around the property. Come. For now, let's go up to the house and leave them to finish their work."

I made no move to go. The police indeed had more to do, such as determining where Mr. Brown had exited the property and in which direction he might have gone from there. "I have work to do as well. I'm going to stay and find out as much as I can about what happened, and where Orville Brown might be now."

"But it's raining." Mr. Berwind turned his face toward the sky, then back at me. "You'll catch your death."

"I assure you, I won't. I'm made of sterner stuff than that."

"She is," Jesse concurred, "not to mention being as stubborn a Newporter as ever was born."

The coroner declared that Zachery Mitchem died almost instantly of a fractured skull and didn't expect to find anything different during a formal autopsy. While Gifford Myers questioned the servants about what had occurred between them and Brown's men, Jesse, Scotty, and several other officers made their way across to the carriage house. Jesse had reasoned that it seemed the most likely route Orville Brown could have taken.

I didn't follow them. The puzzle of why Brown had detoured to the garden continued to nag at me. True, its lower level provided concealment from the upper lawn, but it also effectively cut him off from other avenues of escape.

Or had he gone there looking for something?

I followed the footpath that left the garden and ran to the south-perimeter wall. A fountain stood between me and a pair of gates that led onto Dixon Street. They were secured by a chain, but when I tested them, I found I could open them wide enough to slip through. Could Orville Brown have done so? Was he thin enough?

I squeezed through. From Dixon I continued to Spring Street, effectively stepping from one world—that of opulence and ease—into another, made up of the comfortable homes of some of Newport's more well-to-do families. I glimpsed several policemen who had fanned out into the neighborhood. Walled gardens, raised porches, and shady, narrow lanes offered ample places to hide. Was our quarry even now observing the efforts to find him? I still believed Brown had headed west, toward the harbor, and I saw a few policemen head that way now. How easy it would be for Brown to slip into the confusion of the crowded, bustling waterfront. From there perhaps he hoped to find passage across the bay.

Resisting the urge to join the search, I started back to The Elms property. If the police couldn't find Brown, how would I expect to? No, I believed I might be able to learn more by returning. But I hadn't gone far before someone stepped out from a front yard and into my path.

"My, my, what have we here?"

A sinister chuckle chilled me as a woolen-clad chest filled my view. I quickly looked up into a face I recognized, but its snub, bulldog features brought me little comfort. I surveyed the immediate area, hoping there might be someone else within earshot. The sidewalks were empty.

"Excuse me, please," I said, and tried to step around him.

He smirked, one eyebrow angling above the other in a lined forehead. "Well, if it isn't Emma Cross."

"Yes. Hello, Mr. Dobbs."

"*Mr.* Dobbs. Yes, it's been mister these past several years, hasn't it? Not detective, as it once was."

I let out an impatient sigh. Anthony Dobbs had once been Jesse's partner on the police force, but his double dealings had landed him on the wrong side of the law. An investigation of my own had indirectly exposed his crimes, but in Mr. Dobbs's eyes, his downfall had been entirely my fault. Since then, he had resorted to earning his living doing the back-breaking labor of a dockworker. Or, as perhaps indicated by the workman's belt he wore and the variety of tools hanging from it, a handyman.

"That's years-old news now, isn't it?" I replied with false bravado. I clutched my hands at my waist in my effort to appear composed. If I cried out, would someone inside one of the nearby houses hear me? "Besides, you did me a good turn, didn't you, at Chateau-sur-Mer four years ago? I thought that meant you'd let your grudges go."

A killer had broken into that house—a man I had mistakenly believed to be Anthony Dobbs at the time. But it had turned out that Mr. Dobbs had followed the suspect in and saved me from becoming his next victim.

Now, he shook his head as his scrutiny rained uncomfortably down on me. "Still a loaded pistol, aren't you? Look at you, dressed like a lady reporter, as always. Even your fancy husband hasn't managed to rein you in like he should. That's right. I know you're married. I saw the announcements."

"That's all well and good, Mr. Dobbs, but hardly of any consequence at the moment. So if you'll excuse me."

"Why did the cops fan out over the neighborhood just now? Does it have anything to do with that mess up at The Elms recently?"

"You mean the murder of the young maid?"

He nodded, his expression shrewd. "They're searching the neighborhood, and now here you are, close on their heels. You're looking for somebody, aren't you? Just like you to get involved in something that has nothing to do with you."

I hesitated only a moment before deciding I had nothing to lose by seizing an opportunity. "All right, yes. Do you know Orville Brown?"

He laughed. "Everyone knows that loon. Or knows of him. Can't say I've bent my elbow with him of an evening, but I've heard him spouting off. What about him?"

I wondered, did something of a policeman continue to exist in this man, as had seemed to be the case that night at

Chateau sur Mer? I drew a breath and decided to trust the erstwhile officer. "He turned up today at The Elms, trying to incite a riot and succeeding. When the police came, he made his escape, but not before killing a gardener he encountered in the flower garden. The wharves provide plenty of places to hide. I think he might have headed that way."

"Could be." He rubbed the back of his hand across the bristle on his chin. "There are a lot of wharves along Thames Street."

"Yes, I know. Do you still work down there?"

"Yeah. I work wherever I can find someone willing to pay me." His voice dripped with accusation. I ignored it.

"Then maybe you can help spread the word. If anyone sees Brown, they're to contact the police right away. He's dangerous."

"That your learned opinion?" He laughed. "You really can't stay out of it, can you? One of these days, your luck is going to run out."

"Mr. Dobbs, I only want to see the man brought to justice." I heard the defiance in my voice and wondered how Anthony Dobbs always managed to put me on the defensive.

"This doesn't sound like Brown, though."

"What, to hide out? Obviously, he's a coward and not about to take responsibility for his actions."

"No, not that. Committing murder." Mr. Dobbs's eyes crinkled at the corners as he shook his head. "He's a troublemaker, true enough. But he's all bluster. He doesn't have the stomach for true violence. Not for committing it himself, anyway. That's why he tries to provoke others into fighting his battles for him."

I folded my arms. "That might be true most of the time, but when cornered, it seems Orville Brown is quite willing to resort to violence. If you don't believe me, ask Zachery Mitchem."

"Who's that?"

"The man who died today. Mr. Brown pushed a statue over on him and it fractured his skull."

"And you're sure Brown did it?"

"Who else? He ran off across the lawn behind the house, trying to get away from the police. Zachery Mitchem must have tried to stop him. He might not have known what Brown had done up at the house, but seeing anyone run through the property like that would have set him on the alert."

Mr. Dobbs was silent several moments, his brows knitting. Then he met my gaze. "All right, I'll spread the word if it'll stop you from searching the wharves yourself. You'd only get yourself killed. And annoy a lot of hardworking fellas."

I rolled my eyes at his priorities, but perhaps he had a point. Not all dockworkers were Newporters born and raised, as Derrick and I had already learned. Many hailed from all over Rhode Island and nearby Massachusetts, not to mention faraway countries. They'd feel no kinship toward me, nor see much reason to treat me kindly. "Thank you, Mr. Dobbs."

"I'm not doing it for you. A man like Brown . . . he starts trouble and leaves others to clean up his mess. I don't like that. Was a sad day for the island when he stepped onto our shores."

I left him and slipped back onto The Elms property through the Dixon Street gate. My instincts brought me back to the garden. The body had been moved and the place was deserted, and the pathways once again appeared tranquil and lovely. I wondered if Jesse was still up at the house, speaking with the Berwinds. I sighed. What a trial these last days had been for them, opening their new house with every expectation of passing an exhilarating summer in Newport only to have death shadow them at every turn.

Orville Brown would say that they deserved no sympathy, that they had brought their troubles upon themselves. Perhaps they had, to a point, but in my mind these deaths involved more than the unrest between servant and employer.

What had brought Orville Brown to the garden rather than take a direct route to the carriage house and out the gates onto Spring Street? What possible reason could have induced him to take such a risk? Indeed, he had been caught by poor Zachery Mitchem. But it easily could have been several policemen who had cornered Brown on these footpaths. I scanned the garden to my right and left, and once more ventured toward the Dixon Street gate.

Perhaps Mr. Brown had believed the carriage entrance too obvious, and knew about this secondary gate, used by the gardening crew and for deliveries onto the lawn. In fact, I knew the Berwinds planned an outdoor fete next month.

Methodically, I began going over the details of that morning. Orville Brown might have staged his protest directly at the front of the house, where he would have gotten the attention of the Berwinds themselves, rather than their servants. True, the new servants had taken over the positions of those who had been fired, but ultimately it was the Berwinds whom Brown held responsible for having unfairly dismissed their original staff. He had brought a ragtag group of individuals, each with their own grudge against—well, against the world. Things had easily gotten out of hand when Brown might have used his influence to restrain his followers.

A possible answer came to me: he had purposely staged a distraction. Perhaps he hadn't meant for the police to be called, hadn't wanted matters to become quite so contentious that men fell to blows, but I suddenly saw that he might have wanted the servants and even the Berwinds to be focused on the melee outside the service entrance while he slipped away.

Could he have been searching for something in the garden? I hurried back the way I'd come, back to the footpaths between the flower beds and sculpted hedges, shadowed now by the garden wall, the balustrade, and the pavilions.

So many places one might hide something.

Had Ines come here first that night? Perhaps the garden had been her meeting place. Or perhaps she had hidden the necklace before moving on to Dixon Street for her rendezvous, only to meet with a ruthless killer who refused to negotiate.

Who had she expected to meet? Rudolfo? Orville Brown? Both? Or had it been Rex Morton, whom she had hoped to extort with the necklace she had stolen. After all, she could hardly sell such an item herself—no one would ever believe she hadn't stolen it.

Where to search? The garden wasn't very large but it was intricate. She might have buried the necklace in a flower bed. Here was a question for Jesse: Had there been traces of soil beneath her fingernails? I glanced up at the two pavilions at either end of the balustrade and wondered if they were kept locked. I climbed the closest staircase and peeked through the French doors. Some lawn furniture and a small wrought iron table made up the furnishings. I detected no good place to hide anything. When I pressed the latch, it didn't budge.

My focus returned to the garden. My first thought was to tell the Berwinds of my theory and suggest they enlist some of their gardeners or footmen to search. But I discarded that notion for two reasons. First, one of them might find the necklace and secrete it away. And secondly . . .

What Anthony Dobbs had said played over in my mind: that Brown was all bluster and didn't have the stomach for true violence. What if Orville Brown hadn't been the individual Ines came outside to meet that night? I didn't wish to alert anyone else to the possibility that the necklace could be hidden here. And that included Rex Morton and even Charles Gilchriot.

No, I would speak to Jesse at the first opportunity and see what he thought.

I continued up to the house, intending to take my leave of the Berwinds. The police and Mr. Carver would already have apprised them of the circumstances earlier, but I might be able to add some details, especially since I had taken notes. As I reached the terrace, the French doors into the drawing room abruptly swung open and Minnie Berwind rushed out.

"Emma, where on earth have you been? We've all been so worried." She wore a soft lambswool shawl over her gray silk day gown and pulled it tighter across her arms against the chilly drizzle. The frantic energy wafting off her filled me with guilt. She might have been Nanny scolding me for not taking care of myself. "Look at you, you're soaked through. Ned feared as much when you told him you were staying out to see what the police concluded."

"I'm a bit damp, that's all. It hasn't been raining very hard." I kept my feet still so she wouldn't hear the squelching inside my boots.

"My dear, that's beside the point. Where were you? I was about to send the police out looking for you."

"I'm sorry. I merely tried to answer some of my own questions about what happened with Mr. Brown and that poor gardener."

"But why you, you silly girl?" She fussed with the loose tendrils stuck to my damp cheek. "You're not a policeman."

"I'm a reporter and this is a story."

She shook her head at me as though I were a hopeless

cause. "Well, come inside and have some tea. And we'll find you a change of clothes. You must be shivering."

"I'm fine, but yes, a cup of tea would be heavenly, thank you."

We entered through the drawing room but didn't stop there. Minnie led me up the south side of the double staircase and down the corridor to the left of the spacious upper landing.

"This is my room," she said as we reached the end of the hallway. She opened the door to a well-appointed bedroom decorated in feminine tones of yellow and gold. After inviting me inside, she went through a door into a wardrobe closet. "I'm sure I have something. . . ." She searched through the skirts and bodices hanging from the bars until she came upon a day dress in embroidered cobalt silk with ivory accents and a high neckline. "This should do. It's become slightly snug on me, so I believe it should fit you well enough. It might drag a little, though, as I am a bit taller than you. I'll send in my maid. When you're ready, I'll be in the sitting room. That's the room we passed opposite the landing, directly above the ballroom."

I thanked her. Moments later her maid entered and helped me change. The rain hadn't soaked through to my undergarments, so we made short work of exchanging my damp walking suit for Minnie's lovely frock. We also switched my sodden boots for a pair of house shoes. They were large on me, but Irene, the maid, stuffed tufts of cotton into the toes and that did the trick.

Warm and dry and feeling quite restored, I made my way back down the corridor. Giant tapestries flanked the entrance into the sitting room, making me feel rather regal as I passed through the doorway. A cheering fire crackled in the gray marble hearth, and the room beckoned with comfortable furnishings, bright white trim, and cheery red damask draperies. While perfectly elegant, the room had been designed with more congeniality and far less ostentation than any to be found downstairs, a haven in which the Berwinds could relax. Even the corners of the room were softly rounded, making the room almost an oval, and on either side of me, two additional glass-paned doors curved to fit those corners in the most remarkable way.

"Well, now, don't you look lovely and quite dry, my dear." Minnie sat on a red damask sofa with a low, gilded table before her, a silver tea set at the ready.

"Thank you. I feel much better." After a glance up at the carved plaster ceiling, I stopped examining the room and went to join her. Before I sat, I caught a glimpse out the three tall windows that faced over the lawn. Even with the sheer curtains and the cloudy skies, I saw the dull sheen of the harbor in the distance. "Goodness," I exclaimed, and then said, "May I?"

"Of course." I started at the sound of Mr. Berwind's gravelly voice; I hadn't noticed him ensconced in the wing chair to my right, near the piano. "Take a look and see why I built my house on the *wrong* side of Bellevue Avenue."

His laugh echoed behind me as I went to the middle window. Moving the lace curtain aside, I peered beyond the lawn, gardens, and Newport's rooftops. In the distance, the harbor spread out like a pewter tray beneath the lowering clouds, its surface dotted with myriad sails of all shapes and sizes.

I caught my breath, imaging the splendor of this same view on a sunny day. Indeed, I *had* wondered why the Berwinds had chosen to build their mansion on the west side of Bellevue Avenue—the side without the ocean views most of the Four Hundred coveted. Now I understood. This room, along with any of the bedrooms on the west side of the house, enjoyed spectacular views of Narragansett Bay and the vessels anchored there. Ned Berwind, a former navy officer, would of course find such a prospect irresistible.

Tearing my gaze away, I turned back to the room.

Minnie patted the sofa cushion beside her. "Come and tell us about everything you witnessed today. Was it very horrific?"

"I fail to understand why that husband of yours allowed you to come alone." Mr. Berwind ran a hand over the handlebars of his mustache and harrumphed, as was his habit. "I must have a word with him."

This I ignored as I settled beside Minnie, adjusted my borrowed skirts around my legs, and accepted the cup of tea she poured for me. "Where are your guests?" I asked, wondering if the Mortons and Gilchrists had decided to leave The Elms.

"The ladies are lying down," Minnie told me. "When the police came and told us what had been going on at our own doorstep, and then what occurred in the garden, it proved too much for them. I feared Kay might faint at the news, and Silvie had already been looking pale this morning. I had tea sent up to their rooms and ordered each of them to take a nice long nap."

"A good idea." I made sure to hide my relief that the two couples were still in Newport. "And the gentlemen?"

"The Reading Room," Mr. Berwind supplied. "Poor men needed a break from female sensibilities. One can't blame them."

I was surprised Mr. Berwind hadn't gone with them to Newport's exclusive, men-only club. How easily he passed off the wives' reactions to murder as "female sensibilities." I inwardly shrugged off his indifference and began relating the events of that morning as they had occurred once I had arrived on the scene. I included the jeering, the accusations and flying vegetables, the brawling, and the efforts of the police to bring Brown and his cohorts under control. My theory about the necklace possibly being hidden in the garden nearly rolled off my tongue, but I caught the words just in time.

Once again, instinct told me to keep that to myself for now.

Chapter 15

Derrick arrived before I'd finished telling the Berwinds about my conversation with Anthony Dobbs. Once again, Minnie expressed alarm about my venturing off the property without an escort.

"He sounds like a villain," she concluded.

Not knowing how to respond to that, I only shrugged. In truth, I *had* once considered Anthony Dobbs a villain, even before his greed as a policeman had been exposed. I'd found him rash, judgmental, and a bully. My half-brother, Brady, and I had both seen the foul side of his temper on more than one occasion. Yet, when life had hung in the balance—*my* life—he had chosen the honorable course. The man continually puzzled me.

Derrick crossed the room and crouched before me, taking my hand in both of his. "Emma, you're quite all right, then?" His voice was low, as if he and I were the only two people in the room. The intimacy of it in front of the Berwinds nearly raised a blush to my cheeks.

"I was never in any danger." I smiled down at him, then

gestured for him to take a seat. He rose reluctantly and moved to an armchair facing the sofa. I'm sure he'd rather have sat beside me, but Minnie showed no hint of moving.

"Hogwash," Ned Berwind said in a gruff voice. "Andrews, this wife of yours is far too independent for her own good. She's going to get herself hurt or worse, and you as well, when you must rush in and save her."

I clenched my teeth to keep from speaking out. Mr. Berwind was a gentleman of the previous century—one whose opinions clearly hadn't entered the present one. I darted a glance at Derrick. His eyes held amusement, yet with an undercurrent of something else. Acceptance? Reluctance? Fear? Did I cause my husband undue worry?

If so, I didn't know what I could do about it short of becoming the kind of woman I had long ago vowed not to be.

About a quarter of an hour later, a message came that Irene had returned upstairs with my walking suit, dried by the heaters in the laundry room below stairs. I went back to Minnie's room to change. My boots were still damp, but no longer sopping. When I handed Minnie's day dress to Irene, I thought perhaps I would soon add one like it to my wardrobe.

I was on my way back to the sitting room when, at the other end of the corridor, the service door opened and Silvie Morton stepped out. Carefully she closed the door behind her as if afraid to make a noise. Then, on tiptoe, she started across the hall.

She caught sight of me and stopped. Our gazes held for several seconds. Then, to my surprise, she beckoned to me. I hesitated briefly, then hurried past the sitting room to meet her in the guest wing.

"Emma, a moment, if you please."

"Of course." I longed to ask her what she had been doing

in the service hallway. Had she just come up from below stairs? Or down from the third floor? What business could she possibly have in either locale? But instead, I said, "The Berwinds and my husband are in the sitting room. Why don't you join us?"

"No. Please come into my room, just for a moment."

I followed her through a small anteroom and into a spacious bedroom decorated like Minnie's bedroom, in hues of gold, but in much deeper tones. She shut the door behind us, then turned a pale face to me. She didn't invite me to sit.

"It's my husband. He's worse than ever. I can't understand it. Yes, the necklace, of course, but he's . . . he's been getting up at night and leaving our room. It's happened twice now, and last night . . . well . . . last night I followed him. At least as far as the conservatory, where he unlocked a door and went out."

"Out? Onto the terrace?"

"Beyond it. I'm not sure which way he went—I couldn't see. But I heard voices, his and at least two others."

I schooled my expression not to reveal my sudden excitement. "Did you hear what they were saying?"

"No, I couldn't make out the words, even though I opened the door a crack. I feared to do more than that. I took such a risk as it was in following Rex. If he knew . . . he'd be terribly angry."

"Yes, of course."

"I did hear the sounds of hostility, though." She snatched up my hand. "Emma, I don't know why I'm telling you, but who else is there? The police—they can't do anything. Why, a man is certainly entitled to a breath of air at midnight, isn't he? Except that this was more than that. This is something . . . dangerous. I feel it. What can I do? I fear I'm going to lose my husband."

"No, surely not." I placed my palm against her cheek.

"Your husband is overwrought at losing the necklace, his investment. Are you sure there was more than one other voice?"

She nodded, her eyes gleaming with fear. "Who could they be, do you think?"

I thought back to another time Rex Morton had been engaged in conversation and afterward exhibited anxious behavior. "Could they have been the same men who spoke to him on the golf course?"

"Goodness, I'd forgotten all about that." Her brows gathered in concentration. "I can't be certain. I couldn't see them in the dark."

"Both encounters occurred after your husband discovered the theft of the necklace. Perhaps these men are private detectives he hired to find his necklace."

"Do you think so?" The eager hope on her countenance brought an ache to my throat. "But why the secrecy? Why wouldn't he tell me? Why sneak off in the middle of the night?"

"I wish I could answer that, but I'm afraid I can't. Perhaps he doesn't wish to worry you about the matter any further."

She clutched her hands together and paced to the window. Gazing out, she said, "More and more I grow convinced Rex is involved in something . . . illegal. I'm so frightened." She spun about to face me. "What do you suggest I do?"

I thought it best to be honest with her. "If Rex won't confide in you, there isn't much you can do. If you're right, his silence might be in an effort to protect you."

"I don't wish to be protected," she cried out. Her hands covered her face as she attempted to suppress a sob. Within moments, she seemed to compose herself and raised her face to me. "I just want things to go back to normal, before all this began."

"Silvie, the police and my husband are making inquiries

about Ines and Rudolfo—the worker who disappeared the night she died and was later found dead. Perhaps if we learn more about them, we'll solve the mystery of your husband's missing necklace."

"I do hope so." Despite the words, she sounded forlorn.

"I should get back to the others." Yet, I hesitated, wishing to ask her what she had been doing in the servants' stairwell. Suddenly, I thought of my conversation with the house-keeper, how reticent she had been, and how she had become defensive when I brought up the Mortons. I'd come away with a gnawing sense the woman had been hiding some-thing. About Silvie Morton, or her husband.

She was studying me now with a quizzical expression, un-doubtedly wondering why I continued to linger. I drew a breath and bluntly asked, "May I ask what were you doing on the servants' staircase just now?"

"The servants'...?" She appeared startled by the ques-tion. I waited, trying not to let my impatience show. "Noth-ing," she said. "I didn't go down. I only went into . . . the sewing room right off the landing. To see if my maid had mended something for me." She let go a brittle laugh. "She hadn't. Not yet."

I nodded as if I accepted her reply, even though I didn't. How could I when my question so obviously unsettled her? She could have simply rung for her maid, not gone searching in the sewing room herself. Had she gone below stairs and spoken with Mrs. Rogan?

I left Silvie in her room and rejoined the others. Soon, Derrick and I took our leave and Minnie and Ned saw us out.

"How did you come here?" I asked Derrick as we stepped outside. My buggy, which had been brought down to the carriage house, now stood waiting warm and dry on the drive.

"I was able to catch a lift from George Wetmore, who passed by on Spring Street."

"Good, then we can ride back together."

The rain, for now, had stopped. I took up the reins, ignoring the latest look of shock that claimed Minnie's features before she retreated inside. My aunt Alice never approved of a woman driving her own buggy either.

"I have so much to tell you," I said as I guided Maestro and the gig onto Bellevue Avenue. On the way to town, I explained my theory about the sunken garden at The Elms.

He appeared skeptical. "Why would Ines hide the necklace there? And why arrange to meet her accomplice on Dixon?"

"Because there would have been too much commotion on Bellevue Court." I squeezed around other vehicles and turned onto Bath Road, heading to Spring Street. "Carriages being driven to and from the carriage house, servants in and out, last-minute deliveries. She and her cohort might have been seen. Dixon, however, would have been quiet at that time of night."

"And the chain on the gate allowed enough slack to let her squeeze through," he said, more to himself than to me. He seemed to be reviewing in his mind everything I'd told him so far. "What about the guests? During the intermission, some of them roamed the lawn."

"I don't think any of them went as far as the garden, though. Don't forget, it's a good distance from the house and the grass would have been damp at night. Ines might have taken the same route as Brown, keeping tight to the perimeter wall on the north side to avoid running into any of the guests, and then skirting straight across to the garden, where she hid the necklace and continued to the south gate."

"To meet with the person who murdered her."

I nodded. "And dumped her into the coal chute to hide the body while he made himself scarce."

"Or came back into the house." He turned to me and our gazes met.

"We'll need to search the grounds," I concluded.

His hand rested casually on the side of the carriage, but I sensed his sudden tension. "Do you mean 'we' in the general sense, as in letting the police handle it, or 'we' as in you and I?"

"If the Berwinds will allow the police to do it, then the former. The garden is far too extensive for two people to search."

"I'm a bit relieved to hear that."

"There's more to tell you." We turned onto Spring Street and I held the reins loosely. Maestro knew the way from here as well as Derrick or I. While he conveyed us to the *Messenger*, I told Derrick about my encounter with Silvie Morton, and how she had come skulking out from the servants' staircase. "She said she had only been as far as the sewing room, which is apparently there on the second floor."

"Could she have been telling the truth?"

I gave that only an instant's reflection. "If it had been me, then perhaps. I'm used to doing for myself, so searching through the sewing room wouldn't have been out of character. But a woman like Silvie Morton, born to riches and surrounded by servants all her life?" I shook my head.

"I see your point." Maestro had slowed his steps and now came to a halt outside the *Messenger*. A shout from behind us drew attention to the fact that my horse hadn't moved to the side of the road and now blocked the lane behind us.

I waved to the delivery wagon waiting to proceed and began to maneuver us into an empty space at the curbstone.

Derrick climbed out and then handed me down. "So, she was lying."

"I believe so. Just as I think Mrs. Rogan was lying when I spoke to her in her parlor. She claimed neither Silvie nor Rex had come below stairs."

"And do you think it has anything to do with Ines and the missing necklace?"

My gaze drifted past him, taking in the shop fronts along the sidewalk. "I don't know. But I intend to find out."

Chapter 16

That evening, I discovered Bridget Whalen had left Gull Manor. She had said little to Nanny except that she appreciated what we had done for her, but that she had overstayed her welcome.

"She didn't tell you where she was going?" I watched as Nanny picked fresh herbs from our kitchen garden. It was a task she insisted on doing herself, as she didn't trust anyone else to discern which of the plants had matured to perfect ripeness.

"Not a hint." Nanny sat on a low stool as she pored over the verdant plants and plucked each leaf individually. "I asked her to wait for you, but she wouldn't listen."

"I would have tried to convince her to stay." I sat on the grass just outside the low picket fence, my folded legs tucked beneath my skirts. Patch lay beside me with his head on my lap. I combed my fingers through his fur in long, even strokes that occasionally elicited a rumble of pleasure. This was a stark departure from his usual evening antics around the property and I wondered about his apparent lack of energy. Should I be worried? "Could something have happened to make her go? Had any messages arrived for her? Did she seem agitated?"

Nanny shook her head at each of my questions while she gently separated a sprig of rosemary from the rest of the plant. "She seemed fine. She hasn't been a lick of trouble at all. On the contrary, she's been a big help." She chuckled. "Part of me hoped she'd stay on indefinitely. She certainly lightened Katie's daily load."

"Perhaps she's had word of a new position," I mused. Rose-tinged clouds scudded overhead, pushed by the brisk ocean breeze. The sun hovered over the horizon and spread a swath of flame across the waves. "But if that were the case, it's odd that she wouldn't share that news with us. Perhaps she's gone home to her family."

"That seems unlikely, considering what they said to her when she was arrested." Nanny scooted without rising, stool and all, to another bed of herbs. "I hate to say it, but there's something mighty suspicious about her sudden departure."

I didn't like to admit it, either, but I shared her qualms. I regarded the curling hairs edging Patch's floppy ear, currently having flipped inside out. "Is that why you're not in a mood to run and play tonight?" I asked him. "You're missing your new friend?" I glanced over at Nanny again. "They seemed to get on well together, Bridget and Patch."

"They did at that." Nanny snipped some scallions and placed them in her basket with the rest. "He took to her straight away, and she obliged him whenever he came wanting attention."

That made me smile. I leaned down closer to my dog and slipped my arms around him for a hug. "You're a good host, aren't you, boy? You make everyone feel at home."

"Well, that should do it." Nanny sat up straighter. With a hand at her back, she gently stretched the muscles. Before she could begin the struggle to rise, I slipped out from beneath Patch and stepped into the garden to offer her a hand. She groaned a bit and leaned her weight on me but soon stood squarely on her own two feet. I picked up the basket.

We had started for the house when I heard whistling from our small barn. Derrick came out through one of its double doors, his coat hanging over one arm. He had unhitched the buggy and tended to Maestro, as well as Barney,

When he saw us he grinned and waved and sped his steps toward us. "All brushed, fed, and tucked in nice and cozy." He peered into the basket and raised his eyebrows in surprise. "That all for tonight?"

"No, you silly man." Nanny opened the kitchen door and let Patch scramble in ahead of the rest of us. "They're for drying. Tonight's supper is already prepared."

Derrick waited until Nanny and I had entered the kitchen before following us in. After I set the basket on the counter, we left Nanny and Katie to see to dinner's final preparations and continued to the parlor at the front of the house. Derrick poured himself a brandy, and for me, a spot of sherry.

"Bridget's gone," I told him, as he'd gone straight to the barn after we'd arrived home and hadn't heard the news from Nanny. "She said she'd overstayed her welcome."

We settled together on the sofa. "Shouldn't that have been your decision?"

"One would think, but perhaps she's someone who doesn't like to feel indebted. In fact, from the very first she gave me the impression of being fiercely independent."

"It couldn't have been easy for her to go back to her parents' house, then."

"Indeed not." I thought back to her arrest. "She said she

stole that man's wallet because her family needed the money and she felt guilty about not earning any. But maybe she wanted the money to get away, to find a place of her own."

"A less noble ambition." His gaze scanned the room. In only half jest, he asked, "Have you looked around to see if anything is missing?"

"Derrick," I scolded, but caught myself surveying our surroundings. At first glance, I didn't see anything out of place. Should I count the silverware or run upstairs to check my jewelry? Not that I had much of value. My most prized possession, my wedding ring, sat securely on my finger. I turned it this way and that as I considered Bridget. "Perhaps we're reading more into her sudden disappearance than there is. Perhaps we should take it on face value and not consider it a sign of guilt."

"Can you do that?" he asked, holding his brandy snifter up to the fading light through the window.

I let out a sigh. "I'm not sure. I won't be until I've had an opportunity to speak with her." I took a tiny sip of my sherry, then lowered the glass at the sound of carriage wheels on the drive. Sitting up taller, I craned my neck to see out the front window. "Could that be her returning?"

Derrick had already come to his feet. He held out his hand to help me rise, and together we went to the front door to greet our unexpected visitor.

A man I had never seen before brought his carriage to a stop on the drive, set the brake, and swung down. I recognized the small emblem on the side of the vehicle as being from Stevenson's Livery in town. Beneath his derby the man's hair was pale gold, his eyebrows and mustache darker, nearly red. Before I could wonder very long as to his identity, Derrick strode out with his hand extended.

"Stockwell, this is certainly a surprise. Surely you didn't come all the way to Newport merely to speak about the matter you've been researching for me."

"Yes I did, Mr. Andrews. I thought you'd want to see firsthand what I have for you."

Hearing those words, I went out to join them. "Do you mean about Ines Varella and Rudolfo Medeiros?"

Derrick gestured to me. "Stockwell, I'd like you to meet my wife. Emma, this is Larry Stockwell. He works for my father."

Mr. Stockwell, a man of about thirty, stuck out his hand. "Ma'am, a pleasure."

I placed my hand in his and we shook. "Likewise. Please come in. We're about to have dinner. We'd like for you to join us."

"I don't mean to impose. . . ." He took a step back toward the carriage.

Derrick slapped him on the shoulder. "Not at all. You've come all this distance and we want to hear what you have to say." He stepped closer and spoke as if taking the other man into his confidence. "Besides, our Mrs. O'Neal is the finest cook in New England, in my opinion."

Mr. Stockwell retrieved a case from his carriage and followed us into the house. Once inside, he said, "Have you a table where we can lay out what I've brought?"

"The dining room." I pointed the way and let Derrick escort him in. I continued down the hallway to the kitchen to let Nanny and Katie know we had a guest for dinner.

"There's plenty," Nanny assured me, and I retraced my steps.

In the dining room, Mr. Stockwell opened his case and drew out a stack of papers. "These *might* be about Varella and Medeiros."

"Might be?" Derrick hovered at the edge of the table.

"Those names don't appear anywhere and we don't have any photos. Only a couple of courtroom sketches."

"Courtroom?" I exclaimed. "Then they've both run afoul of the law."

"This particular couple has," he clarified. "We can't prove it at this point, but I've a good hunch they're who you're looking for."

"Let's sit," I prompted, and we pulled out chairs, me at the head of the table and Derrick and Mr. Stockwell on either side. Together, we began sifting through the articles Mr. Stockwell had clipped from archived newspapers at the *Providence Sun.*

"They were married." I pointed to a line in an article. "Look here. Their names are Ruffino and Ilaria Meira."

"Yes, a married pair of scam artists," Mr. Stockwell replied.

Derrick reached for the page I held. "Can we even be certain those were their real names?"

"Yes, fairly certain." Mr. Stockwell slid his now-empty case aside. "Their immigration records were checked. It appears they were married in Portugal."

"At least they were really Portuguese. I was beginning to wonder if that, too, was an act." I picked up a second article. Each of them seemed to be from the same time, March of two years ago. The Meiras had been charged with not only theft but fraud. They'd swindled a well-to-do couple in Boston—I broke off reading. "They were from Boston."

Mr. Stockwell nodded. "Yes."

"I suspected Ines was and while I have no evidence about Rudolfo's origins, I assume he came down to Newport with her." I continued reading. Ilaria had been hired as a social secretary to the woman of the house, while her husband,

Ruffino, had insinuated himself into the husband's finances as an investment adviser. I looked up in surprise. "Rudolfo, an investment adviser? His coworkers at The Elms had described him as rough around the edges, not well educated. The sort one would expect to be a menial servant. They both must have spoken excellent English to be believable in their deception."

"A good con artist can take many forms, like a chameleon." Derrick thumbed through several articles, skimming them quickly. He sighed and shook his head. "The pair of them apparently persuaded this couple to become involved in a fraudulent investment and a nonexistent charity. At the same time, the woman, Ilaria, out and out stole several pieces of jewelry."

I nodded, finding the same information in the article I held. "Without firm evidence that the Meiras knew the financial arrangements were fraudulent, those charges were dropped." I glanced up. "Well, that's ridiculous. Of course they knew."

"Yes, but proving it in court can be tricky." Mr. Stockwell was riffling through the pages on the table. "But they each served several months for theft before being released."

I tsked. "Released to go right back to swindling unsuspecting victims."

"Unfortunately, they were gullible victims." Mr. Stockwell stopped his shuffling, having found what he had been searching for. He slid several papers closer to Derrick and me. "Here we are. The court sketches."

We gazed down at the image of the woman first. An abundance of dark hair was piled high on her head, with curling tresses falling about her face. Her eyes were large, her lips full and lush. At best this was a caricature, with the artist having portrayed her as something of a gypsy. The same could be said of the man, whose hair was long and unkempt, his chin and cheekbones sharp and exaggerated. An attempt had been made to show his complexion as dark and swarthy.

"What do you think?" Derrick murmured.

"It could be them," I said with a shrug. "Or it could be one man's interpretation of any number of immigrants. He seemed more influenced by creating a narrative than presenting the facts." I continued studying the sketches, searching for anything that might definitively identify Ines. But where I had seen sweetness and vulnerability in the young maid's face, this rendering revealed worldliness, arrogance, and a good dose of impudence. She might almost be laughing at the judge and jury.

I set the sketches aside and returned to the articles. "Ines was able to open a safe by reading the combination over a man's shoulder and at a distance. That suggests something to me."

Derrick gave me a curious look. "And what is that?"

"That she, and probably Rudolfo, were much more sophisticated than the average immigrant arriving in this country. They were more than pickpockets or petty thieves who got lucky."

Derrick studied me intently now. "Yes, I think that much is obvious."

"And they might not have been working alone. Someone else was helping them, setting up whatever they needed to deceive their marks, and helping them be in the right places at the right times." I noticed Mr. Stockwell smiling at me. "You think so too, don't you?"

"I'm not the only one. Here's a statement from the chief detective on the case." He slid yet another page before me.

I scanned the missive. "It basically confirms what I just said, that they believe the Meiras were working with someone, but the couple refused to admit it, even though they might have served lighter sentences for the theft." I searched for the victims' names again. "Abel and Rebecca Dunham. I wonder if Jesse knows about them. They could prove important to the case."

"We'll make sure he does." Derrick gathered up the pages and tried to return them to Mr. Stockwell, but our guest held up the flat of his hand.

"Keep them. You might need them again."

"Dinner," Nanny called a moment later from the hallway, and with our habitual informality, we adjourned to the morning room, where it was indeed proved that Nanny was the finest cook in New England.

A trolley accident brought me to Bellevue Avenue and Bath Road the following day. Being close enough to the *Messenger* to walk to the scene, I did just that, and a good thing, too, as the intersection at Bath Road and Bellevue Avenue had been closed, with traffic backed up in all directions.

A carriage had attempted to cross Bath Road in front of the oncoming trolley and the two had collided. The scene had me holding my breath when I arrived. Though the trolley stood on its tracks and appeared undamaged, the carriage sat at an awkward angle across the intersection. The injured had been helped onto the sidewalk, all except for one woman who lay prone in the middle of the intersection. Several people surrounded her protectively. Someone had covered her to her chin with a cloak and had folded another outer garment beneath her head. I searched for blood but didn't see any, but that didn't mean her injuries weren't severe.

As for some of the others . . . I noted one man holding a handkerchief to his bleeding nose, crying children who appeared more frightened than hurt, and a woman holding her forearm in the palm of her other hand. A picnic basket lay on its side, the contents spilled out onto the street. Several hats and more than one parasol had been crushed by either the trolley's or the carriage's wheels. The trolley would have been taking people down to Easton's Beach for what should have been an enjoyable day by the sea.

Several policemen had already formed a perimeter around the vehicles and were restricting onlookers to the sidewalks except for those helping the injured woman. Finding a familiar face, I asked a former neighbor from The Point if she knew what had happened.

Dorothy Holt, a local landscape painter, nodded sagely. "Impatience, that's what happened. See that gentleman over there?"

I followed the direction of her outthrust forefinger to the gentleman sitting only a few feet away from the prone woman. Though he did not appear hurt, he sat on the dusty road, his knees up, his hat in his hands, and a dazed look in his eyes. Every few seconds he rubbed the back of his hand across his brow.

"Was he driving the carriage?" I asked. "Did you see the accident?"

Mrs. Holt, widowed recently but once part of my parents' artistic set, pinched her lips before replying, "Yes, and yes. I saw it all. I had just come out of the dressmaker's"—she pointed over her shoulder—"when it happened. Why, I couldn't help but cry out for that buffoon to stop when I saw him urging his horse right into the path of the trolley. Did he listen?" Her nose went into the air. "His companion, his wife, one assumes, was thrown from the seat onto the road."

"Goodness, I hope she isn't terribly hurt." An agitated whicker floated on the breeze and I turned to behold a policeman standing beside the carriage horse, one hand on the bit, the other stroking the lean, muscled neck. I excused myself to Mrs. Holt and crossed to him. "Is the horse all right?"

"Spooked, that's certain," the officer said with a shake of his head. "The trolley clipped the back end of the buggy and tossed it nearly sideways. Look how the back wheel and axle are bent. Thank the stars the shaft had enough give. Otherwise, it would have splintered and the whole carriage, horse and all, could have gone over on its side."

I glanced over my shoulder. "What about the woman?"

"Might have a head injury. Could have fractured a thing or two as well. The rescue wagon should be here any moment."

"I hope so." The image of Zachery Mitchem popped into my mind. Head injuries could kill. "Do you know their names? I don't recognize the gentleman."

He couldn't enlighten me, so I thanked him and approached another officer, who was attempting to keep people calm and away from the injured. He was able to oblige me by supplying me with the names of the carriage driver and his companion, as well as some of the others who were injured. Then I returned to Mrs. Holt.

"Can you tell me exactly what happened?" I held my notebook and pencil ready.

"Are you going to quote me in the *Messenger*?"

I couldn't tell if she found this a good or bad prospect. "May I?"

"I should hope so. Maybe you could also mention the art show next week at the Redwood Library. I've got several paintings to be exhibited, along with half a dozen other artists. All local."

I paused, regarding her. "I'll put a notice of it in the paper. Separate from this article. Now then . . ."

Mrs. Holt had just left me, after giving me her description of the accident, when a voice called out to me from the southeast corner of Bath Road. I shaded my eyes and made out Kay Gilchrist trotting toward me, the brim of her wide, beribboned sun hat bouncing with each step. Her maid hurried behind her with several bags dangling from her hands.

"Oh, Emma!" She paused to catch her breath and right her hat. The maid stopped several feet away, panting. "Isn't this awful?"

"Good heavens, Kay, were you on the trolley?"

She compressed her lips, one corner of them slipping between her teeth. "I . . . uh . . . yes, I was."

"Are you hurt?" I scanned her from head to toe, then passed my gaze over her shoulder to her maid. "Are you both all right?"

"Fine, thank you, ma'am," the maid said, but I could see the lingering dismay on her features. If nothing else, the accident must have frightened them both.

"I might have bumped my shoulder against the wall of the trolley when we struck the carriage," Kay said. She wiggled her shoulder up and down. "But I'm all right, I think. It was just so jarring. So unsettling."

"What were you doing on the trolley?" It was none of my business, but I couldn't help blurting the question. Women of her class simply didn't ride on trolleys. Another glance at her maid didn't enlighten me, as the young woman merely stared down at the dust around her feet.

"We were going down to Easton's," Kay said after another uncomfortable hesitation. "Please don't mention it to my husband, or anyone at The Elms."

"I won't . . . but . . ."

"You see, I like to get away occasionally. To simply experience what other people do without all the fuss. My husband thinks I'm shopping—which we were." She gestured at the packages in her maid's hands. "But then I wished to see the beach—the real beach, where people stroll the boardwalk and buy roasted nuts and popcorn and . . . I don't know . . . simply be."

"I understand." I smiled. "And your secret is safe with me. I think I have enough information about what happened here. Would you like to join me for a cup of tea? We could go to the tearoom at the Casino."

She looked first relieved and then delighted. "I would enjoy that very much."

At that moment, the ringing of the rescue wagon's bell could be heard advancing in our direction from the north end of town. I lingered at the scene a few minutes more to see if the medical team could tell me anything further about the injuries, but they advised me to check with the hospital later that afternoon, after everyone had been examined.

I rejoined Kay and her maid where they waited for me at the corner and we continued the half block to the Casino. Outside the tearoom, Kay's maid headed toward a bench outside in the shade. Beyond the horseshoe pavilion, a couple of tennis games were in progress, the whap-whap of the rackets hitting the balls echoing along the shingled building fronts. I stopped at the door, regarding the maid, and asked Kay if she could join us inside.

"You wouldn't mind?"

"Of course not. I realize it might seem irregular, but the poor thing experienced the accident too and could probably do with a strong cup of tea."

Kay gave a decisive nod. "Thelma, you may come in with us. Only . . ." She trailed off until Thelma had picked up the packages on the bench beside her and made her way back over to us. Just as we were about to cross the threshold, Kay continued in a murmur, "Only, please don't tell my husband. Understood?"

Thelma nodded eagerly, her eyes widening in comprehension. "Understood, ma'am."

Chapter 17

Mrs. Gilchrist's admonishment to her maid didn't surprise me. I could easily envision the peevish Charles Gilchrist disapproving of his wife allowing such familiarity with a servant. That the word *peevish* had entered my mind to describe him momentarily surprised me. In truth, Charles Gilchrist was outgoing and friendly—with others, but not with his wife. He seemed forever to contradict her and silence her. Yes, I could understand why Kay Gilchrist might decide to ride the trolley and enjoy the beach anonymously among ordinary Newporters, and I could equally sympathize with her not wanting her husband to know she had invited her maid to tea.

I had no intention of telling him, especially when such an opportunity had fallen into my lap.

We ordered a pot of oolong tea and a tray of tiny sandwiches and minuscule pastries. Thelma didn't take anything at first, but silently sipped her tea. It wasn't until I slid the tray closer to her that she questioned her mistress with a flick of her gaze, waited for Kay's nod, and chose a sandwich. The sweets she left untouched.

"Do help yourself, Miss . . ." I hesitated to call her by her first name.

"Rush," she murmured, and bit off a corner of her sandwich.

"Miss Rush." I smiled at her.

Kay said, "You must excuse her. She's terribly shy."

Poor Thelma Rush turned as ruddy as the strawberry compote on our tray as she ducked her chin into the linen collar of her dress.

"There is nothing to excuse," I said, waving off Kay's observation. "Especially considering the accident just now, and, my goodness, everything that's happened since you've arrived in Newport. Miss Rush, did you know the maid who died?"

She regarded me from beneath blond eyebrows so light they were nearly invisible. "Not well, ma'am."

"No, you hadn't been here long enough to get to know her," I agreed. "But had you formed an opinion of her?" Both women looked surprised by the question. I thought Kay might intervene and cut the conversation short, but she remained silent as we waited for Thelma's reply.

"I . . . stayed out of her way, ma'am. She was . . . always very busy."

I tilted my head inquisitively. "By busy do you mean she was brusque?"

A slight smile formed on her lips. "Brusque is putting it politely, ma'am."

"Thelma," Kay said sharply, "we mustn't speak ill of the dead."

The maid once again ducked her chin. "Sorry, ma'am."

"No, please." I appealed to Kay. "The police still don't know what happened to Ines. Any information about her could be helpful."

"Well . . ." Kay looked unconvinced, but once again gave Thelma a nod of permission.

"Mrs. Morton's maid felt the same way," Thelma went on. Her voice lost some of its timidity. "We didn't wish to cross Miss Varella. We both feared . . . she might get even with us."

This concurred with what Bridget had told me. "Did you see her anywhere in the house the night of the musicale?"

"The only place Thelma could have seen the chambermaid would have been up on the third floor, in the servants' quarters." Kay aimed a pointed look at Thelma. "After you helped ready me for the evening, you retired to your room, didn't you? You wouldn't have had any reason to come back down, as I didn't call you to my room again until the following morning."

"That's right, ma'am," Thelma said in a hurry. "I didn't set foot outside my room except to use the washroom. Oh, and to go . . ." She stopped and pressed her lips together.

"To go where?" I prodded when she didn't appear inclined to continue. I stole a glance at her employer, whose gaze was pinned on her.

"Outside," Thelma said after a breath. "On the roof. It's where the servants often go during their time off."

"The roof?" Kay's eyes were round with astonishment. "Aren't you afraid you'll fall off?"

"No, ma'am." Thelma nearly grinned but caught herself just in time. "You see, there's a wide, flat walkway that goes all around the entire house, with a restraining wall so people down below can't see anyone up there. Except, the footmen built a platform you can climb up on, where you can just see over the wall to the ships in the harbor."

Kay gave a *hmph*. "Fancy that."

"Thelma, can you see the rear lawn and down to the sunken garden from this platform?" I wondered, could one of the servants have seen more that night than we'd been led to believe? After all, the police hadn't put any importance on the gardens at the time, since Ines had been found in the coal tunnel.

"I suppose you could, if you went right up to the wall and peered over. But I didn't, on account of I'm afraid of heights. Looking straight down would have made me dizzy."

"Then you didn't see anything out of the ordinary that night?" In Kay's question, I believed I heard an eagerness to close the matter. Thelma didn't disappoint her.

"No, ma'am. I wish I had seen something that could be helpful, but I'm afraid I didn't."

"There you have it, then." Kay turned to me with a satisfied gaze. A nervous bubble of laughter escaped her. "Perhaps one of the other servants glimpsed something. But why do you ask about the garden? That's not where the girl was found, was it?"

"No, but Orville Brown detoured there yesterday when the police were chasing him. You must have heard about the Berwinds' gardener."

"Yes, but what has that got to do with the chambermaid's death?"

"I thought perhaps . . ." I shook my head, once again realizing it might not be the best idea to share my thoughts about where Rex Morton's necklace might be hidden. "Never mind, it was just a thought I had, but I'm probably wrong about it."

"At any rate, we might not be among you much longer." Kay reached for the platter, took a shortbread cookie, and spread compote on top.

My pulse quickened at this news. I didn't like the idea of anyone connected with The Elms departing our shores until the killer was found. "Are you leaving Newport?"

"We're considering cutting our visit short, yes. With all that's happened, we think it might be time to continue our summer travels, with a stopover at home to gather the children, and then off to Westbury on Long Island to visit relatives." She sampled her cookie and took a sip of tea. "The only thing stopping us from going immediately is Charles is waiting to receive a letter from the chief finance officer at one of his investment companies. I do hope he won't have to take another business trip and postpone our plans. Although it would be pleasant to spend some time alone with the children at home in Tarrytown."

I had no evidence linking Charles Gilchrist to Ines's murder other than his flimsy alibi of having spent the intermission during the musicale in the library. He had no witnesses to corroborate or refute his claim, which gave me cause for doubt. But his wife's mention of business trips raised new questions.

"Does your husband often travel for business?" I tried to sound offhand as I used the silver cake server to transfer a berry and cream petit four to my plate.

"All too often, I'm afraid."

"Do you go along?" I darted a glance at Thelma, who was gazing back and forth at us from beneath her lashes.

"No, almost never." Kay sighed loudly. "Charles doesn't like to worry about me when he's at meetings and such."

"Worry about you?" I pretended to find the notion humorous, while in truth I found it rather disturbing. A man who doesn't trust his wife to be alone for a few hours? "What does he think you might get up to?"

"I can't say. Perhaps he doesn't wish me to be bored."

Bored in a new city, where there were usually plenty of sights to see, not to mention shopping and restaurants? But which cities might these be? "Does he go to Boston much?"

She glanced up in surprise. "Why Boston?"

"Only because it's the largest city in the northeast, after New York."

"That's true. I suppose business does occasionally take

him to Boston. Also Philadelphia and Baltimore. Other cities as well."

"I see. He's well traveled. Perhaps when your children are a bit older he'll consider taking all of you along with him."

"I do hope so. As I mentioned, we'll soon be off to West bury, but we were supposed to go this past April. I was so looking forward to it, but another of Charles's business trips forced us to postpone."

April . . . just about the time Ines would have been hired to work at The Elms. Had Charles Gilchrist had something to do with that? "And where was this one?"

She hesitated before answering. A rosy hue crept up her face and she blinked several times. "He . . . uh . . . doesn't always tell me. You see, often he's in such a hurry to go. These meetings can be called so suddenly, and there's barely time for his valet to pack his things, and . . . well . . ."

"I see. Yes, men can rush about in such a flurry sometimes that they forget to tell us things," I said, trying to make light of it. Her distress spoke volumes about the nature of her marriage to the older Charles Gilchrist, and the amount of regard he showed his wife.

"Emma, you must think me a fool," she whispered so low I could barely hear her. I stole a glance at Thelma, who was studying her empty plate as though hoping a door might open in the porcelain and she could crawl through. Kay, too, cast a sidelong glance at her maid, and I realized Thelma was well aware of the state of matters in the Gilchrist household.

My heart went out to Kay. Reaching across the table, I slid my hand over hers. "Not at all. We can't help the actions of others. Only our own." And what could she do to change an indifferent husband, a man who had probably only married her for her dowry and her ability to give him children?

And yet . . . in the past twenty-four hours, I had encountered two wives of the Four Hundred each somewhere she shouldn't have been, strictly speaking. Silvie Morton had strayed into the servants' domain—why? Her excuse of searching for a garment in the sewing room had been flimsy at best. Why not simply call her maid and have her retrieve it? And now, Kay Gilchrist had stolen aboard a trolley headed for a public beach. Again, why? Bailey's, Gooseberry, and Hazard's beaches along Ocean Avenue all served Newport's wealthy summer denizens. Surely her husband wouldn't have objected to her spending a sunny afternoon among their peers.

Had she been going down to Easton's Beach to meet with someone? Someone who should not be seen at The Elms?

Besides these new suspicions, our talk left me wondering whether Charles Gilchrist could be the individual who had guided Ines's and Rudolfo's actions both in Boston and here. Although Orville Brown might also be involved, I doubted he possessed the kind of influence to set up a sophisticated crime.

Until I knew if the same person who murdered Ines had also plotted to steal Rex Morton's necklace, the suspect pool for each crime could not be narrowed. Orville Brown, still at large. Bridget Whalen, also missing. Charles Gilchrist, with his feeble alibi during the musicale. Kay Gilchrist, sneaking off on trolleys. Silvie Morton, stealing below stairs. And, finally, Rex Morton himself, who surely came by his necklace through illegal means.

And then there were the men who had engaged Mr. Morton in conversation at the Newport Country Club, and whom he had met with in the middle of the night. Who were they, and how did they fit into all that had happened?

On the way back to the *Messenger*, I passed a newsboy on the corner of Spring Street and Bath Road hawking papers from Orville Brown's *Advocate*. I spotted the name splashed across the top of the front page even before I heard the lad's shouts, and came to an abrupt halt in front of him.

"Is that today's *Advocate*?" I demanded harshly enough for the youth to scrunch up his nose and eye me askance.

"Fresh off the press, lady."

"Who gave them to you?"

"What kind of question is that? Mr. Brown gave 'em to me hisself."

"Himself." My pulse thumped in indignation, but not due to the lad's bad grammar. "Mr. Brown was at his offices today?"

The boy pushed out a laugh. "If you can call 'em offices, lady. Just a shed on some side street west of Broadway. Got a desk and an old press and stuff. Anyway, you're blocking my business." He started to walk away. I nearly grabbed the back of his collar but decided perhaps that would have been a bit too severe when dealing with a child. I grasped his shoulder instead.

"Wait. I'll take a paper." I dug into my handbag for two cents. He handed me the thin publication, one sheet folded in half with a single-page inset. "Can you tell me *when* you last saw Mr. Brown?"

"I don't know, lady." He was clearly becoming annoyed with me. "An hour ago? Maybe more?" He started away. This time I matched his pace to keep up.

"Can you tell me where I might find this shed of his?"

He paused his steps, narrowing his eyes at me. "Why? You sweet on him?"

"Good heavens, no." In my astonishment at such a question I pressed a hand to my breastbone. "I merely wish to speak with him. I'm a reporter myself, you see, and there's a matter I'd like to confer with him about."

"You, a reporter? That's a good one, lady."

I looked him up and down, surprised he hadn't heard of me since I was the only "lady reporter" in Newport. Then I had an idea. "Do you get steady work from Mr. Brown?"

"Naw. Some weeks there's nothing. I take what I can get."

"Well, I work at the *Messenger*, just down a few blocks from here on Spring Street. Our subscriptions are growing and we can always use another newsboy. Come and see us if you like."

"Okay, maybe I will. Thanks, lady." He balanced on the balls of his feet, ready to bolt.

My hand closed over his shoulder again. "Before you go, the name of the street where I might find Mr. Brown?"

"I told you. West of Broadway. I know how to get there but I don't know the name. Can't read." And with that, he wriggled from my hold and trotted across Bath Road. Once he reached the far corner he stopped again, turned, and yelled, "Besides, he won't be there now!"

With my curiosity fairly pulsing through me, I hurried the rest of the way back to the *Messenger*. Once there, I slapped the *Advocate* on Derrick's desk, practically swatting his nose with it as I did so.

"What's this?" Before I could answer, he leaned, read the paper's name, and craned his neck to peer up at me. "This is today's? How is that possible? Does he actually employ a typesetter and press operator at that rag of his?"

"Yes, it's today's." I folded my arms in front of me. "I ran into one of his newsies on my way back from the accident. There was one possibly serious injury, by the way, the rest looked superficial, although people were shaken up." I slapped my hand down on the *Advocate*. "But getting back to this. The lad told me Brown operates out of a shed somewhere west of Broadway. But he couldn't tell me where. He can't read the street signs."

"Shouldn't be too difficult to find out—just ask around until someone admits to hearing the press running." He frowned. "Then again, I'll wager Brown uses a treadle press. I doubt he's got a steam generator."

I nodded. "So, no rumble. Which is why the police haven't

known where to find him, either. What gall the man has, slinking back to his press to get out a new edition."

"He's a slippery devil, all right. I wish you could have held on to the boy."

"He wasn't the type to be held on to. A bit slippery himself."

"I can imagine. Well, let's see what our brazen Mr. Brown has to say now." He began scanning the front page while I leaned over his shoulder to do the same. Both of us gasped in disgust at the same time.

> Ines Varella is still causing mischief in this city, even from the grave. In addition to causing dozens of servants to be fired from their positions, she has now landed yours truly in the unenviable position of being suspected of murder. I tell you all, there is no truth to it! I was nowhere near the scene of the gardener's death, am entirely innocent of the crime, and, furthermore, have no inkling as to who might have done it. Perhaps our indomitable lady reporter, Miss Emmaline Cross of the *Messenger*, is to blame as she was certainly present at the time.

We raised our heads for a breath of air that didn't stink of lies, and traded glances of incredulity.

"How dare he." It was a rhetorical question I didn't expect Derrick to answer. " He's blaming *me*? And how in the world can he claim to have been nowhere near the scene of the crime when he was right there on The Elms property, leading the police and footmen on a merry chase?"

Derrick pushed to his feet and put his arms around me. "Emma, please calm down. No one is going to take that rot seriously. This is merely Brown being Brown."

"Yes, I know." I drew a deep breath and exhaled slowly. "But it's still infuriating to see him print such . . . such . . ."

"Rot?" He relaxed his embrace and smiled down at me.

"I was thinking of a much harsher term but nothing I should repeat. Ooh!" I clenched my fists until the nails bit into my palms. I glared down at the article, and something else caught my notice. I snapped up the paper. "Look at this. He mentions Bridget Whalen at the end of the article, calling her a heroine of the working poor, a light to Ines's darkness."

I dropped the paper back onto the desk to allow Derrick to read the article to its conclusion.

"Why mention Bridget?" I demanded of no one in particular. "Why not one of the other dozens of servants who lost their jobs that day?"

Derrick didn't answer at first. He stared down at the article, then out the window onto Spring Street. People rushed by on foot and in vehicles, oblivious to the quandary in which we'd found ourselves. "She's special to him, is my guess. Perhaps they're special to each other."

"That could explain her sudden departure from Gull Manor. But if she's trusting him, she could be in grave danger."

Derrick turned away from the window. Leaning against the desk, he clasped my hands until my fingers relaxed. "Do you think there could be something to his denial of killing the gardener?"

"And what? *I* did it?"

He tipped his head back with a chuckle. "No, my darling. But according to Anthony Dobbs, Brown doesn't have it in him to do violence. Isn't that so?"

"Mr. Dobbs said that, but how can he be certain? Besides, Brown might not have meant to kill Zachery Mitchem. He might only have wanted to stop Zachery from pursuing him, and not planned for the statue to strike him on the head." I stopped to give Derrick's suggestion its proper consideration. "If he didn't kill Zachery, who did? None of us saw anyone else on the lawn. Only the police and footmen who were after Brown."

"Are you sure there couldn't have been someone else? You can't see down into the garden until you're right on top of it. Someone could have gone looking for the necklace, having no idea that Brown and the rest of you would come charging down from the house. Or that the gardener would be working there."

Reluctantly, I admitted, "I suppose it's possible. But again, who?"

"Isn't that what we've been trying to figure out? Jesse too? Who wanted to steal the necklace badly enough to hire Ines to take it, and then kill her when she was supposed to have brought it to him? Someone who didn't count on her hiding it before their rendezvous and who is now scrambling to find it."

I didn't answer for several moments as, yet again, I ran through the suspects in my mind. "I believe the same person must be behind Ines's death and the theft of the necklace. But could someone like Bridget or Orville Brown have learned about the necklace?"

"Bridget might have overheard something Ines said to Rudolfo. And she might have passed on the information to Brown."

"True. So neither can be ruled out. But I don't believe either is the mastermind of all that's happened."

Derrick raised a speculative eyebrow at me. "Perhaps they're working for whoever is pulling the strings."

"Perhaps." I considered the others. "Then there's Rex Morton. He might have realized the necklace was missing long before he let the rest of us know. He might have gone after Ines that night."

"And killed her."

I nodded. "Derrick, we need to be staying at The Elms so we can keep a closer watch on everything that happens, both in the house and on the grounds."

"How do we know the necklace hasn't been found?"

"Because they're all still here. Brown, the Mortons, the Gilchrists . . . Kay told me they were thinking of leaving Newport. But they're lingering, waiting for a letter, according to her. If her husband had the necklace, wouldn't they be making immediate plans to depart?"

"What about Bridget?" he asked. "You don't know for a fact that she is still on the island. Or Brown, at this point. This paper was probably printed hours ago."

"That's true," I admitted. "It might be time for another visit to the Whalens' home."

Chapter 18

Leaving the *Messenger* later that afternoon, Derrick and I drove over to the neighborhood behind the Island Cemetery hoping to find Bridget at her parents' house, or that they might be able to enlighten us as to her whereabouts. We pulled up a few doors down from the dilapidated cottage and walked to its side entrance.

A girl of about eight responded to our knock and stared at us with large eyes that reminded me of Patch when he had something important to communicate to me. She said nothing, merely peered up at us.

"Hello there." I crouched down to her level and smiled. "You must be Bridget's sister, yes?"

"She's not here," she said curtly. I heard little evidence of Bridget's brogue in the girl's speech and concluded she must have been born in this country. She started to close the door.

"Please wait." I pushed against the door to keep it from closing. "It's very important. Is she living here? Or do you know where we can find her?"

"Izzy, who are you talking to?" A brogue thicker than

Bridget's drifted to us from another room. Then a woman in a faded cotton day dress shuffled in from the kitchen, judging by the towel that dangled between her damp hands. Those hands were reddened and chapped.

I pushed to my feet, standing in front of Derrick and hoping the presence of a man wouldn't frighten her and put her off. "Good evening, ma'am. I assume you're Mrs. Whalen? I'm Emma Cross from the *Newport Messenger*. I'm hoping I might have a few words with your daughter, Bridget."

"And who is he?" She jerked her chin at Derrick as she swiped strands of brown hair back from her face.

"This is my husband and the owner of the newspaper."

He tipped his hat. "Ma'am."

"She's not here."

I tried not to show my disappointment, or that I had doubts about the truth of that statement. Both mother and daughter seemed to be replying by rote. "Can you tell us where to find her?"

"I don't know that I should."

"Please, ma'am, we only wish to speak with her."

She opened her mouth, and by the look on her face I braced for her insistence that we leave her doorstep immediately. At the same moment, there came a crash from somewhere in the house.

"What the . . ." The woman turned and made her way across the front room, then disappeared through an open doorway. "Good heavens. Help! Please help!"

Her daughter scrambled after her. Derrick and I rushed across the parlor, if one could call it that, and into a bedroom. A case of shelves lay on the floor, with a tangle of clothing, shoes, and hats in a heap around it. The sounds of weeping filled the room.

On their knees, Mrs. Whalen and her daughter were attempting to lift the case from the floor and grunting with the effort. A small child lay half under the shelving, his legs pinned beneath. Derrick ran forward and gripped the edges of the case.

"Stand back," he told Mrs. Whalen and the girl. He put the full strength of his shoulders into lifting the piece, consisting of thick oak boards. Soon he'd cleared enough space for Mrs. Whalen to slide the little boy out from underneath.

"Good gracious, Sammy, what were you up to? There now, you'll be all right." Mrs. Whalen helped the child to sit up and then wrapped her arms around him. I judged him to be about four years old. He wailed loudly against his mother's shoulder, more out of fear, I believed, but I tried to look him over for injuries.

"What on earth were you doing? You could have been killed." Mrs. Whalen's voice had turned stern, then just as quickly softened as she asked him, "Where does it hurt?" She eased the boy away from her and scanned him from head to toe, using her palms to search for bruises and bumps. Finding none, she wiped his damp cheeks with the hem of her frock.

"A weighty set of shelves," Derrick commented as he shoved it closer to the wall.

"My husband built it," Mrs. Whalen informed us, her tone hovering somewhere between pride and regret. She explained, "We can't afford a bureau."

Sammy hadn't stopped whimpering, and now he began to howl in earnest again. His mother held him while issuing an admonishment. "You were climbing those shelves again, weren't you? What did I tell you?" Her gaze shifted to the older child. "And you—Izzy—you were supposed to be watching him. Why else did I keep you home from school today?"

"Please, don't blame your daughter." I watched as tears spouted from the girl's eyes. My heart ached at the thought of one young child having to take care of another. It wasn't right; wasn't fair to either of them. "It must have happened when she came to answer the door. It's our fault, not hers. We distracted her."

"Yes, you did." The woman set little Sammy on his feet and stood. He immediately pressed himself against her leg. She compressed her lips and assumed an apologetic expression. "I'm sorry. Thank you. I don't know how I would have gotten that off him if you hadn't been here." The girl called Izzy began gathering up the fallen items and stuffing them rather untidily back onto the shelves. Soon her brother stooped to help her.

"You're welcome," I said, and hesitated. Derrick filled the silence.

"Ma'am, that's only going to happen again unless it's secured to the wall."

"I'll have my husband do it as soon as he's home again. He's off to sea. Found work on a freighter."

"Have you some nails, or perhaps hooks, and a hammer along with twine or wire?" Derrick waited as her astonished gaze traveled over him. "I'll secure it for you now."

"In those clothes?" Mrs. Whalen very nearly scoffed, but instead she regarded the shelves again, and then her still sniffling son. "I'd be beholden to you. I'll get you what you need."

After she shambled out of the room, Derrick and I both crouched to speak to the children. We asked how old they were, and learned Izzy, or Isabelle as she proudly proclaimed, was eight, and Sammy four, as I had guessed. He held up the required number of fingers. Izzy ventured closer to me and set a hand on my shoulder as if we were fast friends.

"You're pretty. I like your clothes."

"Thank you, darling." I had worn a simple shirtwaist with a lace neckline and cuffs, the collar secured by a silk tie the same color as my skirt. A modest outfit any woman might wear on a warm summer's afternoon. Izzy's faded pink dress had obviously been hemmed and taken in for her, passed down from more than one sister and showing signs of wear. Had Bridget once worn it? "I think you're very pretty, too. Do you go to school?"

"Sometimes. My big sister Emily and I take turns staying home and helping our ma with Sammy when she's got work to do. She takes in washing."

That explained her chapped hands.

"I see," I said, injecting admiration into the words. "You're quite a big girl, aren't you? You must be a big help to your mother." That ache in my heart grew at the thought of this child and her sister missing school to take on responsibilities they were far too young to bear.

Footsteps paused in the doorway, and I turned to see Mrs. Whalen studying me, a suspicious look on her face. She paused another moment before coming all the way in and handing a hammer, twine, and two small hooks to Derrick. The children and I moved out of his way.

Mrs. Whalen sidled closer to me. "I do the best I can."

Surprised, I replied, "I'm sure you do."

"Are you?" The scraping of the bookcase on the floor as Derrick moved it away from the wall again nearly drowned out her words. "You come here in your fine clothes, looking for my daughter with no good explanation, and you expect me to believe you're not judging everything you see? The house, the children, me?"

I shook my head adamantly. "I am not judging, Mrs. Whalen. I promise you that."

"I know who you are and what you do." Her chin came up defiantly as she gathered her dignity around her like a protective wrap. "You take in girls and women, try to change their lives. That's all well and good, but you can't have mine."

Derrick wielded the hammer, driving a hook into the wall. He attached the other onto the back of the bookcase. Each sharp rap echoed in the small room. The siblings stood watching him intently and unconsciously flinching slightly with each blow. I took comfort in the fact that they were not listening to my conversation with their mother.

"I don't want to take your daughters from you, Mrs. Whalen. When you and your husband drove Bridget away, I took her in and tried to help her. Now she's gone. I don't know where, but I'd still like to help her if I can."

"She's a lost cause. Never did have a bit of sense in that head of hers. Best to leave her be."

"I don't believe that and I don't think you do, either."

"Then you're a fool, Miss Cross." With a glance at Derrick, she lowered her voice. "Why this interest in my Bridget? She threw away a good position and then landed herself in jail. What good can ever come of her?"

Rather than answer, I remembered something Bridget had told me the day we walked in the cemetery. "Could Bridget be with her grandmother?"

Before she could reply, Derrick shoved the bookcase closer to the wall, leaving a few inches between them. A few things slid off their shelves and the siblings bent down to pick them up. With a length of twine in his hand, he reached into the narrow gap he'd left and wrapped the twine around each hook, pulled it tight, and then tied it off with a knot that would have made a sailor proud.

"There, that should do it, although you might ask your husband to test it now and again to make sure it hasn't come loose." He set the hammer on a shelf and brushed his hands together. Then he crouched at eye level with Sammy. "But that doesn't mean you should go climbing again. If you wish to climb, find a tree on a grassy spot somewhere. At least a tree won't topple over on you."

"Yes, sir," he managed with an endearing lisp.

He held out his hand. "Shake on it? Both of you?"

One at a time, each child slipped a small hand into his and shook.

Mrs. Whalen's eyes misted. "Thank you, Mr. Andrews. I"—she glanced at me—"I haven't been at all gracious."

"That's all right," I assured her.

"To your question, I honestly don't know. But it's possible Bridget is staying with my husband's mother. She lives on the Point, on Willow Street, just west of the tracks."

"I know the street. It's not far from where I grew up."

As the evening shadows lengthened in the growing twilight, Derrick and I decided to waste no time before visiting Bridget's grandmother. Would we also find Bridget there?

The house wasn't hard to find, being one property away from the train tracks on the north side of the street. We parked the buggy and climbed the three steps to the front door of the two-story colonial fronted in chipped green clapboard. Derrick knocked soundly on the door.

No one came. We waited, then knocked again. The faint sound of voices drifted on the air. I had an idea.

"Follow me." I hopped down from the steps and went round the corner of the house, through a narrow passage overgrown with weeds and wildflowers. This took me to a backyard surrounded by a sagging picket fence. The voices I'd heard grew louder, proving my hunch that someone was home had been correct. Under the shade of a white birch tree, Bridget sat on a wooden bench beside an elderly woman who could only be her grandmother.

Bridget glimpsed me at the same time I spotted her. She jumped up and darted toward the house.

"Bridget, please, I only wish to speak with you. Please don't be afraid."

The kitchen door slammed shut just as Derrick came up behind me. From beneath the birch, the woman eyed us suspiciously. Derrick tipped his bowler to her. "Ma'am."

She surged to her feet with surprising vigor, her gray brows converging. "You've no business here."

"We're sorry to disturb you." I let myself into the yard through a flimsy gate and strode to the back door. "Bridget? We mean you no harm. Please speak with us."

A curtain fluttered, then moved aside an inch or so. I stepped back and saw Bridget peering out at me, and then, to my surprise, behind her I glimpsed a man's white shirt-sleeves and the black of his vest. Then he was gone. Footsteps thudded through the house.

Over my shoulder I called out, "Derrick, I think Brown's inside. He might be running to the front door."

The curtain fluttered back into place and the door opened to reveal Bridget on the threshold. Her eyes shone with triumph. "He'll be gone before you can catch him."

"Stay here." Derrick took off running. The gate slammed shut behind him as he bolted through it.

With no intention of staying put, I grabbed my skirts up and followed in his wake. I swung around the corner of the house to see the front door swaying on its hinges while Derrick raced in pursuit of a scurrying Orville Brown, sans coat and hat. Brown darted into the trees at the end of the street, with Derrick hard at his heels. I held my breath, fully expecting what happened next.

Both men tumbled through the foliage and down the embankment onto the railroad tracks. Brown let out a yowl that made me believe he'd been hurt. When I reached the embankment, shoved trailing branches and overgrown weeds aside, and craned my neck to peer down, Brown lay on his side across the trestles. Derrick, too, was sprawled on the ground but quickly rolled onto his knees and sprang to his feet. He approached Brown cautiously, the dead leaves caught between the tracks rustling beneath his tread. He reached Brown, leaned over him, and said something I couldn't hear.

Brown thrust a fist into Derrick's gut. His arms wrapping around his midsection, Derrick doubled over and sagged to his knees. Before I could shake off my own startlement, Brown was up and running.

"Why can't you leave well enough alone?" Bridget's angry voice startled me, and I whirled to face her. A tide of red engulfed her features. "You have no business here. No business following people."

I opened my mouth to counter her admonishment, but an approaching rumble, accompanied by a chug-chugging and a steady clackity-clack, reached my ears. I spun away from Bridget and looked back over the edge of the embankment. Derrick, one arm still holding his stomach, raced down the tracks in pursuit of Orville Brown, who was gaining in distance. I shouted down to him.

"The train is coming! Get off the tracks!"

Still running, Derrick tossed a glance over his shoulder. I saw the indecision searing his brow and clenched in fear that he might take his chances and continue his pursuit. The ground beneath my feet began to tremble, and the tracks below visibly vibrated as the sounds of the approaching train grew louder. I glanced to my right and through the foliage glimpsed the engine car barreling toward us.

"Derrick, please . . . !" I stepped closer to the edge. Did I intend hurrying down—to do what? Tug Derrick out of the way? Even if that had been my intention, I heard him shout my name, and then saw him scramble off the tracks and onto the embankment on the far side. Here, without the steep incline, he managed to be well out of the way before the train reached him.

I heaved a sigh of relief, only to see Orville Brown keeping to his course along the rails. Was he deaf? Could he not hear the impending danger? Since leaving the depot at Long Wharf, though not far away, the train had picked up enough speed to make a sudden braking impossible. There were no stops along this part of the island, so there was no reason for the train to have ambled along at a leisurely pace.

"Mr. Brown, get out of the way!" I shouted. He neither paused nor turned his head.

Bridget came up beside me, nearly tumbling over the side of the incline in her haste. Grasping a sapling beside her for balance, she, too, cried out. "Orville, get off the tracks! Are you mad?"

I caught one last glimpse of Derrick, safe on the other embankment, and then the train was upon us, streaking by with a clattering and rumbling that drowned out all else.

Except for the screech of the train whistle.

"Sweet Mother of Mercy!" Bridget went rigid, her eyes squeezed shut, her hands pressed to her mouth. The train raised a wind that blew at our skirts, whisked our hair from its pins, and tipped my hat askew. Whipping tendrils blinded me. Around us, the foliage shivered and quaked. The vibrations beneath my feet made me question the ability of the earth to hold me.

Then it was over; the train had passed. It had never slowed, and after that first shriek of its whistle it had gone about its business as if without a care. Had Orville Brown gotten out of the way in time? Or . . .

Bridget started down the embankment, sliding on her heels until her legs gave way and she scooted on the flats of her feet and her bottom. Then she was up again and running. I followed her, taking the hill in several bounds that nearly sent me headlong. But I reached the rails without mishap, my gaze frantically searching for Derrick. He had vanished from the last spot at which I'd seen him. Where was he?

Bridget ran northward along the tracks, following in the train's wake. We could still see its caboose chugging along. Derrick appeared in my line of sight and my heart simply unfurled inside me, though I hadn't realized it had clenched in my fear for him. Picking his way through the brush and weeds beside the rocky track bed, he had started back in our direction. A wave assured me he wasn't injured.

When a sprinting Bridget reached him, he held out a hand as if to stop her. She barely paused to avoid him and kept going. She yelled Brown's name.

"He's gone," Derrick called after her. My heart in my throat, I picked up my skirts and ran to him. My gaze searched the tracks ahead for signs Brown had been struck by the train.

"What do you mean?" I asked when I reached him, while panting to catch my breath. "Where is he?"

Derrick's arms went around me. "I don't know for sure. He disappeared."

"Into thin air?"

"It seemed like it. The train blocked my view. He might have run off into the cemetery, but I don't think so. I'd have seen him. My guess is he boarded the train."

Though the train had by now passed out of view, I stared down the tracks as if I could nonetheless scrutinize it. "But it didn't even slow down. How could he have . . . ?"

"By catching hold of an exterior ladder and swinging himself up. It's a skill most drifters possess, and I don't doubt Orville Brown counts it among his."

"As you said, he's a slippery devil." I peered ahead once more. "But we still have Bridget, whom I don't think is going anywhere soon. Let's persuade her to return to her grandmother's house and have a little talk with her."

Chapter 19

"Perhaps, dear, if you answer their questions they'll go away." Mrs. Whalen the elder, Bridget's grandmother, spoke with a strong brogue, stronger than her granddaughter's. She hovered on her feet beside Bridget's chair in a front parlor that, though modest, showed signs of greater affluence than that of Bridget's family. The woman had offered us tea, but before we could reply, Bridget had waved away her hospitality with a tsk. Because of that, I supposed, the woman seemed all sixes and nines, wondering what to do next.

"I answered their questions before and they haven't left me in peace." Bridget crossed arms in front of her. "Why should now be any different?"

"We keep asking you questions because none of them have been answered to our satisfaction," I admonished. "You've been hiding things."

"You shouldn't lie to the police, Bridget." Her grandmother waved a finger.

"Why shouldn't I?" she shot back, her eyes narrowing, not on Mrs. Whalen, but on me. "You aren't the police. You're like a fever that won't break, a rash that no amount of salve will cure, a—"

I sighed. "Yes, I follow you."

Mrs. Whalen leaned over her granddaughter to whisper in her ear, "You mustn't speak so to our guests."

"They're not guests, Gran."

"Miss Whalen, you're correct in that we're not the police." Derrick stared her down, though she stubbornly refused to meet his eye. "But we can certainly alert them to the fact that we caught you harboring a man suspected of murder. Would you prefer that?"

"Is there no end to your threats?" she mumbled. Her chin sank lower. "Orville didn't kill that man. He's done nothing."

"Did he not incite a riot at the service entrance to The Elms?" I challenged her.

"That's different." She shifted in her chair with an air of defiance. "That was free speech."

I suppressed an urge to chuckle. "I'm afraid there's a world of difference between free speech and encouraging people to throw punches. The man obviously has a violent streak. I will concede he might not have meant to kill the gardener at The Elms, but the poor man is dead all the same."

"You're wrong. Orville had nothing to do with that," Bridget insisted. "He was already off the premises before it happened."

"How on earth can you know that?" I leaned toward her, as if to give more force to my words. "How can Orville have known that? Either he was in the sunken garden or he wasn't. He can't have known what happened there, or when, unless he went down those steps."

"He . . ." She trailed off, her complexion darkening. "You're trying to confuse me. All I know is, Orville is innocent."

"But you knew he was wanted by the police," Derrick said bluntly.

She gave a nod.

"Then you knew you were doing wrong in hiding him here." I gestured toward the elderly Mrs. Whalen. "Had you no thought for your grandmother's safety?"

"I'm fine, truly," the woman assured us. She fussed with a corner of the shawl draped over her shoulders. "I don't know what you're all talking about, but Mr. Brown certainly minded his manners while he was here."

"I'm very glad to hear that, Mrs. Whalen," I said. "Please, won't you sit with us?"

Derrick stood and brought a side chair from the wall. Mrs. Whalen gave him a grateful look as she sank into it. "I do wish you'd let me make tea."

I let that go and folded my hands in my lap. "Bridget, when did Orville first approach you about helping him evade the police? What did he say?"

She scowled as she blew out a breath. "It was early this morning. He came here because he knew I've been staying here—" She clamped her lips shut, her eyes darting from me to Derrick and back. He and I exchanged a surprised glance.

I leaned forward again. "Bridget, how long have you and Orville Brown been sweethearts?"

"What?" Her head swung upward as she met my gaze fully for the first time. "We aren't. We—"

"I think you are," I said quietly. "I think you have been all along. Tell me, was it you and Brown who first cooked up the idea of the servants' strike?"

Her lips formed a tight line.

"Did he put you up to it?" I asked. "Did he persuade you to convince the others a strike would be a good idea?"

"It *was* a good idea," she blurted, "and there's nothing

wrong with a strike. Miners do it. Dockworkers. Railroad workers . . ."

"They have unions. You and your fellow servants didn't. No one to state your case or negotiate for you. It was all too easy for Ned Berwind to simply dismiss you all."

"How could we have known he'd turn a deaf ear on our complaints? That his wife would as well?"

"It was predictable, if you had really known anything about your employers." Derrick spoke matter-of-factly. "You went into it blindly, played with fire, and were burnt."

"Bridget, it was Brown's idea, wasn't it?" I raised an eyebrow at her, sure I already knew the answer. "He talked you into it."

"He had our best interests at heart."

"Did he?" I asked. "Or were his own interests more important? Causing a disturbance, creating a story for the *Advocate*."

"He wouldn't do that," she said between gritted teeth.

"Many a newspaperman resorts to such tactics," Derrick informed her. "If the real news isn't exciting enough, they find ways to embellish it, or even, as my wife says, create it."

Bridget remained silent for a long moment, but I could see her mind working it over, replaying the events of recent days and weeks. Finally, her shoulders sagged as some of the tension and hostility left her. "But to what end? Yes, perhaps to make news for his paper, but that would have nothing to do with Ines's death, or the theft of the necklace."

"Can you be certain of that?" Only now did a possibility leap to life in my mind. If not for discovering this link between Bridget and Brown, it might never have occurred to me. "Could Orville Brown have created the entire confusing scenario to do just that—steal the necklace? He and Ines could easily have been acquainted in the past. We believe she was running scams in Boston along with the handyman who was also murdered—her husband."

"Ines and that Rudolfo fellow?"

"The same," I confirmed.

Her brow creased, not with anger but with perplexity. "Orville and Ines were enemies. She symbolized everything he detested in workers who refuse to stand up for their rights. He had no regard for her."

"That could have been part of their deception." Possible details took shape as I spoke. "If they were in on it together, the strike might have been a ploy to get rid of the regular staff, or at least throw them into disarray. As it happened, a new staff came on board, one that wasn't yet familiar with the house or its routines, making it easier for Ines to sneak into the Mortons' bedroom the night of the musicale and steal the necklace from the safe. After she did, we believe she hid the necklace somewhere on the estate and went on to meet her accomplice—possibly Brown—and renegotiate the terms of their partnership. Perhaps she decided she deserved more of a reward since she did the work. They argued, he killed her, and dumped her body into the coal chute."

"What makes you so sure she hid the necklace, and that whoever killed her doesn't have it?"

I traded another glance with Derrick, this time an uncertain one. Bridget had a point. Ines and Rudolfo could have been working with someone with no prior connection to Newport or The Elms. He or she might have vacated the island that very night, and we would never find the culprit or the necklace.

Derrick gave me the slightest of nods, but what it lacked in motion it more than made up for in confidence. He believed we were on the right track—and so did I. The rest of my thoughts I voiced out loud for Bridget's benefit. "I'm fairly certain of it because otherwise there are simply too many questions concerning people who are still here in Newport."

"Including me," she murmured.

"Yes, including you," I confirmed with a nod. "But not *only* you, either. Or Orville Brown, for that matter. There are others whose reasons for coming to Newport are questionable, along with what they've been doing since they arrived. And despite a murder occurring at The Elms, none of these individuals has left the island."

"You think it's one of the guests," Bridget guessed.

"Perhaps." I raised an eyebrow at her. "Perhaps not."

She sank back in her chair and cast a nervous glance at her grandmother. "What happens next?"

Derrick studied her for a moment. "Can we trust you to stay here?"

She shrugged. "I have nowhere else to go."

I also appealed with a look to her grandmother. "Ma'am?"

"Of course Bridget will stay here. She's welcome as long as she likes."

"Good." I slapped my knees in preparation of ending our little chat. "That settles that. Right now, there's something we must do before we drive out to Gull Manor."

"And what's that?" Derrick asked, looking puzzled. He came to his feet and offered a hand to help me up.

Once on my feet I drew in a breath and let it out slowly. "We have to tell Jesse how we discovered and lost Orville Brown in the space of only a few minutes."

"Just vanished?" Jesse ran a hand through his wavy auburn hair and shook his head. "Just like that?"

Derrick once more explained his theory about Orville Brown jumping onto the train. Jesse had taken the news surprisingly well. I had expected him to chastise us for going after Brown ourselves, except he seemed to understand that it hadn't been Brown we'd gone looking for, but Bridget.

"It sounds like that young woman is headed for serious trouble if she doesn't mend her ways. Reckless and all too trusting," was his assessment of Bridget's actions concerning Mr. Brown. "I should really have her arrested for harboring a fugitive."

"I wish you wouldn't." I placed my hands on Jesse's desk as I leaned toward him. "For one thing, I don't think she's our guilty party. And two, I truly believe her when she says she doesn't believe Brown is, either." Jesse started to respond to that, but I spoke up again, quickly. "And if she *is* guilty, don't we want her where we can watch her?"

"A prison cell certainly makes it easier to watch someone," Jesse pointed out wryly.

"But not if we want to catch someone in the act of breaking the law."

Jesse nodded at the validity of my point.

"Derrick and I have a plan for doing just that," I said.

Derrick, sitting beside me, turned to me with a frown. "We do? I don't remember formulating one."

"Remember when we discussed the necessity of our staying at The Elms, where we can keep a close watch on everyone and their comings and goings on the property?"

He nodded, his eyes scrunching as if searching his memory. "Vaguely."

I turned back to Jesse. "If the necklace is still somewhere in Newport, it's most likely somewhere at The Elms. Have your men been searching the gardens?"

"They have," he replied, "and they've found nothing so far."

"There are lots of possible places." Seeing I had the attention of both men, I hurried on. "Whoever wants that necklace is going to be searching as well. Kay Gilchrist told me she and her husband were planning to leave Newport soon. That could mean he has some idea where the necklace could be. Then again, according to Silvie Morton, her husband has been leaving their room at night. Once she even overheard him speaking to someone else, perhaps two men, outside on the terrace. Who are they, and do they have an interest in this piece of jewelry gotten on the black market? There's Silvie Morton herself, skulking around the servants' areas, where no lady ought to be. Finally, we have Orville Brown—and yes, perhaps with Bridget helping him—creating a diversion up at the house while he runs down to the garden and murders a man."

"All right, these are all possibilities," Jesse conceded. "Except for Bridget. She might be sweet on him, but do you really think she could have had a hand in both the theft and the murders?"

"Bridget all but admitted that the strike was Brown's idea, and that he approached her first about it. Doesn't it seem the strike perpetuated everything that happened after it?"

"Emma makes a good argument," Derrick said with a note of pride. "We've only to narrow our suspects until we have one in our crosshairs. And to do that, as Emma said, we need to be onsite at all times with an eye on all that's going on."

"With your people there too, of course," I added, "unbeknownst to everyone else at The Elms."

"Thank you for including us." Jesse's sarcasm was not lost on either Derrick or me.

"You know it's easier for us to be accepted into the house than for police officers," I reminded him. "And we won't raise the guests' suspicions that the police are any closer to solving the case."

"All right." Jesse ran his hand through his hair again. "How do you propose simply moving into The Elms without it seeming irregular to the staff and guests? And will you inform the Berwinds of your scheme?"

Derrick and I consulted with one another silently. Derrick said, "I think the Berwinds should be none the wiser, for their own safety."

I nodded my agreement. "As for the former of your two questions, I think a roof leak might do nicely."

"A roof leak?" Jesse frowned.

"Yes, with water pouring right into our bedroom at home. It'll necessitate repairs and I simply cannot abide the sounds of hammering. Mrs. Berwind and the other ladies will entirely sympathize with me and question our ruse no further."

"That was certainly easy." Derrick sat his overnight bag on the foot of the canopied bed. "Minnie didn't even blink at the lie you told her."

I turned away from the open armoire, where I had hung up several of my dresses. "White lie," I corrected, "and the beauty of it is that I didn't even have to ask her a thing. She quite freely offered the invitation for us to stay. Eagerly, even."

I gazed around the room, decorated in bright yellow damask with soft gray walls and featuring lovely ball and claw furnishings by Newport's own Townsend and Goddard furniture makers. All were showcased by the light flooding in through the four soaring windows that graced two sides of the corner room, turning the herringbone floor a soft golden hue.

One of the largest guest rooms in the house, it was the one that would be used by Ned's sister, Julia, when she visited. It had been the only one available that would accommodate both Derrick and me, as the two bedrooms on either side of the stair landing contained single beds, meant for the Berwinds' niece and nephew. "A shame they put us here, though, so far from the Mortons and Gilchrists."

"As far as one could possibly be." Derrick opened a drawer in the bureau and dropped in a stack of folded shirts. Indeed, we were at the very opposite end of the second-floor corridor, directly across from both Minnie's and Ned's rooms. "We'll have to be both quiet and quick if we expect to elude the Berwinds and catch the others at anything."

"And good at skulking in doorways." I shook my head wryly at him and regarded his shirts. "They'll wrinkle like that." I took the pile from the drawer, shook out each shirt, and began hanging them in the armoire beside my own clothes.

He eased himself onto the striped and floral settee beside the armoire and reached for my hand. Once he had it, he gave a tug that landed me on his lap. "So, who gets first watch tonight?"

"I wouldn't mind," I said without hesitation, then let out a little squeak of pleasure when his lips nudged the side of my neck. Such gestures still had the power to speed my pulse and stir my desires, and I was glad Derrick hadn't grown tired of bestowing them.

"You understand the meaning of 'watch,' don't you?" His lips continued their exploration of the tender skin beneath my earlobe. I arched into him, enjoying the warmth of his touch and the scent of him, musky and woodsy, something I surely never would tire of. When I didn't answer him, he went on to explain, "'Watch' does not mean follow alone, or confront alone, or anything else of the sort. It means just that—watch—and if anything unusual happens, we follow, confront, or do anything else *together*."

"Hmm," I agreed, and tipped my head to give him better access to my throat.

He pulled away, grasped my shoulders, and glared at me.

"Emma? Do we have a thorough understanding of how this must go?"

"Yes, quite thorough."

"Emma."

"Fine." I slid off his lap and stood before him. "Of course I won't go running off half cocked and put myself in mortal danger. I've learned a thing or two in recent years."

He glared a moment more before his lips curled in a smile. He came to his feet and reached for me. "I believe, madam, that we have a good hour or so before dinner is served."

"Goodness, I do believe you're right, sir." I grinned back at him. "However shall we pass the time?"

With a look that sent chills across my shoulders, he swung me into his arms.

As I had told Derrick, I chose to take the first watch once everyone had retired. Luckily, no one decided to linger alone in the upstairs sitting room. With only the moonlight through the tall windows over the grand double staircase to guide my way, I slipped past the sitting room and down the hall to the doorway of the linen closet. It was recessed just enough to allow me to conceal myself with the help of the shadows.

I was fully dressed, though comfortably, in a tea gown that allowed me to free myself of my corset. Instead of outdoor shoes or boots that would have given me away with their tread against the flooring, I had donned a pair of house shoes in soft leather, the soles pliable and without heels.

Minutes passed and I began to question the wisdom of remaining where I was. Why hadn't I considered that I might be there more than an hour or two, with nothing to sit on and not a crumb to snack on? It had always been my habit on nights when sleep eluded me to steal down to our kitchen at Gull Manor, warm a small pot of milk, and find something sweet to go with it. I had no such comforts now as I leaned as fully as I could in the doorway.

The room closest to me was inhabited by the Mortons. Next door to that was the Gilchrists' guest room. On the opposite side were two storage rooms, and directly across from the Gilchrists' room was the door onto the service landing and sewing room. At the very end of the hallway lay a bathroom with a small anteroom that housed cupboards on both sides of the doorway. The Mortons' room also sported such an anteroom leading into the main room.

In the silence, the ticking of the sitting room clock ricocheted along the corridor, seeming as loud as the clip-clopping of an approaching horse. Several times I had to shake myself from ensuing slumber, my legs sagging and my back sliding downward against the doorjamb. That same clock startled me by chiming the half hour, yet I couldn't remember it striking the hour thirty minutes prior. What was it—one, two in the morning?

Just as it seemed none of our houseguests were going to stir from their beds, the bedroom door closest to me creaked. Though I'd fallen into a half doze, I came fully awake and pressed myself against the doorway. There came another creak, this time not the door but a footfall against the herringbone floor of the room's vestibule.

Was it Rex Morton? Silvie? Gingerly I leaned until I could peer with one eye around the corner of the doorway. There came the light click of a slipper heel against the hallway's marble tiled floor. A swish followed, and I spied a sheen of pale satin billow out behind the figure that stole toward the end of the hall.

I moved farther out of my hiding place. Silvie Morton's hair fell in a gleaming dark river between her shoulder blades and swayed slightly from side to side as she made her way down the hall. To the bathroom? Or . . .

She reached for the latch of the service door and pushed her way through.

I started forward but stopped on the balls of my feet, Derrick's admonishment from earlier sharp in my ears. Watch, but do not follow. Do not confront.

Now I saw the fatal flaw in our plan. If I ran back to our room to alert him, I might lose track of Silvie. Would she go up or down? What errand had she set out upon? No, I had to follow her now or I might never learn her destination, or the reason for it.

Besides, it was only Silvie, and in her nightgown, no less. I'd seen no sign of a weapon in the flowing satin of her robe.

I pressed forward. She had closed the outer door of her room, leaving Rex slumbering alone inside. I hurried past and followed her through the service door and to the stair landing. There I paused and cocked my head, listening. A silence as deep and profound as the midnight sky permeated the staircase. Above me, each servant would lie asleep behind a closed and locked door, muffling any snores or sleep mumbles within.

An echo from somewhere below reached my ears and I started down. At the first landing, I passed the upper level of the butler's pantry, locked up tight at night. Halfway down the next flight, I paused again to lean over the railing, just in time to see Silvie's robe fan out as she reached the first floor. She kept going and so did I.

I reached the delivery hall in the basement just in time to see the door into the cold-preparation kitchen close behind her. I pressed my ear to the door and waited, not wanting her to catch me following her. I wondered again about the time. If it was indeed about two-thirty in the morning, in another hour or two some of the kitchen staff would be up and preparing for the day's meals.

Carefully I pushed the door open. Silvie was just then

going through the next entrance, a pair of wood-framed glass doors. I didn't wonder where she would turn next. If she continued straight, she'd enter the laundry room, and I doubted very much that Silvie Morton was concerned with her laundry at this time of night.

As I expected, she scurried to the left, through another door—directly toward the housekeeper's parlor and accommodations. Once the door closed behind her, I followed as far as the threshold, carefully turned the knob, and cracked the door open an inch or two.

Chapter 20

Their voices echoed along the tiled walls, filtering back at me with an eerie, ghostlike quality. As I stood in the dark in my thin-soled shoes, a chill from the terrazzo floor seeped into my feet. Until this moment, I hadn't realized something, but now it dawned on me so startlingly I flinched and almost let the door fall closed.

Mrs. Rogan, the housekeeper, had expected this visit from Silvie. Otherwise, why had so many doors, especially those leading from the delivery hall, through the cold-preparation kitchen, and to the area in which I now stood, have been left unlocked? No, in a house of this size, especially on a property where crimes had already been committed, security was of the utmost importance. But in this instance, Mrs. Rogan must have unlocked those doors herself.

Why? What did she and Silvie Morton have to discuss that was such a secret they had waited until the middle of the night?

Only snippets of words reached me, and I couldn't piece together their meaning. I opened the door wider and stepped through. Another staircase occupied a squarish, open hall, lined with bright white tiles that caught gleams of light from the streetlamps beyond the high-set windows. The terrazzo floor continued here. There were a few doors ranged around the hall. Two were ajar. One I guessed to be Mrs. Rogan's bedroom, and the other I knew to be her parlor. It was from the latter that the contentious notes of Silvie and Mrs. Rogan's conversation emanated.

"This is the best I can do," Silvie said in a plaintive tone.

"And just what am I supposed to do with this?" The house-keeper's voice oozed with contempt. She sounded very much like the housekeeper she was, but instead of addressing a superior, she might have been admonishing an underling.

"Sell it, of course."

"Where? At one of our local jewelry shops?" Mrs. Rogan scoffed. "And be accused of stealing? A servant appearing anywhere with such a valuable piece is sure to be accused. There'd be a scandal, and even if I cleared my good name, I'd lose my position here."

My heart raced, sending my pulses throbbing. Were they speaking of the stolen necklace?

Silvie's voice, suffused with hope now, interrupted my speculations. "They wouldn't know you're a servant."

"Don't be ridiculous. My dear, I don't have the wardrobe to pretend to be anyone grander than I am."

"I could lend you something."

Mrs. Rogan laughed softly. "Again, don't be ridiculous. No, take this back and get me the money I asked for."

No, I thought, it couldn't be the missing necklace. If Mrs. Rogan expected a cash payment for whatever sort of black-mail this was, Silvie would hardly offer up something so priceless. Nor was Mrs. Rogan likely to have demanded a fortune, especially of another woman. Rather, someone in her position would ask for what she believed she could get, and what would make her life relatively more comfortable.

"I can't." Silvie choked on a sob. "I told you, I can't ask my husband for it, and I can't get hold of that much on my own. I simply cannot."

"Then you have a problem, don't you?" A cold chuckle followed those words.

"And you do as well," Silvie said. A hint of confidence had entered her voice.

"I do not see why. Because, my dear, if I should go to your husband with what I know, he will undoubtedly pay me what I want to avoid the scandal and humiliation of being cuckolded by his wife."

"It's your word against mine."

"Is it?" Mrs. Rogan chuckled again, a snide little snort. "All I have to do is plant the seed and your husband will start looking at your son—the shape of the nose, the color of the eyes, the slant of the chin—and then, goodness, he'll remember he wasn't even in the country when the boy was conceived."

"You wouldn't."

"I assure you I would."

"What about my son—think of *him*. He has the most to lose—and he's done no wrong. He's completely innocent."

"More's the pity. But I expect he'll land on his feet, one way or another."

"You're despicable. I wish you'd never been born."

Another laugh, this one lighter, with genuine amusement. "A bit late for that, I'm afraid." A tense silence filled the hall around me. Were they finished? Would Silvie retrace her steps now? I hurried over to the staircase, wondering where it went. I tiptoed up as far as the first landing, into deeper shadow, and met with a closed door I assumed to be locked.

I didn't bother trying it, but instead hung over the railing, continuing to listen.

"Go on now," Mrs. Rogan ordered. Her voice sounded louder now, closer. I assumed she had opened the door to her parlor wider as she dismissed Silvie. "Take your trinket with you. The next time we meet, you had better have the money. *Money*, Mrs. Morton. Nothing else will do or I'll go straight to your husband."

Footsteps clattered across the terrazzo floor, then stopped. "Why do you hate me so? What have I ever done to you?"

"Why, nothing, nothing at all," Mrs. Rogan replied as if the question had taken her by surprise. "I worked in your home as the housekeeper's assistant and discovered an indiscretion on your part. There is nothing personal in any of this, my dear. It's merely an opportunity—for me. Pure and simple."

Another pause, a lengthy one, and then, "Miss Varella apparently saw an opportunity as well. Have a care, Mrs. Rogan, or you, too, might end up in a coal cart."

I remained where I was while Silvie made her way back into the main hall. Then a startling thought occurred to me. What would I do should Mrs. Rogan follow her and relock all the doors?

Holding my breath and careful not to make a sound, I eased my way down the stairs, stopping partway to listen. I could hear Mrs. Rogan humming to herself, and then the sound of running water hitting metal.

She was making tea, I thought with relief. Perhaps that would give me enough time to hurry back to the staircase. Then again, what could happen if she caught me—she, a housekeeper in the midst of blackmailing one of her employers' guests?

Unless it was Mrs. Rogan who had murdered Ines, perhaps after Ines discovered the older woman's treachery. Could Mrs. Rogan have stolen the necklace?

Upon reaching the bottom of the stairs, I stood still again to listen. Hearing the clink of crockery and seeing no shadow fill the parlor doorway, I scurried across the hall and out through the door. I didn't stop my racing, albeit tiptoeing, steps until I reached the service staircase. I heard no footsteps on the treads above me. Silvie must have been back in her room by now. I kept going.

Finally emerging onto the second-floor corridor, I saw that the Mortons' door was closed. Good. I had a lot to think about and I intended returning to my own room and waking Derrick, if he wasn't already awake. But as I reached the open gallery at the top of the double staircase, a hand reached out from the sitting room doorway and grabbed hold of my forearm.

I very nearly screamed except that Derrick tugged me against him and whispered in my ear, "Where the devil have you been?"

In my momentary confusion I stammered, "Silvie . . . she . . . went down. I followed. . ." Seeing the puzzlement on his face, I began again. "I saw Silvie sneaking across to the servants' staircase, so I followed. Turns out she went to see Mrs. Rogan about a little case of blackmail."

"You weren't supposed to go anywhere without me." But even as he scolded me, he was easing me out of the doorway and to one side of the double staircase. "Come on."

"Where?" I asked in a whisper, even as I followed him readily.

"After Rex. He's got a penchant for nighttime wandering just like his wife, it seems."

We paused on the half landing and listened, hearing Rex Morton's footsteps grow fainter off to our left, in the north wing of the house. It couldn't have been a footman, I knew, because the night staff carried out their duties at a subdued pace, painstakingly checking doors and windows as they went. These steps were hurried—one might even venture to say troubled.

"The conservatory," I whispered to Derrick. He nodded. We went the rest of the way down.

When we reached the conservatory, we found it empty but for the mythological statues ranged at intervals around the room. Then, a telltale pinpoint of light revealed where Rex had gone: outside. The light flared bright orange again as whomever Rex had gone outside to meet with drew on a cigarette. Like stealthy cats we darted diagonally across the stone floor without a sound and took up position at the French door near the corner of the room, which overlooked the side terrace where it gave way to steps down to the walkway.

Rex had gone down, drawn as if a moth to the tiny flame we had seen from across the room. They must have been whispering, as we could hear nothing through the glass-paned doors. We exchanged a glance, and then Derrick reached for the latch. As the door eased open, a perverse thought ran through my mind at how aghast the Berwinds would be if they saw how many doors had been left unlocked tonight, how all their security measures had gone to waste.

"You have until noon Thursday. *This* Thursday, you understand," drawled a voice I didn't recognize. The end of his cigarette burned brightly.

"But I might need more time."

"No." I heard a whoosh of breath, saw wisps of smoke curling blue against the moonlight. "You've had enough time. Thursday, noon is your deadline."

Or . . . what? Again, Derrick and I traded glances, each of us wondering what was going on.

"But . . . I've been trying. I've had a run of bad luck. . . ."

"Doesn't matter. Thursday, noon. That's it. Good night, Mr. Morton. Do not contact me again. I will send a note Thursday morning telling you where to meet me."

"Please . . . I . . . I just need a little more time. *Please.*"

"Good night, Mr. Morton. I won't say it again." Footsteps crunched on gravel. Derrick peered out as far as he dared, then pulled back in.

"He's just standing there," he informed me. "As if he's one of these statues." He gestured to the one beside us, a woman in loose, flowing robes holding a sheaf of wheat at her shoulder.

He grabbed my hand and pulled me along. I thought we were about to make our escape before Rex could reenter the room, but Derrick surprised me by leading me only as far as one of the wicker settees.

"What are we doing?" I murmured as he pulled me down beside him.

"Waiting—for Rex. It's time for a confrontation."

"Do you think this meeting was about the necklace?"

"I do. I think Rex is supposed to hand it over to this man, but Ines Varella got in the way and thwarted their plans. Shh." He gestured toward the corner door. "He's coming in."

We sat facing Rex as he slithered in through the terrace door. Even by moonlight he looked like a man defeated by his own game, sunken and stooped. After locking the door behind him, he started toward us; he hadn't yet noticed us in the darkness. Beside me, I felt Derrick brace, his indrawn breath indicating his intention to surprise Rex by announcing our presence.

A click heralded a flood of electric light. I blinked in the abrupt glare and I'm sure Derrick and Rex did, too. This time, we all three were rendered motionless, just like the marble statues watching us from their pedestals.

Silvie's voice echoed against marble and glass. "Rex, what on earth is going on here?"

Rex stumbled to the middle of the room, nearly tripping over Derrick and me. It wasn't until he teetered to a halt that he seemed to notice us. He frowned down at us as if we constituted the most puzzling quandary ever presented to him, until he looked up at his wife.

"Silvie."

"Yes, Rex. Whatever do you think you—" As she spoke, she plodded closer to him before pulling up short. Her gaze landed on Derrick and me and her eyes went wide. "What are you two doing here?"

"What are we all doing here?" Derrick corrected her, one eyebrow raised quizzically. He came to his feet. I did likewise.

"Good evening, both of you," I said. I gestured to the two wicker chairs facing the settee across a low, glass-topped table. "Why don't we all have a seat?"

"I don't think . . ." Rex rubbed a hand against his chin, raising a chafing sound against his nighttime growth of beard. "I don't wish . . ."

Derrick faced him head-on. "Have a seat, old man." Then, softening both his expression and his tone he said, "You too, Silvie."

"What on earth is going on here?" she repeated as she crossed the room and then sank into the chair closest to her. She allowed her spine to curve against its sloping back and gripped its hand rests. Her gaze darted to me, the whites of her eyes forming wide rings around the irises in a show of fear. Had she realized I'd followed her earlier? Did she fear I'd expose her own midnight jaunt?

For now, I had no intentions of doing so. I wished to hear what Rex had to say first.

Her scrutiny passed from me to Derrick, and then finally

back to her husband. "Are you going to explain what you're doing down here yet again?"

A look of surprise entered his eyes. "Yet again?"

"Yes, Rex. I'm aware of your nocturnal wanderings. It's high time you told me what you've been up to." Once again, she glanced at Derrick and me, only this time she suddenly appeared more composed. "If you two would excuse us, please."

Before either Derrick or I could react to that, Rex held up a hand. "No. Let them stay. Oh God, what's the use of hiding it any longer?" His hands went to his face, and he seemed to collapse in on himself.

Silvie appeared genuinely startled. "Rex, whatever do you mean?"

"It's over, my dear."

"Rex, you're not making sense," she replied, and then demanded, "What's over?"

"Everything." He whispered the word against his palms. "I'm sorry, Silvie, but I've made a terrible mess of things."

"What *things*, Rex?" A wariness came over her as the color slowly leached from her complexion. "What have you done?"

"I thought I'd make a killing. Then, when it didn't pan out, I thought I could fix it, pay everyone off with no one the wiser. I truly believed it could work, and then everything would be all right. But, Silvie, it's *not* all right. It never will be, and if you have any sense, you'll divorce me immediately."

"What?" Silvie's hand went to her throat while the remaining color drained from her face. "Rex, no. Surely nothing is as bad as all that."

"No?" He shot to his feet. "If I had any sense of honor, I'd take a gun to my head."

"Rex!" Silvie pushed to her feet as well, but before she

was fully standing Rex took off running toward the long gallery. "Rex, where are you going?! Derrick, stop him!"

Derrick had already sprinted in pursuit, and the sounds of a scuffle echoed loudly in the empty corridor. Silvie and I ran toward them, and suddenly the entire length of the hall was ablaze with light. Two footmen ran toward us. Before they reached our end of the lengthy corridor, Rex had stopped struggling. Derrick's hold on him eased, and he held up a hand to the servants.

"It's all right. Everything's under control here."

The pair in livery hesitated. One said, "You're quite sure, sir?"

"Quite," Derrick said with a nod. "You can go about your duties or go back to bed, whatever it was you were doing."

The two young men summarily turned about and put distance between themselves and us.

Derrick leaned to speak into Rex's ear. "You *are* through making a scene, yes?"

Rex nodded.

"Good. Then let's all go back into the conservatory. Or better still, Ned's library." Derrick pointed the way. "I happen to know he keeps his liquor cabinet unlocked. It's a kind of test for his night footmen."

The men pulled chairs closer to the leather sofa and once again we all sat. Derrick poured brandies for all of us, which both Rex and Silvie accepted gratefully. We gave them time to sip their liquid fortitude and settle their nerves.

Finally, it was Silvie who asked the first question, or made the first demand, I should say. "Rex, you have prevaricated long enough. What were you doing up, not only tonight but the other nights you sneaked away from our bed, and why are you in such a state?"

I could have asked Silvie the same question, but I left it for another time.

When Rex attempted to hide once more behind his hands, Silvie vacated her chair and sank in front of his. She pried his hands away and forced them to his lap. "Tell me," she commanded him in no uncertain terms.

He let out a long, loud groan. "We are ruined, Silvie. Utterly and irrevocably."

She sank back on her heels. "*What?*"

"It's true."

"*How* can it be true? You're a banker. A financier. You make fortunes for a living."

"I am also, my dear, a fraud, a cheat, and a fool."

Chapter 21

"There have been two of them, but the one I have to worry about is Smith. He's going to kill me if I don't pay him a hundred and twenty thousand dollars by this Thursday."

"A hundred and . . ." Silvie's hand rose to cradle her throat. "How . . . why . . . what did you do . . . ?" Before he could answer, she surged to her feet and slapped him across his right cheek.

Derrick and I were on our feet in an instant. We flanked Silvie, ready to stop her from striking Rex again, although in truth, after what he'd just admitted, I wasn't sure he didn't deserve another slap or two.

But Silvie did not raise her hand again. Rather, she stood glaring down at her husband, panting as if she had just run a race. "That's . . . an impossible sum to simply hand over to someone. You'll have to close out several investments. You'll—"

"There are no investments to close. I'm afraid we're quite ruined."

"We can't be," she insisted. "We could sell off a property or two."

"Mortgaged," he said succinctly, then added in case any question remained, "To the hilt."

"*What?*" She glanced around as if lost, as if looking for something that simply wasn't there, until her gaze landed on the chair she'd vacated. She took one step toward it before her knees gave way and she started to sink to the floor. Derrick swiftly caught her beneath the arms and helped her shuffle to the chair.

I crouched before her. "Silvie, are you all right? Do you need some water?"

Instead of water, Derrick poured more brandy into her glass and held it up to her lips. "This will fortify you."

She sipped, then wrapped her trembling hands around the glass and took it from Derrick. Some of the color returned to her face. "Rex, explain. Leave nothing out."

Silvie's slap had left a welt on his cheek. After fingering it gingerly, he let his hand fall to his lap. "There was an investment opportunity. A new automobile manufacturer just outside of Pittsburgh. They were poised to make a killing in the industry." He closed his eyes. "Or so I believed."

Derrick and I returned to the sofa. Derrick asked, "What happened?"

"It was all a sham." Rex stared down at the floor and shook his head. "I toured the factory. Reviewed the plans for the motorcars. They were..." He scooted forward to the edge of his chair, hands dangling between his knees. "They were to be the first that ran on both gasoline *and* electricity. It was astounding."

Silvie's face twisted with loathing. "And impossible. No automobile can run on both. Why would anyone even want such a thing? Rex, how could you have been so taken in?"

"Don't you see? It was innovative. The motor would start out on gasoline, and when that ran low, the driver could simply switch over to electric power. The car could go twice as far before refueling or recharging. They were the only manufacturers to come up with this idea—"

"Except they didn't, did they?" Silvie scoffed and turned her head away.

"What was this company called?" Derrick asked him.

"The Bryce-Hall Automobile Company."

"I've never heard of it," I said.

"Why would you have?" Silvie downed the last of her brandy and then held out her glass for Derrick to refill. "As my husband said, it was all a sham."

"I saw the factory," Rex repeated miserably.

"You saw *a* factory." Derrick hefted the bottle of brandy and stood to oblige Silvie's request.

"He wouldn't know an automobile plant from a cotton mill," she said with contempt. "What's next, Rex? A diamond mine in Poughkeepsie?"

Rex groaned and dropped his head into his hands.

I attempted to restore his focus. "So you invested in this business, yes? Then what happened?"

"I didn't just invest my own money. I invested countless funds of Morton and Sons Mutual customers."

Even as my stomach sank, Silvie's eyes went wide. "Without their knowledge?"

Rex nodded. "I bought low. We were poised to make a fortune several times over."

"What were you going to do when your investors wanted access to their money?" I quietly asked him. "If they wished to buy or sell off stocks? Or withdraw their funds entirely?"

"I accommodated them."

"How?" Derrick eyed Rex warily, as if he already knew the answer, and it wasn't good.

"By accessing other investors' funds."

Derrick, having leaned forward, now collapsed back against the sofa. "You stole from Peter to pay Paul?"

"As new investments came in, yes, I used those funds to pay dividends on the older investments. But it was only supposed to be for a short time," Rex said in a pleading tone. "Until the first Mortons were unveiled to the public. Orders would have started pouring in and their stock would have soared."

"The first *Mortons*?" The situation suddenly became clear to me. Still, incredulity made me demand clarification. "This is how they persuaded you to invest? By naming the auto after you?"

"Good Lord, Rex." Silvie groaned. "That's in bad taste even for you."

"One can't help but wonder how many others they've fleeced." Still leaning back, Derrick crossed his arms over his chest. "My guess is they've long since vacated this factory you saw."

"Who is this Smith?" I asked, realizing we hadn't yet gotten the entire story. We needed to stay on track. "And what is he threatening to do?"

Rex snorted a laugh. "He hasn't been terribly clear on that. Kill me, maybe, if I don't raise the funds to reimburse the investors he represents. Or maybe he'll have me arrested." He held up his hands and shrugged.

"It was Smith and a couple of his cronies at the Country Club that day, wasn't it?" I remembered how shaken Rex had been after his conversation on the course, and how he and Silvie had made a hasty departure before they'd finished the game. "And whom you've met here tonight."

He shot an accusing look at Silvie, then admitted in a small voice, "It was."

"And whom does he represent?" Derrick asked.

"About a dozen investors who've gotten wise to what I've been doing. Big names, most of whom you would recognize.

They hired Mr. Smith to rough me up and shake me upside down, as it were."

"You deserve it," Silvie muttered.

Another realization struck me. "The Marie Antoinette necklace. It was your attempt to recoup what you'd lost with Bryce-Hall."

Rex confirmed this with another of his brooding nods.

"My guess is you got it cheap on a private, anonymous bid," Derrick said. "Not sure how you managed that, but one assumes some form of extortion was involved. Your purchasing agent must have had some knowledge about the seller that the seller didn't wish to be made public." Looking at me, he explained, "Things like that happen fairly frequently in Europe, where the old families are often desperate to raise cash for their crumbling piles." Turning back to Rex, he concluded, "Buy it cheap, and sell it at an enormous profit here in the States."

Rex inhaled deeply and let it out slowly. "That was the general plan."

"And now it's gone," Silvie snapped. "You let it slip through your fingers. And with it, our very lives."

He gazed over at her, his eyes glimmering with moisture. "Silvie, my darling, can you ever forgive me?"

She came to her feet and stared down at him for a long, silent moment. I don't believe Rex drew a single breath during that time. But then, Silvie's shoulders neither rose nor fell, either. "I'm going to bed. Sleep somewhere else tonight."

I followed Silvie upstairs, but Derrick remained in the library with Rex. In the upstairs gallery, I called softly to Silvie just as she was about to turn into their room. She stopped, seeming surprised to see that I, too, had turned into the guest wing.

"It's very late and I've had a terrible shock," she said when I reached her. "Can whatever it is wait until morning?"

"It won't take long." I walked past her into the bedroom. As she followed me in, I turned to face her. "I know where you went earlier. I know you spoke to Mrs. Rogan."

She gasped and looked as though she might flee. Instead, she switched on the dressing table lamp. Myriad emotions flittered across her face, the final one, the one that persisted, being anger. "You followed me. How dare you."

"Yes, I followed you. It wasn't the first time you'd stolen below stairs, though you'd have me and everyone else believe otherwise. Did you think I believed you when you claimed to have been searching in the sewing room for an item of your own clothing?"

Her mouth skewed, her expression admitting that she'd been caught out. "So, what do you want? Are you going to blackmail me the way Mrs. Rogan is doing?"

"No, Silvie. But I am going to ask you a blunt question. Did you kill Ines?"

"Good heavens, no. Why would I?"

I raised an eyebrow and stated the obvious. "Because perhaps she also knew about your secret. The one that is allowing Mrs. Rogan to blackmail you."

"As far as I know, she didn't. She'd have no reason to have known." Her lips flattened and her nose flared. "Are you going to tell my husband?"

"Again, no. I'm not interested in the state of your marriage or what you might have done in the past. At least, not in the days and years before you came here."

Her posture relaxed, in relief I supposed. "You can't know what it's like having someone know the one secret that can destroy you. If it ever came out that my son isn't Rex's . . ." She gave a soft laugh. "Not that Rex hasn't already destroyed our lives."

"You mustn't lose hope. People have recovered from worse than this."

"I don't see how. And I don't see what could be worse than being penniless."

I could think of many things, but I guessed the suffering of others was beyond her comprehension, at least at the present moment. "You and Rex are well connected, from good families, and you're both clever. I'm not pandering to you when I say I believe you'll emerge from this intact. What is Mrs. Rogan demanding?"

"Five hundred dollars."

I nearly whistled between my teeth. By the standards of my Vanderbilt relatives such a sum might not seem vast at all, but to an ordinary individual, it was a small fortune.

"I offered her a bracelet." She smiled without parting her lips. "In case you were wondering, I was not offering her Rex's missing necklace. I don't have it, and if I did, I wouldn't see it in the hands of that woman."

"I believe you. At some point, Minnie must be made aware of her housekeeper's true nature. It wouldn't do for her to be blackmailing the guests on a regular basis."

"No! If you tell her, then there will be questions about who she's been blackmailing and why. Those questions will lead directly to me—and my son."

I grasped her hand to calm her. "We'll worry about that later. Don't worry, I have no desire to divulge your secret. As you told Mrs. Rogan, your son is innocent and doesn't deserve to suffer."

She slipped her hand from mine. "You were listening quite closely, weren't you? Where were you hiding?"

I shrugged away any chagrin I might have felt for eavesdropping. "In the corridor outside Mrs. Rogan's parlor, and then on the staircase."

"I would never want you for an enemy, that much is certain." Her eyes narrowed. "There is no work being done on your home, is there? You're here chasing this story for your newspaper."

My chin came up. "I'm chasing the truth of who murdered Ines Varella." Did I say truth? Some of the bravado slipped from my posture. "And yes, that truth will be reflected in the article I write for the *Messenger*."

Derrick came up to our room shortly after I returned from my conversation with Silvie. He wasn't surprised to see me still awake, or that I hadn't yet changed into nightclothes. As soon as he closed the door and locked it, he crossed the room and took me in his arms.

"Thank goodness we are not *them*," he whispered passionately. I had no doubts as to whom he meant, or why his relief caused his hold to tighten as he kissed me soundly.

"We'll never be like them," I whispered back just as fervently. "We'll never keep secrets from each other. Never make decisions alone that should be made together."

"No, never." We stepped apart, and he worked the knot of his tie free. "He's still denying having anything to do with Ines's death."

I helped him undo the buttons of his vest. "I believe he's desperate enough to have resorted to extremes, but ruthless enough to commit murder? I'm not so sure he has it in him. Just as Anthony Dobbs doesn't believe Brown has it in *him*. You saw how Rex cowered once he realized he'd been discovered."

Derrick nodded. "I half expected the man he met with tonight to be Brown, but he didn't sound at all like him." I nodded my agreement and he went on, "What about Silvie? You said you followed her earlier. What was that about?"

"Good heavens, in all the kerfuffle, I haven't had a chance

to tell you what happened earlier." I went on to describe the conversation I'd overheard outside Mrs. Rogan's parlor.

"Good grief," he exclaimed when I'd finished. "Rex and Silvie make quite a pair, don't they?"

"I don't know that Silvie is very much to blame."

"Not to blame for having a child with a man who isn't her husband?" His eyebrows went up.

"Considering the kind of man her husband is, should we judge her for seeking solace in the arms of someone else? I very much doubt this current fiasco is the first time Rex has shown a miserable lack of wisdom."

His hands stilled over the buttons on his shirt. "Any idea who that someone was?"

I shook my head. "I didn't ask, and she certainly didn't offer up the information."

"We're only slightly farther along than we were," he pointed out, his disappointment palpable. I shared his frustration over our lack of true progress in discovering who had murdered Ines and Rudolfo.

Still, I reminded him, "We do know the reason Rex bought the necklace and brought it to America. And I know why Silvie has been skulking about below stairs."

"Yes, but that doesn't mean either of them didn't dispatch Ines, and later Rudolfo, for having learned their secrets and applying a bit of blackmail."

I couldn't argue with that. We slipped into our night-clothes and between the covers, but sleep was still a long way off for both of us.

In the morning, Rex failed to turn up in the Chinese breakfast room. When Silvie came in I questioned her with a look, but she merely shrugged, reminding me that she had ordered her husband not to return to their room last night. It was Ned Berwind who solved that particular mystery.

"Appears Rex slept on the sofa in the library last night,"

he said with a show of amusement. "Silvie must have given him the heave-ho."

"Ned!" Minnie was returning from the sideboard with a plate full of the lighter breakfast offerings, while Ned piled on eggs, sausages, and plenty of potatoes. When he took his place at the table, she admonished him further with a glare that promised a dressing-down later. He shrugged and picked up his fork.

"He's been snoring horribly lately. He was kind enough to allow me a good night's sleep last night," Silvie said calmly, though her cheeks glowed with embarrassment.

"Of course, Silvie dear." Minnie patted her hand. "I do hope he wasn't too uncomfortable. Had he mentioned his intention of sleeping elsewhere, we'd have seen to it he had all he needed. He might have used our little nephew's room."

"He didn't wish to be a bother," Silvie murmured, and raised her teacup to her lips. I silently acknowledged that Rex wouldn't have had access to Ned's brandy had he slept in the Berwinds' nephew's room.

"What's this about Rex?" Charles Gilchrist led his wife into the breakfast room, both looking refreshed and, for once, not at odds with each other. He held her chair for her, kissed her cheek, and asked what she'd like for breakfast. When he returned to the table, he held a plate for each of them. Kay's look of gratitude, tinged with surprise, made my heart both swell and ache for her.

It also raised my guard. Where did this sudden solicitude come from, and was it sincere, or an attempt to distract his wife from something she might object to?

Derrick and I left The Elms shortly after breakfast. We said we were going to the *Messenger*, but in truth we drove in our carriage past the building and to Marlborough Street, where we met with Jesse.

After we grouped ourselves around Jesse's desk, we reviewed the past couple of days.

"There's been no sign of Orville Brown," he told us, "but we don't think he's left the island. Now, tell me what, if anything, you two have learned."

I described Silvie's late-night jaunt below stairs, and then Derrick explained about Rex meeting the man named Smith on the terrace outside the conservatory. I added that it had been Smith at the Country Club the day the Berwinds and their guests played golf, and between the two of us, we painted a picture of Rex's financial woes and his attempt to fix them with the stolen necklace.

"And the Gilchrists?" he asked when we were finished.

We both shrugged. Derrick said, "They seemed composed and more harmonious than I've ever seen them."

"Yes, which makes me wonder," I said.

Derrick glanced at me in surprise, but Jesse nodded thoughtfully. "An act?"

"I don't know. On his part, perhaps. It could be as simple as his having met recently with a mistress. Or planning to soon. Kay, on the other hand, looked so happy to have his attention my heart went out to her."

"Theirs isn't an easy marriage," Derrick concurred. "She's much too young for him. They have very little in common."

Jesse leaned back, his fingers threading together. "Or perhaps her husband has done something that drives fear into Mrs. Gilchrist's heart. Watch them all," he said, "closely. And contact me the moment one of them does something suspicious, no matter what it is." I started to speak, but he cut me off. "That includes late-night conversations with housekeepers and terrace meetings with strangers. The pair of you have been taking too many chances. If you keep it up, I'll have to detain you both."

"And then who will you have inside The Elms?" I asked in an admittedly saucy tone. "One of your men? Assuming the Berwinds allowed it, a man in uniform would be highly conspicuous among their guests."

"Just keep a sharp eye out," he said with a dismissive wave of his hand. Derrick and I took that as our cue to leave.

Chapter 22

To make good on our claim of going to the *Messenger*, Derrick and I headed there next. The presses were running smoothly, and Ethan had been covering local matters in my stead with ease, if not enthusiasm.

"There's no joy in it," our society columnist complained, pointing to the sheet of paper currently inhabiting his typewriter. "No glitter. How does one report on the news day after day with no break for life's more resplendent occasions?"

I laughed. "Poor Ethan. Don't worry, as soon as this case is solved, I'll be back full-time to free you of everything mundane and gloomy."

"It won't be too soon for me." He typed a few words, then swept a glance upward. "Sorry, Miss Cross—I mean Mrs. Andrews—"

"Emma," I reminded him with a smile.

He nodded. "Sorry to complain. I shouldn't. Don't take me seriously."

"I won't, Ethan. Now, where are the Associated Press

wires?" I found them and got to work selecting which out-of-town and out-of-state news stories would be included in the next day's edition, today's having already gone out. I didn't see Derrick again for several hours, time that passed quickly as I buried myself in my work and he in his.

It wasn't until the window in my office, facing the building next door only feet away, became draped in long shadows that Derrick knocked at my open doorway. "Ready to go back to The Elms?"

He might have said, "Once more unto the breach." I slapped my pen into its holder, stoppered my jar of ink, and pressed to my feet. "Ready and able."

We returned to find Rex still avoiding the others. "I did try coaxing him down for lunch," Silvie told me in an aside, "not that I've forgiven him, mind you. But I suppose being at odds with each other won't solve a thing. Besides, he doesn't deserve to mope. He'd better well come up with a solution."

"Perhaps that's what he's doing as we speak."

She quirked her lips in a show of doubt. We stood by the windows in the upstairs sitting room, gazing out at the forest of masts in the harbor, their sails tightly furled. Clouds had moved in to block the sunset, and the wind swept the trailing branches of the European beeches in wild swirls. As we watched, drops began splattering the window.

"Perhaps the other men can help him," I said. "Has he confided in Ned and Charles?"

"That I don't know. They persuaded him to accompany them to the Reading Room this afternoon, although I'm told he didn't stay long. I hope it was discussed. Although, one must admit, the very notion of one's poverty being paraded so openly is rather demoralizing."

I pressed a hand to her shoulder. "Not if they solve the matter and your poverty becomes a thing of the past."

"What are you ladies whispering about?" Ned Berwind chuckled and said to the others, "Women. Always plotting."

Silvie and I exchanged ironic looks and returned to the group. In contrast to the Mortons' tenuous marriage, Charles and Kay still appeared to be enjoying uncommon harmony. They sat side by side, their fingers entwined, and anytime she reached for the tray of canapes on the sofa table, he snatched one for her and set it on her plate. Could something have happened to awaken his affections? Had she plucked up the courage to speak to him about the state of their marriage?

During dinner and the rest of the evening, I kept an ear open and attempted to overhear any words that passed between them. Oddly, very few did, whether of an affectionate nature or otherwise, yet Charles's attentiveness continued.

When Rex failed to materialize for dinner, Silvie expressed mild concern but assumed embarrassment kept him at bay. After a lavish meal in the equally opulent dining room, the ladies retired to the drawing room while the men remained around the table for brandy and talk of business. Or were they discussing Rex and his difficulties in his absence? Once again, I wished I could listen in on their conversation, but no opportunity would possibly present itself. Only Derrick's faint nod assured me I'd hear all about it later.

Before the men joined us in the drawing room, Silvie came to her feet with a rustle of silk and taffeta. "Do forgive me, but I believe I'll retire now. Perhaps Rex slipped in while we were dining and went straight up." The wistful note in her voice produced a pang of sympathy beneath my breastbone.

Not long after she left, the men rejoined us. My thoughts still on Silvie and Rex, I only half listened to the conversation around me until Kay, who had been doing a circuit of the room, sat down beside me. "I do hope they find a solution." She leaned closer. "Silvie and Rex, I mean."

She needn't have clarified. I offered a small smile. "Have you known them long?"

"I've been acquainted with the Mortons since before my marriage. We know many of the same people, but I cannot claim to know Silvie well at all. She's a difficult person to become close to. At one time, earlier in our acquaintance, we seemed to be getting on rather well. Then she . . . I don't know . . . pulled away. Rather suddenly. It was after she had her son."

Good heavens. My pulse leaped at this bit of information. Could Silvie's sudden reticence toward Kay have been due to her son—more specifically, to her son's father being Charles? Had Silvie and Charles had an affair, with Silvie putting distance between her and the other woman to prevent Kay from becoming too close to the boy, in whom she might recognize traits he had in common with his father?

"But Charles and Rex have been doing business for years," she went on, oblivious to my revelations. "Since before Charles and I were married. Rex has advised Charles on some of his financial matters."

"I see." Could Silvie and Charles's affair have begun before he married Kay? "Is that why you're all here together? For the men to discuss business?"

"No. I believe I told you that Charles and I are here to see the house." Did she sound a trifle impatient with me? "Charles has a great interest in the workings of the electrical system. I believe he wishes to build a house like it on some property we own in the Catskills."

"I see." Another, entirely different, thought occurred to me. Could Charles be either a victim of Rex's financial scheming . . . or, perhaps, an accessory? Just as I opened my mouth to ask if Charles and Rex ever took business trips together Silvie appeared in the doorway, flushed and out of breath.

"Rex is gone," she said in a rush, her face pale and her eyes large.

"You mean he hasn't come in yet," Minnie attempted to clarify, but Silvie shook her head.

"No, he was here, I know he was. But now he's gone." In her hand she held a sheet of paper. The Berwinds' combined initials emblazoned the top; it was stationery they provided for their guests' use. I could see lines scrawled across the top half. She thrust it toward us, then let it drop to her side. "I just found this on his pillow. He says he's gone to the Cliff Walk to clear his mind."

Kay and I both pressed to our feet, as did the others. Minnie went to her and drew her farther into the room. "He's gone for a walk. Is that so terrible?"

Silvie rustled the paper in her hand. "The cliffs in the dark? I fear what he might be thinking. Planning. Perhaps his financial troubles have proved too much. . . ." She wadded the page between her hands. "I fear he's lost his mind. Please, Ned, summon every available footman in the house and go search for him. Oh, perhaps we should summon the police as well."

"There should be officers patrolling the perimeter of the property," Ned said. "I'll send for them."

"Ned, no." Minnie placed her hands on Silvie's shoulders. "My dear, you don't want Ned to involve the police. Not yet, at least. There will be such a scandal if what you fear is true. Let the men here handle it. They'll find him and bring him safely back."

"What if it's already too late?" Silvie whispered.

Minnie shook her head. "You mustn't think like that. If he didn't wish you to know where he went, would he have told you in a note? You see? He only means to walk somewhere and think."

"The cliffs are so dangerous at night," Silvie persisted in a strangled voice.

"And our husbands will find him before any harm comes to him," Minnie said with a firm nod. She looked over her shoulder at her husband. "Won't you, Ned?"

He hesitated only an instant. "Yes, of course, my dear."

Ned pressed the necessary call buttons and enlisted the help of four footmen who had already gone to bed for the night. Nonetheless, they assembled in the main hall within minutes, carrying lanterns and wearing cloaks to ward off the rain.

As they all prepared to set out, I followed Derrick to the entry hall and took him aside. "Do you think Rex would harm himself?"

"I don't know. I don't even wish to venture a guess." He embraced me. "I just want to find him as quickly as possible and set his wife's mind to rest."

"Perhaps I should go with you," I suggested, but he shook his head before the words were out.

"Please stay here." He pressed his cheek to mine. "Look after the ladies. Keep watch and listen closely," he added, perhaps seeing the necessity of giving me a sound reason for remaining behind.

I nodded and released him to the rainy night.

I returned to the drawing room to discover Silvie absent.

"She's gone back upstairs to lie down," Minnie told me. "I offered to sit with her but she insisted on being alone. I've had a pot of tea sent up along with some sandwiches, not that I think she'll touch them."

"Poor dear. This must be entirely too much for her," Kay remarked.

Minnie nodded her agreement. "I shall check on her in a little while. She mustn't be alone for too long at a time. How sick with worry she must be."

"Yes, poor thing," Kay essentially repeated. "I do hope the men won't be too long in finding Rex. They'll all catch their deaths in this rain."

"They'll be all right," I assured her. "Odd, though, that Silvie didn't want to wait for their return downstairs, where she would know all the sooner once her husband is safely found."

"One never knows how one will respond to distressing events." Minnie offered me the tray of teacakes brought up a little while ago by a maid who'd apparently been roused from bed to serve us.

I waved them away, not in the least hungry. Despite my assurance that the men would come to no harm, I worried about them searching the cliffs in the rain and dark. The rocks would be slippery, the earth wet and unstable. Would Rex, once found, go with them docilely, or would he put up a fuss, further endangering them all?

With a shake of my head I attempted to banish such dismal thoughts. But Silvie's absence continued to niggle at me. Besides this most recent upset with Rex, she also had the pressure of the housekeeper demanding payment to keep a secret that would ruin her. Could Silvie herself be depended upon not to attempt to harm herself in any way? Or would she, like her husband, attempt something reckless and ill advised?

That thought brought me to my feet. "I'm going to go up to check on Silvie. I know she wishes to be alone, but I'm just going to see if she needs anything. You never know, she might want to talk."

"She might at that." Minnie smiled kindly up at me. "You go now, then, and I'll take a turn in a little while."

On my way up the stairs, my foot slid on one of the marble treads, forcing me to grip the banister to keep from going down. Gingerly I stepped back onto the step below it and inspected the surface. The light from the hall chandelier behind me gleamed on drops of moisture, and not only on that step. I followed them all the way down, then noticed the trail coming in from the front door. Had the men returned? Surely not, or they would have made their presence known to us immediately. Unless they were so wet they'd gone upstairs to change first?

I glanced out the glass front doors, framed in filigreed iron. The rain had lessened considerably, was down to a drizzle. I shook my head. No matter how drenched they might have been, they would have alerted us women to their return.

I continued my climb. By the half landing, I noticed no more drops, suggesting the shoes of whoever had entered the house had dried by then. At the gallery at the top of the stairs, I stood listening a moment. There was nothing, not a sound other than the faint hum of the electric sconces and chandeliers that lit the way. I started down the guest wing.

There was no answer at Silvie's door when I knocked, but I heard quite clearly, even through both the outer and inner doors, the sounds of someone within suddenly going still. She must have wanted me to believe she had fallen asleep, but I wasn't fooled.

"Silvie, please let me in." I tried the knob of the outer door, which turned in my grip. I opened it and went into the small foyer that housed a wardrobe closet. The inner door, as I had suspected, was locked. I knocked again. "Please, Silvie. I heard you moving about. I only wish to see that you're all right. I know you're upset, but sometimes it does wonders to talk to someone. You shouldn't wait alone."

Silence met my entreaty until I heard the key turning

slowly in the lock. The door opened a few inches. "I'm fine. Truly."

Even through that scant space, I could spy the room behind her. Clothes were heaped on the bed, and a steamer trunk stood open. "You're packing."

"Uh . . . yes. I am determined that Rex and I should leave tomorrow. Newport is having disastrous effects on my husband."

"I cannot argue with you about that. May I come in?"

She huffed, stepped aside, and widened the door. "I suppose you might as well."

"I could lend you a hand," I offered, scanning the disarray. "Or perhaps you'd like to call your maid down?"

"Let her sleep. I can manage for now. It's giving me something to do besides fretting over Rex."

"The men will find him," I said, but my conviction lagged considerably behind my reassurance.

"Yes," she said after a hesitation. She turned away and began pulling garments out of a chest of drawers.

I paused beside the open trunk. "Silvie, were you outside recently?"

"Outside? Goodness no. I haven't left this room since I came up."

I nodded, and still puzzled about those wet footprints, looked about to decide where to start. "Are there things in the closet?" I pointed into the tiny anteroom. "I could bring them in for you."

"Yes, thank you." She spoke tightly, as though her composure was brittle at best. "That would be a help."

We worked in silence for some minutes. Then, as I stepped up to the bed to gather a bundle of folded skirts to put in the trunk, I heard a crackling beneath my foot. "What's this?"

Silvie lurched to my side, and we bent at the same time to

MURDER AT THE ELMS   287

retrieve the crumpled paper I'd stepped on. Our heads missed colliding by a fraction of an inch. When we straightened, I held the paper in my hand.

After smoothing it open, I glanced at it and realized immediately what it was. "I'm terribly sorry. I didn't mean to pry. It's Rex's note."

I was about to hand it back when the slant of the lettering caught my eye. The familiarity of the handwriting took my breath. I had seen it before. Studied it. Pondered it.

Ines's letter of reference when the Berwinds hired her. The same handwriting sprawled across this piece of paper, I was certain of it. Written by Rex . . . ?

The realization of the truth must have etched itself across my face, for as I looked back up, I discovered Silvie watching me closely. She had recognized *my* moment of recognition.

What would she do? More to the point, what should I do? Run? Scream? Wrestle Silvie to the floor?

In the corner stood a door I had forgotten about since the last time I'd ventured into this room. It opened now and Charles Gilchrist stepped in from the adjoining bedroom, the one he and his wife shared.

"What the devil is going on in here?" As he spoke, he crossed the room and seized my arm. I started to protest—loudly—and he gave my arm a sharp yank to silence me. "Silvie, why on earth did you let her in?"

"She was being insistent," Silvie replied, and pursed her lips in distaste. She pointed at the note I still held. "And now we have a problem."

Charles swore under his breath and slid a pistol from his pocket. The elegant silver weapon fit snugly in the palm of his hand. The end of the barrel fit equally snugly against the small of my back. "What are we supposed to do with you now, my dear Mrs. Andrews? We can't let you walk back downstairs and tell the others what you know."

"That's certain." Silvie shook her head at me as one might when vastly disappointed in a child. She even tsked. "We'll need to keep her quiet and compliant."

"We wouldn't have this problem if *you* hadn't insisted on such an elaborate ruse," he countered. Silvie scowled in reply.

"What ruse?" I couldn't help myself from asking.

"The theft of the necklace, what else?" Silvie went to her dressing table. Leaning close to the mirror, she smoothed her hair and straightened the strands of pearls around her neck. Her reflection regarded me. "Did you think I only now found out about the disaster Rex made of our finances? I've known for months. Since before we went to London. And I knew all about his illicit purchase of that necklace."

"*You* hired Ines and Rudolfo," I said in disbelief.

"No, *I* hired them," Charles corrected me. "And that little witch double-crossed us."

"She hid the necklace thinking she'd get the better of us," Silvie added, then laughed. "Not a very profitable bargain for her, though."

"Except that you don't have it either, do you?" I couldn't keep the triumph from my voice. "And now you'll have so many tracks to cover, you're both sure to be found out."

"No, my dear Mrs. Andrews." Charles jabbed the pistol into my spine. I bit back a cry, not wishing to give him the satisfaction. "The only tracks leading to us right now are yours. And I'm going to see to that presently."

I tried to break free of his hold and bolt for the door, but Charles grabbed the hair coiled at my nape before I'd completed a single stride. When I continued to struggle against him, he wrestled me to the ground, and slapped me for good measure. My cheek exploded in fiery pain that spread through my skin in waves. My hair fell like a tattered curtain around me.

"Hand me that scarf," he commanded over his shoulder. Before I could blink away the fog in front of my eyes, he had bound my hands behind me. Silvie supplied another scarf and Charles wrapped it around my head and over my mouth so tightly I thought my jaw might crack. The floral taste of her perfume permeated my mouth and lungs.

When he finished the task, he pushed to his feet and stared down at me with murder in his eyes. "That should hold her for now, but we'd better move fast."

"And go where?" Silvie's arms went out in supplication. "We had planned to leave in the morning, you, me, and Kay. How will we explain a sudden departure in the middle of the night?"

Kay? Was she a party to this, too?

"Let me think. . . ."

Silvie ignored his implied request that she remain silent. "Are you certain you took care of the other matter properly?"

"I'm positive," he snapped. "Stop worrying."

"And you made it look as though . . ." Silvie coughed. "You know."

"Yes, yes, Silvie. I left his hat and cravat there on the rocks where the others will be sure to find them. Now, will you be quiet?"

"His cravat?" She chuckled with derision. "Why did you bother doing that?"

He huffed. "Because it will look like his despair was such that he couldn't breathe, so he tore the necktie from around his collar and tossed it to the ground."

There was a pause, and then, "Hmm, I see. Yes, a good touch, that."

Some of the tension left Charles's posture and he gave a laugh. "Thank you, my dear. Now do be quiet and let me figure out a solution to our current dilemma."

Sickening realization roiled in the pit of my stomach. They had set it up to look as though Rex, despairing over his finances, had jumped from the Cliff Walk. But in reality, Charles must have pushed him. And yet, something about that didn't seem possible. How had he managed it without any of the others seeing? Wouldn't Rex have called out for help? Surely he wouldn't have simply stood still while Charles took his necktie from him. And how could Charles have known exactly where to find Rex in the first place? It made no sense, none of it. . . .

Unless Rex never went to the Cliff Walk at all. No one had seen Rex since he'd left the house to go to the Reading Room with Charles. Silvie had written that note, not Rex. Perhaps the entire matter had been a ruse devised by the two of them to set everyone on the wrong trail.

Then where was Rex? The ice running through my veins suggested an answer, not to that question, but to whether Rex Morton was alive or dead.

Charles regarded me in silence for several moments. "I've an idea. . . . First, I have to get her out of this house, and I have to do it before the other men get back. Silvie, check the corridor."

She stuck her head out the door. "All clear."

"All right. I'll take care of her. You wait a few minutes and then go downstairs to rejoin Minnie and Kay. When they ask about her, as I'm sure they will, tell them she seemed suddenly to think of something and said she had a matter to see to. Act surprised that she hadn't yet returned to the drawing room."

"Take this." Silvie opened a compartment in her trunk and drew out a military knife. She handed it to Charles. "You can't very well fire your pistol in or near the house. Where do you plan on taking her?"

His smile chilled me. "There'll be another coal delivery in

the morning. There's a cart already in place beneath the bulkhead doors. By the time they fish her out from beneath all that coal, and Rex along with her, we'll be long gone. And if all goes well, Orville Brown will take the blame."

Those last words turned that chill into an arctic freeze. Charles had answered my question. Rex was indeed dead, having met a fate similar to Ines's. And now I would follow. . . .

"Get up." When I didn't move, Charles reached down and wrapped his hand around my upper arm, the fingers digging in cruelly. The silk covering my mouth swallowed my cry of pain as he yanked me to my feet.

Silvie checked the corridor again. "Still clear."

His hand clamped around my arm, Charles hurried me across the hallway and through to the service staircase. With my bound hands compromising my balance, I nearly tripped as he started us down. We'd gotten as far as the first landing when voices from below drew Charles to a halt.

He stood so close to me his breath fanned the back of my neck. The knife lodged firmly against my side. "Damn."

We hovered another moment. Charles obviously pricked his ears to judge where the individuals below were headed. A familiar voice echoed up at us.

"We'll have to let Silvie know immediately." My heart leapt against my stays at the sound of Derrick's deep tone.

"Nothing is yet certain," Ned Berwind replied. "And where the devil is Charles? It's like he vanished into the mist. Good God, Derrick, you don't think he also . . ."

"Lost his footing and went over? Let's not even think it. It's more likely he's here in the house."

Other voices spoke, and Ned said, "Yes, you men go down to the kitchen and have something warm to eat. And dry off."

Before I could hear another word, Charles roughly turned me about and impelled me upward. The presence of the re-

292 <i>Alyssa Maxwell</i>

turning footmen had foiled his plan to take me out by the service driveway. Up we went, the tip of his knife penetrating the layers of my clothing. I tried to bring my heels down with a clatter that might claim the attention of those below us, but after the first clack Charles's knife pricked a sharp warning against my skin.

We passed the second-floor landing and kept going, all the way up. Without loosening his hold on me, Charles again spun me around as he opened the door into the servants' quarters. He stuck his head in, looked up and down, and dragged me through. I sent a desperate glance along the hallway's length, hoping someone would be up and about, but as far as I could see, the bedroom doors were closed. According to Mrs. Rogan, they would be locked as well, each servant safe and sound in their own room. Working such long hours as they did, the only ones who would be awake now were those called to help find Rex. But they were headed down to the kitchen. I could no longer hear their voices echoing in the stairwell.

We had barely set foot in the hallway when Charles opened a door behind us, forced me up a few steps, and shoved me outside, onto the roof. "Have you seen the view from up here, Mrs. Andrews? It's quite spectacular."

Chapter 23

Once again I hoped for the presence of servants—that some of them would be out on their rooftop gathering place. But the only sound was the breeze and the rain dripping from the drain spouts. Charles forced me around a corner and along the walkway until the platform the servants had built came into view.

Was he planning to throw me over?

He took me to the platform. I could see he was thinking it over, trying to decide what to do with me. Would he wait it out and take me down to the service entrance later? I believed him to be in quite a quandary, one he hadn't expected. I tried to speak, to question him and get him talking, but he had secured the scarf too tightly to allow my lips to move or much sound to come out.

A lamp came on behind the thin curtains in one of the rooms behind us, tossing an orangey light over us. *Please*, I thought, *open the curtains and look out!* Charles flinched and tugged me back into the shadows. He brought me close to the retaining wall, pressing my back up against it. His hand came up, and the blade of his knife lodged against my throat. I barely dared to breathe.

"I think I'll have to kill you right here, my dear. It's less than ideal, but I see no other way. I'll hide your body beneath the platform. At least then you won't be found till morning. Silvie and I will have to leave ahead of schedule tonight, but it can't be helped. *Why* didn't you mind your business?" This last he hissed between his clenched teeth. "No one was meant to die. No one. Not Ines or Rudolfo, not the gardener, not even Rex. Certainly not you. Would none of you simply cooperate?"

He emphasized that last word with a shove at my shoulder that knocked my back and bound arms hard against the wall. The knife pressed, and with rising terror I wondered if it was rain or blood dripping down my neck into my collar.

Yet, I hadn't missed his admission to yet another crime. The gardener's assistant. It appeared Bridget had been right about Orville Brown, who had told the truth when he'd proclaimed his innocence in the gardener's death. Had Charles been rooting through the garden, hoping to find the necklace, when the gardener came upon him? Even if the young man hadn't challenged Charles in any way, Charles would still have wished to silence him, especially if he had been caught sifting through the foliage. In his effort to cover his tracks, Charles had left a trail of death in his wake.

As for Orville Brown . . . Charles had said with any luck he would take the blame for all of this. How? Had Charles left clues pointing erroneously at the newspaper owner?

"All of my efforts—*all*—for nothing," he spat as if reading my mind. He gave me another shove that knocked the back of my head against the wall. "Damn you all, and damn Silvie for her scheming. Never trust a woman to get it right."

My head pounded and stars danced before my eyes. In other circumstances I might have pointed out that since he had followed Silvie's lead voluntarily, she couldn't be entirely blamed. But even if I could have spoken then, I would not have risked sending him into a blind rage. Through a haze of pain and fear, I forced my mind to focus. My feet were not bound. I could fight with my legs. Years ago, Derrick had taught me certain techniques. But could I launch an attack quickly enough to avoid him slashing the knife through my throat? Even if I did, then what? Throw myself against a window and hope someone heard and looked out before Charles stabbed me to death? Either way, I might die. I therefore had little to lose. Except that he still had his pistol in his coat pocket. Would he turn it on whoever came to help?

"I'm sorry, Emma. . . ."

Without thought, I kicked upward, jamming my knee first into Charles's thigh, then into the juncture of his legs. He doubled over and the knife came away from my throat, but when I thought he'd go down, he hung on, using my shoulder for leverage. His forehead knocked painfully against mine. He released my shoulder only to tangle his fingers in my hair to hold me fast. The hand with the knife pulled back. . . .

"No, Charles!"

I heard footsteps, a female voice. Had Silvie had a change of heart? A blur of clothing filled the edge of my vision, and then a thud sounded. Charles's hands went slack and fell to his sides. The knife clattered to the ground. I heard a second thud, and Charles fell over backward.

Kay Gilchrist stepped quickly out of the way before her husband landed on her. In her right hand she gripped a golf club, a heavy driver made of wood and brass. Charles wouldn't be stirring anytime soon.

In my relief, I sagged to my knees. Kay hurried to me, her arms going tightly around me. "Emma, my dear Emma, are you all right?"

She crouched behind me and went to work unknotting

the scarves around my mouth and wrists. When she had freed me, I twisted around and put my arms around her. We embraced, rocking back and forth.

"Did he hurt you?"

"I'm all right, I think." I pressed my fingertips to my neck and glimpsed traces of blood on them when I pulled them away. How close he had come to . . . "Thank you, Kay. Thank you. But . . . how did you know where we were?"

"You went to check on Silvie, and when you didn't return downstairs, I went up to check on you. Right before I knocked at the Mortons' bedroom door, I heard the oddest thing: Charles's voice coming from inside. So I hid in the lavatory at the end of the corridor and peeked out as he forced you through the service doorway."

I studied her face, her expression. Many emotions flitted across her features, but shock wasn't one of them. "You knew about Charles and Silvie, didn't you?" She nodded and I asked, "How long?"

"For months. Ever since I laid eyes on her son during the Christmas holidays. *Charles's* son. But even before that. They way they acted around each other, the looks, the whispers . . ." She shrugged. "What was I to do about it? Nothing. Charles has always made it quite clear to me that I was to endure whatever whims struck his fancy." She absently raised a hand to rub at the opposite shoulder, as though to massage away a pain. I guessed it wasn't actual pain, but the memory of one.

"Kay, I'm so sorry."

"Yes, well. Come, we must get you inside." She rose and grasped my hands to help me up. Then she gazed at her husband's prone form without a hint of remorse. "He might regain consciousness at any moment. We must find someone to subdue him when that happens. I suppose we could use these scarves to tie him. . . ." She looked at me in question.

I shook my head. "As you said, let's go in and find some-one. You and I would be no match for him should he awaken." My gaze fell on the golf club where she had dropped it. "Then again, perhaps we are. At least, *you* are." I shook my head. I would never have believed timid Kay Gilchrist had it in her to knock her husband—or any man—out cold. She saved my life. I would never underestimate her again.

As Kay and I approached the drawing room, we could hear Silvie's voice. There was also the rumble of male voices whenever she paused.

"I truly don't know what she had in mind," Silvie was saying. "Merely that some thought had occurred to her and she needed to see to something important. I'm sorry, Der-rick, I don't know what it was."

She was giving the excuse for my whereabouts Charles had suggested. I hurried across the hallway and turned in. Silvie held her arms out to her sides in a shrug of puzzlement—until she saw me. Then her arms wilted slowly downward while her mouth hung open.

"Emma. Darling." Derrick rushed to gather me in his arms. "I was so worried to discover you gone. Where did you go?"

From over his shoulder, I held my gaze pinned on Silvie. "I never went anywhere. I was here all along. Wasn't I, Sil-vie?"

Derrick suddenly released me. "I'm sorry. I'm getting you wet."

"I'm already wet," I replied, and held out my skirts. "From being on the roof."

"What were you doing on the roof?"

My gaze slid past him. "Silvie knows, don't you, Silvie?"

She stood up from her chair with such force it scraped

backward over the herringbone parquet floor. "I'm sure I don't know what you're talking about."

"Then I'll explain." I turned back to Derrick and included Ned and Minnie in my gaze. "Charles took me up to the roof after he and Silvie realized I'd discovered what they had done. It was they who killed Ines and Rudolfo, and Rex as well."

"Rex?" Ned stepped toward me. "My dear lady, we were just about to break the news to poor Silvie that it looks as though Rex jumped from the Cliff Walk."

Silvie let out a cry of distress whose false note made me shake my head. "Charles and Silvie schemed to make it look as though he had, but in truth, he was already dead before Silvie ever wrote that note. Have someone check the coal chute. I believe you'll find his body there. And your gardener? It seems he came upon Charles digging through your sunken garden, searching for Rex's stolen necklace. And Charles couldn't have him wagging his tongue about that."

"She's lost her mind." Silvie clutched the neckline of her frock, attempting to play the part of a frightened, grieving wife. She stepped around her chair and continued backing away from the rest of us.

"Emma's mind is quite clear, Silvie." Kay came to stand at my side. "I watched as Charles dragged her into the service staircase and up onto the roof. I heard him admit to killing Rex and the others, and I heard him tell Emma he was going to kill her next."

All gazes converged on Silvie, who now stood with her back pressed against the Louis Quinze commode against the wall. I imagined the carved gold-leaf cherub at its center must have been digging into the small of her back. Fear filled her expression. "Charles did this, not me. I'm innocent. I swear it."

"You are not." Kay raised an arm to point, her expression as fierce as an avenging angel's. "Charles fathered your son, and Rex never knew. You and Charles learned of Rex's financial straits and how he planned to remedy matters. You knew about his purchase of the necklace and conspired to steal it, making it impossible for Rex to ever pay off his debts." Kay placed both hands on her hips. "Charles alone could not have achieved so much without the help of someone close to Rex. Very close. His wife, for instance."

"His wife . . . who knew the combination to his safe and told it to Ines," I took up when Kay left off. "And while you've been in Newport, how could this Mr. Smith have known where to find Rex without someone telling him? Again, it had to be someone close to him. Which of you told Mr. Smith about the outing to the golf course—you or Charles? Not that it matters—you were operating as a team." I turned and said to the Berwinds, "You need to send someone up to the roof to apprehend Charles when he wakes up. We don't want him slipping away. And the police must be called. Mustn't they, Silvie?" I couldn't help adding.

"Goodness," Minnie said with a gasp, "and to think I advised against that earlier. Yes, I'll have the police summoned immediately." She pushed a call button on the wall. A moment later a footman arrived. Minnie murmured a series of instructions to him, and he hurried away.

"No, don't bring the police here." Silvie shoved backward against the commode as if to move it out of the way of her retreat. The china figurines on its marble surface rocked precariously. "You don't understand. Rex *ruined* us. How were we to live? What was I supposed to do?"

"You were supposed to *not* scheme to murder people," I said bluntly. "Ines double-crossed you by hiding the necklace and attempting to coerce you and Charles to pay her more for her efforts. My guess is it's still hidden, or you and Charles would have been gone by now. And Rudolfo? Why did he have to die?"

"He and that little harlot were in on it together." Silvie

scowled so fiercely I feared she might spit as well. "He was never supposed to be here at all. The pair of them thought they'd extort *us*. He ran when he saw what Charles did to Ines, but he couldn't run far or fast enough. The pair of them had no idea whom they were dealing with."

"No," Derrick said, his hand slipping around mine, "none of us did."

"None of us could have imagined it," I agreed.

When the police arrived, they discovered Rex's body where Ines's had been—in the coal chute. And tucked into his coat pocket was a typewritten note, supposedly signed by Orville Brown, bidding Rex to meet him out on Dixon Street if he wanted certain information. Jesse had scoffed at the ruse, asserting it wouldn't have fooled anyone even if the truth about Charles and Silvie hadn't come out.

Then Jesse spoke with me alone. He and I were in Ned's library, where Silvie's cries of protest could be heard only minutes ago as the police escorted her out of the house. Jesse had had the foresight to arrange for the ambulance wagon for Charles, who had been brought down from the roof on a stretcher. He'd been conscious, but dizzy and weak. At the time, a fretful Kay had asked Jesse if she would be arrested for assault, but he had assured her that acts of self-defense against an admitted killer were not criminal.

After I'd described everything that had happened to me, Jesse sent for Kay. It took her longer to join us than one might expect, and when she finally arrived, she held a black velvet bag in her hands, about the size of a lady's small handbag. She came into the room slowly, her chin tucked low, as if facing a tribunal. What could the dear woman possibly fear now?

"Detective," she murmured as she reached Ned's desk and stood beside my chair. Though Jesse had placed a second chair at the desk for her, she remained standing.

"Thank you for joining us, Mrs. Gilchrist," he said. "Please let me express how sorry I am for the way matters have turned out. I'm sorry I had to arrest your husband."

"I'm not sorry," she said, surprising us both. She placed the bag on the desk and without another word pushed it toward Jesse.

"What's this?" He raised a questioning gaze to her face, but when she didn't respond he worked the drawstring open and looked inside. His eyes widened. "My word."

I leaned forward, trying to see. "What is it?"

Jesse reached in and drew out a strand of glittering diamonds set around a centerpiece larger than any I had ever seen. Even my aunt Alice didn't own such a gem. "My word," he said again, looking dumbfounded.

"The Marie Antoinette necklace." I reached over and fingered the priceless center diamond, reflecting the lamplight as though a flame danced at the stone's core. "Then Charles *did* have it."

Kay avoided my gaze. "No, he didn't."

"I don't understand." I studied her features as she continued to look away from me. "How long have you had it?"

She clutched her hands and bit her lip as her eyes filled with tears. "Since the night of the musicale. Since the night my husband murdered Ines Varella."

Jesse and I traded looks of astonishment. My breath left me in a whoosh and I fell back against my chair. "But . . . how?"

"Wait." Jesse stood up and crossed the room. When he returned, he carried one of Ned's decanters and a crystal liqueur glass. He beckoned Kay to the chair beside mine. "Sit, please." He poured a measure of amber liquid into the glass and passed it into Kay's hands. "Now, take a couple of sips, and then tell us, slowly, how you came to possess this necklace."

And why you didn't tell anyone you had it? Especially

when you knew how important it was, I burned to know.
But I kept the question to myself, for now, not wanting to
frighten her off. She surely must be wondering if her actions
would lead to her arrest, as did I.

With trembling hands, Kay brought the glass to her lips
and took two good swallows. Then she lowered it to her lap,
clasped in her two hands. "During the intermission that
night, I fled upstairs to escape Charles, just for a few minutes. He was being so nasty, criticizing my gown, my hair,
my very self." She looked down at the glass and swirled the
liquor slightly. "So, as I had told you, Detective, I went up
to use the facility in the guest wing. I had a little cry, actually, and then splashed water on my face. As I was about to
leave, I saw Ines stealing into Silvie and Rex's room. Realizing she had no business there at that time of night, I slipped
into my room and opened the adjoining door just a crack.
Did you know the two rooms connected?"

Jesse shrugged and motioned for her to continue.

"There was Ines, crouching in front of Rex's safe. It didn't
take her but a moment to open it and take out that bag and
the box inside it." She pointed to the velvet jewelry pouch
on the desk. "She left the box, closed the safe, spun the dial,
and hurried out."

"What happened next?" Jesse prompted when Kay paused.
She took another sip.

"Ines entered the service staircase." She ducked her head
and blushed. "And I followed her. All the way out onto the
service drive and across the back lawn. I couldn't imagine
where she was taking that bag, or what was in it. But I
guessed it was important. She stopped at the fountain, the
one near the Dixon Street gates."

My curiosity soared. "What did she do when she stopped?"

"She tucked the bag into the ground at the base of the
fountain. As I watched, I could see that a hole had already

been dug. She placed the bag in, covered it up, and used the bottom of her shoe to pat it down. Then she hurried out through the gate."

"I'll wager Rudolfo dug that hole in advance for her," I mused.

Jesse pursed his lips, regarding the necklace that sat glittering on the desktop. "And you immediately dug up the bag, yes? And looked inside?"

Kay nodded, her head down once more. "I was astounded. I thought to return it to Silvie and Rex, truly I did. At first. But as I hurried back to the house, I began to think about what Silvie had done to me, her and Charles. *Their son*." She spoke those words bitterly. "And I realized that with those diamonds, I could finally be free of Charles. Free to go where I pleased and live as I wished."

"And when you learned that Ines had been murdered," Jesse said, "did it not occur to you this might be valuable evidence in the case?"

Kay tightened her hands around the cordial glass to stop their shaking. "It did occur to me. But I had no idea Charles or Silvie could be involved in her death. I only knew I longed for an escape. And that necklace presented me with one. I'm sorry, Detective." She turned to me. "I'm so sorry, Emma."

What she had done was wrong, no mistake, but her reasons captured my sympathies. I reached over to place my hand over hers. "I believe I do understand."

She offered me a tremulous smile and turned back to Jesse. "Will you arrest me now?"

He blew out a long breath. I held my own as I waited for his answer. In my mind, Kay was yet another victim of her husband's vile nature. And of Silvie's.

Lifting the necklace from the desk, Jesse turned it this way and that to catch the glow from the electric lamps. The diamonds flashed with near blinding light; the center diamond sparked a flame that seemed to originate from deep within it. Despite that illusion, I knew the stone would yield no warmth, would never be anything but hard and icy to the touch.

"Jesse," I whispered, "please."

"No, Mrs. Gilchrist," he said evenly, "I don't think an arrest will be necessary. But I will be taking this into evidence."

"Of course, Detective." She smiled. "I'll be happy never to lay eyes on it again."

Derrick and I drove home in our carriage by moonlight. Minnie and Ned practically begged us to stay until morning, but neither Derrick nor I wished to wait that long to indulge in the peace and comfort of home. Kay would remain at The Elms for the next few days, in case the police needed to speak with her again.

Home this time meant Gull Manor. Nanny would be overjoyed to see us. Even if she had already turned in for the night, she would hear the carriage coming up the drive and rouse herself. She always said she had learned to sleep lightly while I was a child, so she would always be at hand when I needed her. I had few doubts she already had something savory waiting in the larder, and perhaps something sweet and fruity in the pie cabinet.

Yet, as we approached the house on Ocean Avenue, Derrick didn't slow the carriage to turn onto the drive. To my surprise, he drove us past, to the next parcel of property. No house had yet been built here, and Derrick carefully pulled us onto the rocky, weedy turf.

"What are we doing?" I gazed out to the ocean, rolling in long waves that foamed blue in the moonlight. The rain had cleared, though the breeze still wafted in forceful gusts, pushing the remaining clouds across the sky to momentarily blot out the constellations as if someone were flipping an electric switch off and on. "Stargazing?"

"I thought we'd take a look much closer to home than the sky." He reached his arm around me and pulled me to his side. "It's a nice, relatively flat piece of land, isn't it?"

I nodded my agreement. "I'm surprised no one has built here yet."

"How about if we do?"

With a start, I pulled far enough away from him to be able to look him fully in the face. "What do you mean? We already have a house, right next door."

"Yes, but that house, as lovely as it is, isn't *ours.*" He drew me close again and nuzzled his lips against my temple. "Isn't that what's been bothering you? That we don't really have a home to call our own?"

Again, I pulled away, dumbfounded. Too dumbfounded to attempt to deny it. "How on earth did you know?"

He smiled, the moonlight kissing his cheeks as they rounded. "My darling Emma, after everything you and I have been through these past several years, do you really think I haven't come to know you as well as I know myself?" He kissed me, then smiled again. "Or very nearly so?"

I tipped my head back and laughed—from sheer relief coupled with the joy of this man. Of his being in my life. Of his knowing me and accepting me for all that I was. I threw my arms around his neck and laid my cheek on his shoulder. "But what about Gull Manor? I couldn't possibly sell Aunt Sadie's house."

"Well, I thought . . ." He lifted my hand and brought it to his lips. "I thought Gull Manor might make a wonderful school for young ladies. And Nanny, if she is willing, might help oversee it. And you, of course. It would need your wisdom and vision to be the right sort of school, one for this new century we're living in, where women will be doing things they never dreamed possible. But there's plenty of time to plan while the new house is being built." He fell silent. We sat listening to the wind and waves, watching the clouds scudding overhead. Finally, he turned to me, lifted my face in his hands, and gave a hearty laugh. "Well? What do you think?"

"It's wonderful. *You're* wonderful." I gulped away a lump in my throat and blinked away a tear. "And I can't wait to get started."

Author's Note

While the names Richard Morris Hunt and McKim, Mead & White were practically synonymous with Gilded Age architecture, there were other equally talented architects contributing to the legacy of conspicuous consumption. The Elms was designed by Horace Trumbauer, known for his palatial residences, hotels, and office and university buildings. The Elms was modeled after and bears a striking resemblance to the Château d'Asnières near Paris, built in the mid-eighteenth century.

Edward Julius Berwind, or Ned, was the son of middle-class German immigrants and enjoyed a career in the navy before joining his brother, Charles, in the coal business. Together they and partner Allison White founded the Berwind-White Coal Mining Company, where Ned would make his vast fortune. At the turn of the twentieth century, the Berwind-White company was one of the largest coal producers in the world. In addition, Ned had a hand in developing New York City's subway system and served as director of the parent company of the White Star Line, under which the Titanic would sail.

Herminie, meanwhile, enjoyed life growing up in Italy as the daughter of U.S. consular agent and sculptor Franklin Torrey. Although I portray Minnie's childhood as one of privilege but not great wealth, her father's family were part of Bowker, Torrey & Co. of Boston, Massachusetts, a leading marble manufacturer, and owners of marble quarries in Carrara, Italy. Ned and Minnie met and married in Italy.

They would never have children of their own but enjoyed the company of their nieces and nephews, who were frequent visitors at The Elms.

As in the story, Ned Berwind proudly refused to negotiate with his employees, whether it be his household staff or workers in his coal mines. Thus, when his household servants went on strike, insisting on more reasonable working hours and time off, he summarily fired them all. As I also have it in the story, the Berwinds then hired all new staff and, adding insult to injury, allowed them time off on a rotational basis. However, I did take artistic license with the timing of the strike, which occurred in 1902, during the Berwinds' second summer at The Elms.

In keeping with her husband's demanding nature when it came to employees, Minnie had timers installed next to her call buttons to assess exactly how long it took servants to answer her summons.

The Elms, which opened for its first summer in 1901, was indeed one of the most modern houses in America at the time. While other "cottages" such as The Breakers and Ochre Court boasted electrical power, gas fixtures were installed as well. Electricity was still so new in those days that most people didn't trust it to be a reliable source of power. Ned Berwind didn't agree. Coal from his mines was delivered via the coal tunnel that opened onto Dixon Street just outside the property's south wall, and shoveled into the three massive furnaces in the subbasement twenty-four hours a day, in eight-hour shifts.

With the exceptions of Gertrude Vanderbilt and her husband, Harry Whitney; Mamie and Stuyvesant Fish; and Harry and Elizabeth Lehr, who all make brief appearances at the Berwinds' "musicale," the rest of the houseguests are fictional. So, too, are Orville Brown and Bridget Whalen, along with the rest of the servants. The platform on the roof outside the servants' quarters exists but is a modern installation for the benefit of visitors who tour the house nowadays, yet I couldn't help imagining that some innovative servant might have erected just such a structure to enjoy the night views with his fellow employees. Likewise, the sunken garden at the bottom of the lawn near Spring Street also exists but was not there in 1901. It was part of a slightly later project as the grounds were further developed in a Classical Revival style between 1907 and 1914.

I must take a moment to acknowledge, once again, The Preservation Society of Newport County. The Servant Life Tour at The Elms, the information available during the house tour, and the virtual house tour available on their website are treasure troves of information and proved invaluable to the writing of this book. I especially encourage all readers to take advantage of the latter, which is available for most of the other Society properties as well, which will allow them to follow my characters throughout the houses room by room as they read the Gilded Newport Mysteries.